BLONDE
DUST

BLONDE DUST

TATIANA DE ROSNAY

GRAND
CENTRAL

New York   Boston

Grand Central Publishing
Hachette Book Group
1290 Avenue of the Americas, New York, NY 10104
grandcentralpublishing.com
@grandcentralpub

Originally published in 2024 by Albin Michel in France

First US Edition: June 2025

Grand Central Publishing is a division of Hachette Book Group, Inc. The Grand Central Publishing name and logo is a registered trademark of Hachette Book Group, Inc.

The publisher is not responsible for websites (or their content) that are not owned by the publisher.

The Hachette Speakers Bureau provides a wide range of authors for speaking events. To find out more, go to hachettespeakersbureau.com or email HachetteSpeakers@hbgusa.com.

Grand Central Publishing books may be purchased in bulk for business, educational, or promotional use. For information, please contact your local bookseller or the Hachette Book Group Special Markets Department at special.markets@hbgusa.com.

Print book interior design by Taylor Navis

Library of Congress Control Number: 2025932833

ISBNs: 9781538770962 (hardcover), 9781538770986 (ebook)

Printed in the United States of America

LSC-C

Printing 1, 2025

To Nicolas

In loving memory of Eric D, my cousin.

1957–2023

BLONDE
DUST

"How do you find your way back in the dark?"

"Just head for that big star straight on. The highway's under it; it'll take us right home."

—Arthur Miller, *The Misfits*

SUNDAY, JANUARY 30, 2000

Virginia Street, Reno, Nevada

To see the Mapes again. To gaze at it one more time, and to watch it fall. The hotel had been in full construction on the corner of Virginia Street and the banks of the Truckee River when Pauline arrived in Reno in 1946 at the age of seven. She'd seen it go up brick by brick and reach its culmination for its grand opening in December 1947 when it proudly dominated the small town as the western United States's first-ever skyscraper after the war. Dazzled, Pauline, a little French girl, had never laid eyes on such a magisterial and pristine building.

Publicity about Reno's new hotel flourished in all the local gazettes, raving about the orange-red hue of the Art Deco façade, its twelve floors, three hundred rooms and forty suites, air-conditioning, two restaurants and two cocktail bars, casino, barber shop and beauty salon, but especially the Mapes's crown jewel—the famed Sky Room right at the top with its bay windows offering unrivaled views of the Sierra Nevada mountain range. There, noteworthy evenings ensued with wining and dining, concerts, performances, and after-dinner dancing.

Pauline still remembered the odor floating in the Mapes's vast lobby: a distinctive combination of cigarette smoke, felt fabric, and room fragrance called Sweet Desert Rose, which tyrannical Mildred had sprayed there morning, noon, and evening. She also recalled the less pleasant aromas, in spite of Sweet Desert Rose, persisting in the main floor restrooms where she cleaned up: whiffs of drains, bleach, and scouring products, not to mention the often-excruciating reek left by hasty guests who didn't cast a glance her way, while others bestowed her with a smile, a word of thanks, or a coin.

In those days, Mildred Jones—the one they dreaded, housekeeper in charge of the twenty or so maids hired by the Mapes Hotel—had been her boss and the cause of the pit in her stomach each morning for three years. *Would she be there today?* Pauline wondered. *How old would she be now?* Back in 1960, Mildred was in her forties, so she would be well into her eighties now. She might very well be there, after all. Just as Kendall Spencer might be there too, a septuagenarian with tribe in tow—a frosty wife who would look askance at her even after all this time, and their children and grandchildren, those well-to-do, respectable Spencers.

Today, with her dear friend Billie-Pearl by her side, Pauline knew she would undoubtedly identify figures from her past within the throng amassed to watch the Mapes's spectacular collapse. And, she wondered, *Why had they all planned to come?* To remember, to rejoice, to get closure? Or, like her, to pay one last homage?

The entire district around the Mapes had been cordoned

off. East Second Street, Center Street, and North Sierra Street were closed, but Billie-Pearl managed to cross the river through Arlington Avenue and, at the last minute, was able to park by West Liberty Street. They hurried along to join the crowd gathered by the south banks of the Truckee River. From there was a perfect view north over Virginia Street Bridge toward the doomed hotel.

They had to elbow their way to reach the forefront, about two hundred feet from the Mapes. Pauline couldn't get over the number of people: How many, a couple of thousand? Much more, offered Billie-Pearl, just as impressed. She pointed out numerous television cameras and reporters on site. *The fall of the Mapes was a public affair*, thought Pauline. Everyone wanted to see it.

Facing the camera, a journalist explained in detail how the Mapes was coming down. A hundred pounds of explosives had been inserted through four hundred holes drilled into support columns on five floors. The building, which stood tall at one hundred and thirty-three feet, was going to dissolve in midair. The crowd listened, awestruck.

Here and there, with a quick pang, Pauline spotted a couple of familiar faces, but felt incapable of putting names to them. She settled for sharing a smile or a nod.

Next to Pauline and Billie-Pearl, a young woman wearing a blue beanie seemed tearful. She told them her father worked at the Mapes Casino for a long time, and she used to accompany him when he picked up his paychecks. A historic chunk of Reno's past was to vanish forever and deserved better than turning into a pile of rubble.

"It's such a pretty building," she almost sobbed. "Look at it! Preservationists fought till the bitter end," she added. A cluster of them were there, still shouting, "Save the Mapes!" minutes away from its destruction. A wake with a bagpiper had even been organized.

Another woman behind them shrugged and sighed as she eavesdropped—she was in favor of letting go of the past. The decrepit old Mapes had been shuttered for twenty years. It certainly wasn't pretty anymore, and it was time for a fresh start for this part of Reno! A nearby group of friends added they had come up from Auburn, California, especially for skiing, the Super Bowl, and the implosion.

"It's going to be phenomenal!" tittered one of them. "Better than the movies!"

Pauline noticed a number of people proudly brandishing large red bricks and certificates of authenticity bearing the Mapes's cowboy logo she immediately recognized: two cowboys riding mustangs. They were going like hotcakes for a dollar each on the street corner.

"Do you want a brick as a keepsake?" asked Billie-Pearl.

"No," murmured Pauline, wondering if she shouldn't be saying yes.

All around them arose snippets of conversation caught in flight: *Remember?...What floor were we on?...On the seventh, there!...No, more like the fifth...My, oh, my, those unbeatable Coffee Shop milk shakes...I preferred the Coach Room vibe....That's where we celebrated Kathleen's thirtieth....Oh, it was such fun!...And that nice Addie, who worked with the operators....Thank God Miranda is no longer with us, she'd be in tears...Barbara and Josh's wedding reception was a ball, we partied all night...Such a classy place...Remember when Rick got a lucky hand at the Casino?...I'll never forget!...*

It was impossible not to listen to them, each and every one, like the old lady clutching her caregiver's arm, pointing a wobbly finger up to the Sky Room, saying she met her husband there for the first time, at a prom ball. Pauline noticed a dignified elderly man standing alone, clutching a red rose to his heart. He observed the façade in silence. What was his story and why had he come here today?

A pudgy sexagenarian came up to her, politely asking if her name was Pauline. He had come with his wife and kids. Pauline had no memories of him, but pretended she did, so as not to offend him. His name was Nate and he worked back then with Max at reservations. Pauline vaguely recalled a Max. Nate made a face: But hey, in those days, he used to be in shape and had a head of hair! She laughed along with him.

"It's coming back to me, they used to call you 'Frenchie,'" clucked Nate.

"That's right, I was born in Paris, after all," replied Pauline, amused.

The sky, low and ominous, was loaded with fast-approaching snow; people huddled close to each other trying to beat the cold. Pauline glanced at her watch. It was coming up to eight o'clock. The inexhaustible Nate was going on about how the Mapes's proprietors were on-site as well, inconsolable. They hadn't been able to rescue their beloved hotel.

While Pauline was wondering how to give Nate the slip, a sturdy bearded man stationed himself in front of her. Elated, she recognized her half-brother, Jim. He had been positive he'd find her here, but she should have warned him, he protested, all smiles. Billie-Pearl intervened—this was her fault; she had dragged Pauline to Reno, a last-minute plan.

"How's it going?" asked Jim softly, wrapping an arm around his sister. "Are you happy to be here?"

He was the spitting image of his late dad, Doug Hammond—same playful grin, light blue gaze, stocky build—and whenever Pauline laid eyes on Jim, she was reminded of the beloved stepfather she still missed. Doug burst into her mother's life in the haphazard and tumultuous times following the liberation of Paris. She had no recollection of her own father, Jacques Bazelet, who died of cancer in 1939, the year she was born. Doug Hammond, her mother's second husband, was the one who brought her up, here in Reno. Against all odds, the graft had been a success.

Jim lowered his voice to whisper in her ear—he wanted to warn her. She mustn't turn around; Kendall Spencer was nearby. Pauline paid no heed to his words and looked behind her shoulder. It didn't take her long to pick him out. He had certainly aged, but his blue-blood posture hadn't. He still held himself upright with that complacent expression she hated. His thick hair was silver, and she had to admit he looked good. He always had. How young and gullible she had been then, and how naïve.

Kendall Spencer eventually sensed the gaze directed straight at him through the gathering. He seemed uncertain. Did he recognize her? Four decades was a long time, after all. She too, no doubt, had changed: The long brown hair was gone—now short and strewn with white. But she'd kept her slim figure. When Kendall's eyes remained glued to her, she reckoned he had spotted her. Almost bashfully, he raised his hand.

"Forget it," muttered Jim. "Don't even go there."

"Odious prick," hissed Billie-Pearl.

They were interrupted by another TV crew. A few minutes from the event, a nonstop news network was seeking to interview more people who had worked at the Mapes.

"Hey! Here!" yelled Billie-Pearl, motioning toward Pauline. "Right here!"

A camera zoomed in on her and a mike was shoved under her chin before Pauline, taken aback, could protest. A young woman fired away:

"Hi, what's your name?"

"Doctor Pauline Bazelet," she faltered.

"Are you from Reno? What's your current job?"

"I'm a vet. I live in California, but I grew up here in Reno."

"When did you work at the Mapes Hotel?"

"Between 1957 and 1960."

"And what was your position?"

"I worked as a cleaner on the ground floor and in the rooms. I was young, then."

"And what's it like to be here today and watch it go down?"

Pauline's eyes flickered over the ramshackle Mapes looming above them with unfazed pride. Her throat felt tight.

"I can't help feeling emotional. That hotel was like an entire world to me. So many of us worked there, and it was full of guests. It was the busiest place. There was always something going on."

The journalist checked her notes.

"So you were there in the summer of 1960 when John Huston and his actors came for the filming of *The Misfits*?"

Why did Pauline's lips tremble so? Undoubtedly stage fright.

"Yes, I was there. I remember it all."

"We are minutes away from the hotel imploding. Could you briefly tell us what the Mapes was like in all its glory, when you worked there?"

Pauline hadn't prepared a speech; she hadn't expected to be interviewed. She felt tongue-tied. But much to her surprise, she managed to overlook the secret episodes in Kendall's office, Mildred Jones's hectoring, and the unpleasant smells left by customers in the main floor restrooms.

She only saw the curvaceous silhouette standing in front of the windows of Suite 614, champagne glass in hand.

And with a steady voice, she said, "In the summer of 1960, at the Mapes Hotel, I met someone who changed my life."

"Great! Can you tell us more?"

"With pleasure."

But the journalist was informed through her earpiece that the time had come. She was told to interrupt the interview and take it up again afterward.

The Mapes was about to fall.

THURSDAY, JANUARY 20, 2000

Ten Days Before
Mount Shasta, Siskiyou County, Northern California

Pauline was sitting on a stool at work in Starling's box, the wounded yearling who was giving her such a hard time, when her daughter, Lily's, stride was heard at the entrance of the building. Wide-eyed with fear, Starling flinched and Pauline had to murmur soothing words in a low voice to calm the colt. Ever since a tractor had skidded on black ice, crashing into him and shattering his radius, Starling remained in a constant state of alarm. He was her most frightened patient, the one getting the most attention.

"Mom! Phone!" Lily hollered.

"Can it wait?" Pauline asked, cheek resting against the colt's shuddering flank. Under the golden hide, she could feel his heart pumping away.

"No, it can't," retorted Lily.

Intrigued, Pauline detected a grin lurking in her voice, and she got up to study her expression: Lily was all smiles. Pauline checked the poultice and splint fastened around the colt's limb one last time and ran a reassuring palm along his muzzle.

"Way to go, buddy. You got this."

She washed her hands at the tap situated by the stalls and caught up with her daughter. Why all the mystery? Couldn't Lily just tell her right now who was on the phone? Was it Nick, her partner? Lily shook her head, comically clamping her lips, walking her to the central office by the stables.

Pauline still hadn't succumbed to the lure of mobile phones, unlike most of her vet colleagues. She preferred to remain "old school," and she laughingly confessed there was no way she would give in to a Nokia or a BlackBerry! She believed in the virtues of a good old landline and answering machine, which was, after all, normal at her age. Soon to be sixty-one, when teased about her vintage habits, she brandished the unbeatable fact of cell phone coverage being second-rate up in the craggy heights of her veterinary clinic.

Lily handed her the receiver with the same playful smile.

"Doctor Bazelet," stated Pauline, brushing away a salt-and-pepper lock of hair, and expecting to hear Nick's voice.

"You mean, 'the' Doctor Bazelet? The one and only Doctor Bazelet?"

This wasn't Nick's husky rumble.

Pauline's smile mirrored her daughter's. That voice! Her whole youth came back in a flash.

"It's you!"

"You bet it's me, Mademoiselle!"

Only Billie-Pearl would ever call her that—they were the same age and grandmothers several times over. They had been friends since their early teens.

Lily had gone, leaving her mother alone in the large room. Outside through the window, night fell like a curtain, blotting out the snow paling Mount Shasta's peak: a view Pauline had not grown tired of; green in spring, golden by summer, white during winter, crimson in fall, reminiscent of the volcano it still was.

Billie-Pearl went straight to the point; it was in her character and Pauline was used to it. "Are you hard at work right now, Mademoiselle? Lots of lame horses to tend to?"

"A whole bunch," admitted Pauline. "Why?"

"You need to get your pretty face back to Reno on January thirtieth. In ten days. A Sunday, in the morning. When I saw the news, I thought of you. You can't miss this, no way."

"Miss what?"

"You can find a vet who can step in for you, right? And your daughter will help out, like always?" Billie-Pearl mischievously enjoyed keeping her hanging on.

Pauline was used to that too. She lit a cigarette, putting away the stuff cluttering her desk. "How's Dansa?" she asked, teasing her in return.

That was Billie-Pearl's favorite mare, granddaughter of her beloved stallion, Commander, who had passed away years ago.

Billie-Pearl lowered her voice.

"Dansa's fine. Hey, listen. On January thirtieth, they're going to blow up the Mapes. Blast it to pieces."

Surprised, Pauline asked her friend if they really intended to raze it entirely. Billie-Pearl confirmed they certainly did; the luxury hotel had not stopped losing money since it closed in December 1982. The place, which had been empty since then, was in a bad state of disrepair and had nothing in common with the glory of its debut back in the forties, when its elevated outline was Reno's pulsating point of reference. Many people had tried to save it; petitions had been launched, added Billie-Pearl, but that hadn't been enough. It was going to be replaced with parking spaces and a skating rink, and Pauline couldn't believe her ears. Still, in the grip of an unexpected wistfulness stirring within her, she went on listening to her friend.

"That Sunday, the thirtieth, is Super Bowl Sunday," Billie-Pearl went on, "which means roads will be packed like crazy. You could come on Saturday, get here in the afternoon, settle in. I'll introduce you to the yearlings. And the next morning, Sunday, we'll go together. You'll be back home on Monday."

Pauline said yes, even if she was aware it would be tricky getting someone to stand in for her. She would be gone only two nights, a weekend, moreover, and she knew she could trust Lily to manage the clinic. Her daughter was not a vet, but she handled invoices and clients. Lily's husband, Howard, and she had two children, a son, ten, and a girl, eight. The family lived nearby, which meant she saw them often.

Sometime later, as Lily was getting ready to head home, Pauline told her she was planning to be away the weekend of January thirtieth. Lily made a face: She reminded her there were several operations scheduled for Monday morning, which meant arrivals on Sunday. Pauline promised she'd be back as early as possible on that Monday and that she'd be replaced by her friend and neighbor Doctor Merrill. She'd give him a call this evening. Lily grumbled, she had a couple of outings planned with her husband and kids. Wasn't this kind of last-minute?

"Is Billie-Pearl hosting a memory-lane party, the kind where you listen to Carole King and watch your old mustang slides?"

Then she glimpsed the turmoil on her mother's face and came around, placing a compassionate hand on her shoulder.

Pauline lowered her head. She was silent for a moment, then she said, "They're going to raze the Mapes. I just want to be there."

Lily didn't have to ask her mother why she was going. She hugged her close, said she understood.

SATURDAY, JANUARY 29, 2000

——≫≫≫·——

Mount Shasta, Siskiyou County, Northern California

Pauline reversed the Dodge Dakota out of the garage, taking care not to scratch the ancient blue Ford Thunderbird sleeping there, slipped her favorite CD—French singer Françoise Hardy—into the drive, and took off. The trip to Cold Springs, where Billie-Pearl's ranch was situated, would take over three hours, possibly more with traffic. Her friend was expecting her later in the day. Pauline hadn't been to Reno in a while. When was the last time? She couldn't remember. Probably to see her younger brother, who no longer lived in the Hammond family home on Washington Street that had been leveled months ago. Jim had done well in the real estate business and had moved to a pretty home in well-heeled Old Southwest Reno.

Each time she returned to Reno, she found herself entangled in a net of nostalgia and regret, dominated by memories of her mother, Marcelle. Her relationship with Lily's father remained ambiguous, even though forty years had gone by, Lily's age. She knew Kendall Spencer had not left Reno. His name still filled her with a sense of unease. For fifteen years he had sent a check with a Christmas card. Nothing much on the card except his signature and a few scrawled words she could hardly decipher. He hadn't seen Lily again either. And Lily had moved on a long while ago. The years had gone by and he was not part of their lives. He didn't even know his grandkids. *How was it going to feel if Kendall turned up?* she wondered. Uncomfortable. For her. And, no doubt, for him.

Pauline made her way carefully along the sinuous road as it curved down from Mount Shasta, but she knew the way by heart: down CA-89, then on to Feather Lake Highway until Route 395. Luckily, last week's snowfall had not affected travel. She kept thinking of Nick and what he had said to her that morning over breakfast. He had warned her about the full force of her feelings taking over when the hotel came tumbling down in front of her eyes. Even the passage of time wouldn't be able to obliterate what she had undergone there; the good and the bad, all the stuff she had told him, little by little, everything she had held back for so long. Nick was a newcomer in her life, but she trusted him more than most of her good friends. She had opened up to him, completely. She was in love. And it felt marvelous.

Two hours later, when Pauline reached Feather Lake Highway, more and more cars appeared. She had to slow down. She didn't mind; she enjoyed being on the road. Before she opened her equine clinic, she had spent countless hours behind the wheel, visiting her patients around the area. She lit a cigarette, turned on the radio, and concentrated on the road.

Pauline had not set foot in the Mapes Hotel after the fall of 1960. Everything had changed at that moment, and she'd left, not looking back. She remembered holding out her hand for the envelope, seeing her name written in the unmistakable slanted, irregular handwriting, and holding her breath. And the guy at the front desk (what was his name, Lincoln?) saying with a touch of awe, "She left this for you." His grin. Yes, you, Pauline, the maid. The cleaner. The girl with a mop and a pail, the one scrubbing toilets on the ground floor. That girl.

Every mile drew her closer to Reno, bordering on a past she couldn't forget or erase, a past that had shaped her into the woman she was today, as Nick had pointed out. He was right. Often, in her mind, she could see herself racing mustangs at full speed with Billie-Pearl, like they used to in their youth at Pyramid Lake, coated with sweat and dust, mouths parched, skin burned by the sun, limbs shattered by the exhilarating gallop. And, later, her mother's reproachful tone: Where had she been? What was that stench? Had she been horseback riding? With that girl from Wadsworth? Again? Was she crazy or what? Her mother had fought so hard to get them settled in Reno, to turn her into a decent young girl with a proper education. Had Pauline forgotten where she was from? Where she was born? The City of Light. Paris, France! Just because they'd landed smack in the middle of nowhere didn't mean that Pauline should allow herself to turn into a redneck American.

On Route 395, an hour or so away from Billie-Pearl's place, Pauline parked at a busy rest stop near Honey Lake for a cup of coffee and a bite to eat. The weather was dreary, with an icy wind blowing. Seated in the smoker's area, impervious to the din around her, Pauline observed her hands curled around the mug, reddened by cold and toil—a far fetch from anything ladylike. How often had her mother chided her about her hands? Hands she'd not protected from unflinching sun nor relentless labor with horses; hands with veins that showed, speckles, and short unvarnished nails. She did, however, wear a slim silver band on her left ring finger that had nothing to do with matrimony, but rather happened to be a recent present from Nick, and it never left her. Nice, slender fingers, though.

Sitting there, sipping her coffee, she realized she was still physically in California, the state she'd called home for the past forty years, where she had gone to college, raised her daughter, opened her clinic; in a few moments, though, she'd enter the Silver State, and she'd be back in Nevada.

Near Cold Springs came the signposts showing the way to Wild Pearl Ranch & Mustang Rescue and, when she spotted them, Pauline couldn't help her heart swelling with pride toward everything her childhood friend had accomplished. Leaving the town behind, she followed the steep, narrow road, climbing through undulating meadows sprinkled with fresh snow, going over a ravine dug into craggy rocks bordered by hills planted with thick pines, and ending up in a large green clearing. It was nearly five o'clock and the pale winter sun lit up the scenery with a final pink glow before dusk. Pauline halted for a minute by the open gates. Here, she felt the world belonged to Billie-Pearl: She could see the stables and paddocks nestling in the elbow of the hill to the right and, farther on, the ranch dominating the valley toward White Lake. The air she breathed in seemed pure and icy, colder than back home.

As she came nearer, in the fading light, she was able to distinguish the horses frolicking with the snow in the pen, one of them even rolling in the whitened grass. How she loved them, those fierce mustangs Billie-Pearl fought so hard to preserve—some of them descended from horses they had known when they were girls. She identified the lustrous dark coat belonging to Dansa, Commander's granddaughter, the black stallion who had made such an impact on her in her youth. Pauline didn't often have mustangs to treat in her Californian clinic, as her patient base consisted chiefly of quarter horses, well-honed for racing, equestrian events, or farm labor.

Puffs of gray smoke billowed from the ranch's bulky chimney, and Pauline knew her friend was waiting for her in that cozy place dear to her heart. She drove on, waving at two members of Billie-Pearl's crew bringing the horses in for the night. She didn't know them personally as she hadn't visited lately, but she was aware of how the mistress of the premises, year after year, was able to rally around her keen and united teams of young people propelled by the same drive: saving the mustangs.

Pauline parked the Dodge near the other cars, grabbed her travel bag, and went up the few steps to enter the house without knocking. The front door was never locked. Pinned proudly in the entry was a poster of a renowned Nevadan activist astride her horse, Hobo. Velma Johnston, nicknamed "Wild Horse Annie," passed away in 1977—Billie-Pearl had collaborated with her since the fifties in the fight to defend wild horses.

The large living room was in undeniable disarray, which neither surprised nor disappointed Pauline. Her friend might not be a domestic goddess, but she knew how to break in a mustang like no one else on earth. An unfinished jigsaw puzzle and some coloring books lay on the low table in front of the stone fireplace, and a couple of disheveled Barbies and toy cars were flung on the sofas, traces of Billie-Pearl's numerous grandchildren who often came to stay.

"There's my little Mademoiselle! Was your drive smooth?" sang Billie-Pearl, leaving the nearby kitchen. The enticing smell of vegetable soup and herb-roasted chicken wafted to Pauline's nostrils—probably recipes from one of Billie-Pearl's daughters-in-law.

At five feet nine inches, Pauline towered at least six inches over her friend, but she was amused at being dubbed "little." With her mop of curls and round freckled face, Billie-Pearl did not look her age. She was wearing her customary winter garb, a pair of 501 Levi's, a woolen sweater, and cowboy boots. Her summer attire varied little—a denim shirt replaced the sweater. Pauline had not seen her slip on a dress or a skirt since the sixties.

Billie-Pearl's eldest son came into the room, cradling his newborn. Pauline hadn't yet met this latest adorable addition to her friend's growing clan. The family meal that followed was a merry affair: fourteen of them crammed around the long table, joined by a few ranch staff members, and the thick log walls echoed with laughter, shouts, and jokes and, mostly, discussions about horses. This could go on for hours, Pauline knew, and she reveled in it: which mare got colic and the way the new vet did a great job healing her; that fiery-tempered yearling wreaking havoc in the barn; Dansa behaving exactly like her grandfather, the same pluck, the same panache; how Eagle looked uncannily like Dustin; and Nancy, Billie-Pearl's younger daughter, brilliantly breaking in a rebellious stallion.

———⟫———

Later, when everyone had retired for the night, the two friends nestled in front of the fire with mugs of herbal tea. Billie-Pearl sensed her friend's mixed feelings that going back to Reno had resurrected.

"We don't have to talk about the Mapes," said Billie-Pearl, at last.

Pauline reassured her: It was okay, they could talk about it; she couldn't quite believe it was coming down. For so long, the Mapes had represented Reno's glory days before its fame dwindled in the eighties, eclipsed by the spellbinding lure of Las Vegas.

"I want to picture the Mapes in its heyday, when the Sky Room at sunset was the place to be. Remember?"

"So it was!" exclaimed Billie-Pearl. "And that young bartender? He was so nice to us!"

He was called Dan, Pauline pointed out, and he sneaked them cocktails even though they weren't twenty-one. She also remembered how her fussy mother had been won over by the Sky Room's wine list because it boasted a Sauternes from France.

"Dan had a crush on you, Billie."

"Well, the elevator guy swooned over *you*, Mademoiselle."

They both chortled.

Then Billie-Pearl said carefully, "You know Kendall could be there tomorrow, right?"

Oh, yes, Pauline was well aware Kendall Spencer could be there. She was ready, bracing herself to see him. It had been forty years, and she still felt like slapping him, she said.

"Cheers," said Billie-Pearl. "But I know you won't."

"I won't. And besides, the Mapes isn't just about the awful carpet in Mr. Spencer's office. Other, more beautiful things come to mind. Like Suite 614."

"Indeed. The memorable Suite 614..."

"Hey," said Billie-Pearl, interrupting her brief reverie, "do you still have that blue Ford?"

Pauline grinned.

"The Thunderbird? The apple of my eye."

SUNDAY, JANUARY 30, 2000

—⫸—

Cold Springs, Washoe County, Nevada

She got up early to see the horses before the drive to Reno. As daylight broke, Billie-Pearl, her Stetson pulled down to her eyes, was already busy astride Dansa in one of the corrals. The frost didn't seem to bother her. She waved to her friend. Next time, she yelled, they'd go for a ride up in the hills, and Pauline could mount Arrow, or Sweetbriar, but this morning, there wasn't enough time: They couldn't miss the implosion of the Mapes, scheduled for eight o'clock sharp.

In this sanctuary, the horses seemed content. Here, Pauline knew, they were taken in, cared for, gently broken in and then sold, but to owners handpicked by Billie-Pearl, who followed the matter closely. There were still people in 2000, fumed Billie-Pearl, who went on hunting mustangs despite the laws to protect them, who frightened them, caught them, and penned them in horrific circumstances.

In another paddock, a little farther off, a young man was breaking in a beleaguered, bucking yearling; Billie-Pearl watched him from the corner of her eye.

"Easy does it!" she shouted. "You're asking too much of him."

She rode over to Pauline and dismounted nimbly.

"Come on! Have a go on Dansa. We can make it if it's quick."

No matter how much Pauline tried to tell her that her horseback-riding days were over, that she had passed that age, that her job was curing horses, not riding them, that she probably had forgotten how, Billie-Pearl wouldn't listen. Pauline placed her palm on Dansa's neck and gazed into the glow of those lovely, gentle eyes; she dithered still, then took the plunge, encouraged by her friend, sliding her left foot into the stirrup and landing in the saddle.

"There you go, Mademoiselle!"

Compliant, the mare showed no resistance; she probably knew she was dealing with an antique, joked Pauline to her friend, who rolled her eyes.

Dansa headed slowly forward, following her rider's halfhearted instructions to the letter; and how bored she no doubt was, thought Pauline sheepishly, feeling the warmth of the powerful shape moving beneath her. This was Commander's granddaughter, after all!

They ambled along, swathed in elegant placidity, as if they were on their way for a cup of tea with other staid ladies, and it was Billie-Pearl who startled them, atop a silver yearling, barging in straight ahead on the other side of fence, like a bat out of hell. With a bloodcurdling whoop, waving her Stetson about, just like she did when they were girls, she signaled to the young man who opened the gate, letting Dansa and Pauline out, urging her horse up the earthen track. The mare shot off like a rocket with Pauline hanging on for dear life.

"Have you lost your mind?" yelped Pauline, panic-stricken, doing her best to keep up with the piston pump of those long dark legs, until she noticed the deep-rooted instincts kicking in despite herself: her back shifting to an upright position, head high, the supple motion of her hips accompanying Dansa's gallop. The fear fizzled away and sheer joy took over.

Billie-Pearl steered her horse at breakneck speed around the premises, Dansa and Pauline on her tail, while the entire team, overjoyed by their unforeseen cavalcade, cheered them on every step of the way. Dazed by the rush of it all, Pauline no longer took in the landscape, sky, or soil—only the mare's quivering ears and the yearling's bouncing hindquarters; she heard only her own gasps, Dansa's powerful breathing, and the other mustangs' neighs. The memories of Commander came soaring back—his verve, splendor, and flair—all the stuff that made him into the stallion still lingering in her dreams.

They came to a halt at last, short of breath, and bursting with laughter. Wheezing, Pauline no longer had the heart to scold her friend. How could she possibly resent her after this moment of shared bliss? Just like the old days.

"See? I was right. You haven't forgotten a thing," teased Billie-Pearl.

She considered her friend's red and shining face.

"Oh, and by the way, Dansa is not into funeral marches," she added, winking.

"I figured."

Billie-Pearl swiftly turned her horse around so Pauline could see his startling blue eyes.

Pauline exclaimed, "By golly, that's the yearling you mentioned last night. Dustin's grandson?"

"That's him all right; his name is Eagle. He is as amazing as his ancestor." As she listened to Billie-Pearl singing his praises, she couldn't help thinking back to the first time she laid eyes on Commander, Dustin, Hook, Tundra, and Rocket, the mustang herd that played such a large part in her young life.

"Goodness, have you seen the time? Got to get going!"

Billie-Pearl whistled using her fingers (Pauline longed to do it too, but had never learned how), and a young woman sprang forward to take over the horses. The two friends rushed into Billie-Pearl's Beetle; Reno was only twenty minutes away, and the Super Bowl match being broadcast live from Atlanta, pitting the St. Louis Rams against the Tennessee Titans, wasn't scheduled until three thirty local time. Route 395 took them right to the heart of the city, where they would then branch out toward downtown and Virginia Street.

On the way, Billie-Pearl teased Pauline about the new boyfriend, whom she knew nothing about. Pauline admitted that, yes, it was all rather recent, she didn't talk about it much, but Nick was already taking up quite a bit of room in her life. He was a bit younger, a landscape gardener, divorced, father to a twenty-year-old son, and living in Dunsmuir, fifteen minutes away from her place. Billie-Pearl wanted to know what he looked like. A tall, silent guy, with hazel eyes, lovely hands, and a great sense of humor, not very good in the saddle, that was true, but...

"Oh, I get the picture," chuckled Billie-Pearl.

"And what about you?" asked Pauline. "Are you still seeing that rancher you fancied? . . . Ah, that's already over?"

Billie-Pearl's love life was steeped in complications. Without interrupting, Pauline listened.

They soon reached the outskirts of Reno.

"I know what you're going to say, that you no longer recognize *your* Reno," said Billie-Pearl, pointing to the endless progression of high-rise buildings.

She was correct. The little town hosting ten thousand souls Pauline discovered as a child in the forties had been drastically transformed: It now seemed sprawling and crowded, swarming with cars. Roughly two hundred thousand people currently lived here, and a large number of the quaint clapboard houses, like the one belonging to Pauline's stepfather on Washington Street, had been razed and replaced with apartment blocks, office spaces, and malls. As far as Pauline was concerned, the Reno of 2000 had lost its erstwhile charm. Only the distant snowcapped mountains hadn't changed.

As they drew nearer to Virginia Street, Pauline already knew that when the Mapes crumbled, it would be those sixth-floor corner windows she'd be watching closely, especially the four facing southeast over the Truckee River.

How was it possible that a place could be blasted to smithereens and leave nothing but dust behind?

SUMMER 1960

—⟫⟫⟫—

Reno, Nevada

Pauline was running late, and the image of Mildred Jones's puckered-up mouth and horrid frown was already plaguing her. Mrs. Sheldon, the nice neighbor whose car she shared every morning from Washington Street to Virginia Street, had been late too, and that's how it all started. The Mapes Hotel was only a forty-minute walk away, but for Lily, barely three, that was an impossible feat. Sometimes, but not frequently, Pauline and Lily rode in with Marcelle. However, Marcelle's beauty parlor had later opening hours, which did not coincide with the beginning of Pauline's shift. For the trip home, at four o'clock, Pauline and Lily took the bus.

"Did you have a nice vacation, dear?" asked Mrs. Sheldon, who seemed to drive even more slowly than usual this morning, her chin glued to the wheel. She worked in a hosiery shop on Ryland Street.

"Yes, it was wonderful, thank you. We went to Lake Tahoe for two weeks and just got back last night. Lily loved it."

Mrs. Sheldon beamed down at the toddler sitting on Pauline's lap. Such a sweet little girl! Was Pauline still getting someone to watch her while she went on working at the Mapes? Pauline cleared her throat. Yes, Lily was looked after by a seamstress on Pickard Place. She had another child in her care. Pauline didn't add any other details and didn't point out that Lily's father had made this arrangement, and it was financed by him as well, but she was aware that Mrs. Sheldon knew who Lily's father was. Everyone in Reno seemed to know, to Marcelle Hammond's despair, and a child born out of wedlock to her then-eighteen-year-old daughter was still the bane of her life.

Lily was humming along to the catchy song on the radio, "Cathy's Clown" by the Everly Brothers. Pauline held her child close, kissing the top of her head, singing along with her. Lily had a sunny disposition, and even Marcelle had relented in the end, becoming a doting grandma despite herself.

"And how is your mom doing?" asked Mrs. Sheldon prudently. "I guess she enjoyed Lake Tahoe as well?"

If only Mrs. Sheldon could drive faster, thought Pauline with anguish. It was already nine. There was no way she was going to tell their neighbor her mother had spent most of the break moping around, complaining, and topping up her glass of bourbon, even if most folks close to them knew about Marcelle's drinking problem.

"She had a marvelous time," lied Pauline glibly.

"Marcelle must be tickled pink about Gable being in town! She idolizes him."

Pauline's forty-five-year-old mother still harbored teenage-like crushes on movie stars.

"She's hoping he'll come for a trim at *Marcelle ze Hair Stylist from Paris*," Pauline said with a heavy French accent and Mrs. Sheldon laughed along with her, but not unkindly.

Marcelle Hammond's beauty parlor had been situated on Winter Street ever since she opened it in 1948. It had been doing quite well, despite the founder's occasional hangovers. Many clients enjoyed the idea of having their hair done by a bona fide *Parisienne*.

"Clark Gable might visit the john for a last-minute tinkle!" added Pauline. "That way, I'll get to see him as well."

Mrs. Sheldon's double chin jiggled in delight. But when she glanced over at Pauline, there was pity in her eyes. Pauline couldn't stand being pitied. *Stand up for yourself, Mademoiselle,* Billie-Pearl always said. *Don't let them get the best of you.* Luckily, they had now reached Virginia Street Bridge. The conversation came to an end.

Once Lily was dropped off at Mrs. Abigail's, Pauline dashed to the Mapes and went in using the staff entrance in the back by East First Street. The hot summer sun was already pounding down mercilessly. She clocked in at the foyer, mumbling quick hellos to colleagues, praying her ten-minute tardiness would go unnoticed. No sign of Mildred Jones by the elevator where she usually lurked in the mornings, watching out for her "girls." She ruled over all the maids at the Mapes.

Pauline rushed to the ladies' changing room on the basement floor, where she wriggled out of her jeans and T-shirt to slip into the burgundy-colored uniform she loathed. It felt prickly and coarse on her skin, and she found its cut unflattering, with its loosely adjusted waistband and low hem making her seem taller and bonier than she really was, but the worst thing about it was the ridiculous frilly white apron. She tied her hair back, pinning it swiftly into place, and stepped into the black leather oxfords she also disliked. They made her feet look tremendously large.

A young woman came running in. She was late as well. It was Kitty, also a cleaner, a bit older, twenty-three, married, with two children, who had been working at the Mapes for longer than Pauline. She cleaned the higher floors. So now they were both in trouble, Kitty panted. As she donned her own navy blue uniform in haste, almost tearing it in the process, Kitty told Pauline about the thrilling events she had missed because of her vacation. Glamor had at last hit Reno—and the Mapes was where it was all happening. It was darn exciting, really. And to think Marilyn Monroe was under the same roof—good gracious, that was nuts. Well, she hadn't been seen yet; when she wasn't out shooting, she kept to her rooms with her crew, coach, masseur, secretary, hairdresser, makeup guy, wardrobe person, and whatnot. But Kitty had caught a good glimpse of Clark Gable: Holy smokes, what a handsome man, even at his age. And apparently the director, John Huston, was already spending time in the casino, coming in every evening. The night team over there was shocked at the amount of booze he knocked back. She also ran into Montgomery Clift briefly in the elevator, such a cutie! She hadn't seen Eli Wallach or Thelma Ritter, but they were less well-known actors.

As a result of all the pizzazz, Mildred Jones had turned into even more of a despot. Kitty imitated her pursed lips and wagging head, making her coworker giggle. Pauline had to be careful, keep an eye out for old Jones, but in a way, she was better off tucked away in the restrooms. No one was going to bother her there, certainly not old Mildred, too busy intimidating the cleaning ladies because Hollywood had come to the Mapes! A true nightmare. Pauline couldn't even possibly imagine. Already, Mildred was breathing down their necks the whole blessed day, chiding Pilar, Linda, and herself about the smallest details they already knew by heart: the welcome amenities, flower deliveries, turndown service, as if the Mapes had—lo and behold!—become the Beverly Hills Hotel. Then Kitty grinned as she pinched Pauline's cheek. "I'm forgetting you don't care a fig about movie stars. You only think about mustangs, right?"

Kitty wasn't far from the truth, but Pauline added that her daughter was the first thing on her mind. When they had time, she'd tell her about Lake Tahoe and how Lily spent all her time splashing about in the water. As soon as the photos were developed, she'd show them to Kitty.

In front of the staff elevator, they hastily said good-bye. From the basement, Kitty would be riding higher up, while Pauline returned to the main floor restrooms. Pauline still had to get to the maintenance closet to fetch mops and cleaning products.

Pauline noticed how busy the lobby was this morning, even more so than usual. With its Art Deco atmosphere, six square pillars cased in rosewood and luminaires, this was the Mapes's nerve center, and she loved taking it in. Here, guests arrived, sapped by their trip, mountains of luggage in tow, but there were also those checking out, waiting for taxis or to speak to the concierge, and those who were simply meeting up with someone. Because it remained the first place visitors saw, the lobby was crucial, as Pauline knew. Here, perfection was the rule.

No doubt the morning whirl had something to do with that movie being shot, thought Pauline. Reno had been abuzz with stories for the past weeks, and it was almost becoming tedious for those like her who weren't riveted by Hollywood. She picked out several people equipped with photography equipment and remembered her mother mentioning the shoot was to be covered by an internationally renowned photo agency. Would she ever catch a glimpse of the actors, like Kitty had? She didn't think so. She'd heard they were shooting on location during the day and didn't come back until late. At her level, she'd see no one.

Luckily, she didn't have to deal with the large aqua-green carpet in the lobby—that was Fern's job, and she was already diligently going at it. Pauline nodded to her and to Marty, one of the bellboys on duty today. Both winked back at her, as did Ernesto, the doorman. She walked by the front desk, making eye contact with Lincoln, who was dealing with a bossy lady. The restrooms were mercifully empty but already needed cleaning. Down on her knees, she scrubbed away at a soiled toilet bowl, the first one of the morning and definitely not the last.

How long was she going to be able to carry out this position, to put up with it? In the beginning, she had been assigned to clean on the higher floors with Linda, Pilar, and Kitty. She had started out with them in the rooms, just after Lily's birth. Kendall Spencer had kept his word: He had found her a job at the Mapes so as not to leave her and Lily in the lurch, and he had paid for a wetnurse so Pauline could clock in. Kendall was always promising bigger and better things, and she had trustingly believed him. That lasted for a year, but as the months slipped by, nothing bigger and better came along, and Pauline had been unable to find a higher paying, more interesting job. After all, she hadn't graduated from high school because she got pregnant in 1957. Who was going to hire a single mother with no qualifications?

Mildred Jones had banished her to the restrooms a year later.

No matter how much Kendall tried to tell her it wouldn't last, she no longer believed him. She had to face facts. Ever since they met at the Mapes back in 1956, she had fallen under his dark spell. And it seemed she was still stuck there. Coincidentally, Pauline's downgrading corresponded with the date of Kendall's glitzy wedding to his longtime fiancée, Evaline Steward, heiress to and member of one of Nevada's most prosperous lineages of ranchers and landowners, going back to the nineteenth century. She figured the new Mrs. Spencer had found out about Baby Lily and had been incensed. This was her retaliation. Meanwhile, Pauline suffered in silence, still living at the Hammond home, sleeping in the same room as her toddler. She couldn't afford to move out.

The clicking of heels pounding the tiled floor heralded Mildred Jones's arrival. Pauline barely had time to stand up before finding her already there, filling the place with her discontent. She expected to be given an earful about not being on time and inwardly braced herself. The admonishment usually lasted four or five minutes, not more. She just had to bear it. She knew how: summoning images of Commander. The black stallion gave her strength and resilience. Even with her eyes open, Pauline was able to break free from the present situation, imagining herself at his side, a hand on his massive neck. Sometimes Commander even took off, Pegasus-style, endowed with large wings, and she flew away with him to freedom and peace.

But this morning, it appeared Mildred wasn't acting like usual. She seemed flustered, her mouth twitching and, instead of telling Pauline off, she wrung her hands in silence. *There was no need to summon Commander's magic powers*, thought Pauline, surprised. Mildred made Pauline stand up straight by placing two hands on her shoulders, fussed with her apron, which was crooked, smoothed down her collar, and tucked in a loose strand of hair.

"There, that's better," Mildred said in a low voice, which was also unexpected.

She went on with the same odd whisper: Pauline had to leave the restrooms, now, and go straight up to the sixth floor. Her key pass gave her access to the sixth-floor housekeeping store-room. Pauline had to do this right away. She remembered how to clean the rooms, right? Mildred had taught her herself. It wasn't such a different protocol for the suites, just a longer one. Pauline was a good cleaner. All she had to do was tidy up one single suite in less than two hours, on her own. That meant the living room, dining room, kitchen, bedroom, and bathroom. Pauline had to get the job done on time and come back down to the main floor for the rest of the day.

Pauline tried not to look bewildered. Never had she seen Mildred in such a state.

"W-w-why me?" she finally asked, as the older woman led her to the elevators, making their way through the packed lobby. Pauline sometimes stuttered when she felt anxious.

Mildred tiptoed to speak in her ear, leaning in close, and Pauline caught an acrid whiff of her perspiration. "Because Pilar has broken her wrist! She won't be coming in for Lordy knows how long. Talk about disaster. I'll have to do some serious reschedul-ing. And you're my only solution for this morning."

They rode up silently in the elevator, Pauline avoiding the lift-boy's ardent gaze. Young Casper had a crush on her.

When they got to the sixth floor, Mildred stepped out with her and handed her a set of keys.

"Suite 614. They're out for the day. It's up to you, Pauline. Get to work."

Mildred left her standing on the honey-colored carpet in the middle of the long corridor. Here, everything was quiet—a stark contrast with the hubbub in the lobby. Only the faint hum of the air-conditioning could be heard. She let herself in to the maintenance storage room to fetch Pilar's cleaning cart. She felt sorry for Pilar. Breaking a wrist, what bad luck!

Pauline had not yet been in a prestigious corner suite at the Mapes. When she used to clean rooms in the beginning, she was given the standard ones: smaller, simpler, and more numerous. The instructions were the same, however, and she reviewed them mentally as she made sure the cart was properly stocked for the work to be done.

The first step was to air the room, opening the windows wide even during a heat wave or a snowstorm. Then, stripping or making the bed. Placing dirty linen in the laundry bin by the house-keeping cart. Removing all trash, emptying ashtrays, fitting in new bin liners. Replacing used glasses and cups. Checking items taken from the minibar. Dusting each and every surface. Vacuuming carpets, upholstery, curtains, and furniture. Cleaning and wiping them down as well. In the bathroom, removing used towels and mats and placing them in laundry bags. Tidying guests' belongings carefully. Cleaning the bath and shower area. (Mildred was obsessed with hairs. Her "girls" had to hunt down all the "short and curlies.") Cleaning the sink and faucets, cleaning the toilet (no mystery for Pauline). Wiping down the towel rail. Restocking soap, shampoo, and toilet paper. Hanging clean towels. Sweeping the floor, vacuuming it, then using the mop. Closing the windows and shutting the door behind her as she left.

Diving into the private lives of perfect strangers still held a strange appeal. When she used to tidy up rooms, she had often let her imagination run wild. Most of the time, there was nothing romantic about it all. She had quickly discovered, gagging, that sheets were able to give away far too much information about afternoon trysts (condom wrapper residues, or sometimes, worse still, the used condom itself), honeymoons (a bevy of stains), sleepless nights (cigarette ash, splatters of liquor), breakfast in bed (crumbs, coffee spills), nocturnal mishaps (leakages, wet dreams, benders, stomach bugs, menstrual flow). Pauline also scrutinized—how could she not?—beauty products used by guests: their perfume and makeup as well as their clothes, which she put away in the closet or folded with care.

She promptly knocked three times on the double doors of Suite 614, the way Mildred had taught her.

"Housekeeping!"

One had to check if guests were still inside, she had learned the hard way. Once, without taking that precaution, she had walked in on a couple in the throes of making love.

Pauline couldn't hear a sound behind the panel. She knocked again. Still no response or noise. Mildred had specified the suite was vacant, so Pauline used the set of keys her boss had given her and entered with the cart, which she set aside in the vestibule.

The wallpaper was pale beige, with a discreet fern print, and the thick carpeting was of a similar hue. While she moved forward through adjoining rooms plunged in semidarkness—the curtains were still drawn—she realized, dismayed, the place was one heck of a mess: glasses here and there, empty bottles littering the carpet, brimming ashtrays, plates still laden with bits of food, and clothes strewn on chairs and on the floor.

Two sea-green sofas faced each other, lined with pastel-colored cushions. There was a glass coffee table, which wasn't going to be easy to clean, she thought; a drooping bouquet of white roses standing on it needed to be changed. The dining area was just beyond, leading into the kitchen.

A heavy smell lingered here, a blend of pipe tobacco and feminine perfume. It wasn't unpleasant, but she remembered the instructions to ventilate and so opened the drapes and windows. The view from here was magnificent: all of Reno at her feet, with the Truckee River snaking away like a blue ribbon as far as the eye could see.

She decided to tackle the living room, dining room, and kitchen first, finishing with the bedroom and bathroom. Indeed, the suite was a lot larger than the smaller rooms she had been used to—and to think she only had two hours to do all of them! How was she going to get it done on time?

She quickly cleared up dishes and glasses, washed, rinsed, and dried them, and put them away. She emptied the ashtrays, disposed of the dead bottles, folded the clothes (women's dresses, blouses, and pants) and put them aside, meaning to place them later in the bedroom wardrobe. At the foot of the turntable, she found a jumble of unprotected vinyl records. She sorted out the proper sleeves and filed them, noticing albums by Elvis Presley, Frank Sinatra, Ella Fitzgerald. With the feather duster and rags, she went on with her task, fully focused on what she was doing. She was going to meet the deadline. Mildred would be pleased, for once. From time to time, she heard the phone ringing. She knew not to answer. If Mildred wanted a word, she'd come up.

She then plugged in the vacuum cleaner, an older model she didn't like. It was heavy and loud, and she had to push it with all her might to get it to slide under the furniture. She was in the middle of wondering how poor Pilar was going to manage with her broken wrist when she understood she was no longer alone.

A stark-naked woman with short, tangled hair was standing in front of her. Pauline let out a yelp of shock and leaped to turn off the screech of the vacuum cleaner. She stammered, saying she was sorry, she had no idea someone else was here. She must have woken the guest. She wasn't used to dealing with suites and had not thought to check the bedroom first. Mildred hadn't instructed her to do so.

"That's okay," the lady mumbled, rubbing her eyes. She seemed out of it and could hardly stand.

Pauline panicked. Her face reddened. She didn't know what to do. Should she get out of here, give up cleaning the rooms? Or should she get on with the vacuuming and the rest? Meanwhile, she was wasting time. She could already imagine Mildred's wrath.

"Hey," came the soft whispery voice. "I'd like a Bloody Mary."

"Certainly, ma'am," Pauline said.

Shoot—what was the number for room service? This guest was going to think she was the dumbest maid ever. She suddenly had an idea. As the naked lady wandered over to the bathroom, still in a sort of trance, Pauline let herself out of the suite and called the elevator. Before the smitten Casper had time to say anything, she pleaded for help.

"Coming right up!" sang Casper. "A Bloody Mary for Suite 614."

The woman was now lying on the sofa in the living room, still nude. Pauline had rarely been more embarrassed in her life. She had a closer look at her. Had she ever seen such white skin? It was like thick cream, almost luminous. Her hair, however, was in a pitiful state, and Pauline wondered what her mother would have to say about those short, dry strands, hanging there like wisps of hay.

She lay there, resting her head in her palm, staring out to nowhere. At one point, she looked up at Pauline. The whites of her eyes were bloodshot, and there were mascara stains leaking down her cheeks. Her body was plump, with heavy pendulous breasts.

"Sh-sh-shall I go on cleaning, ma'am?"

The woman made a little gesture with her hand as if to say go on. Pauline went into the bedroom. It was pitch-black and stifling. The air-conditioning had been turned off and occulting blinds fitted over the windows. She was trying to peel them off when the doorbell rang. She rushed to open it: Pedro, one of the guys from room service, stood there with the Bloody Mary.

"Hey, Frenchie!" he said, sotto voce. "What are you doing on the sixth floor? Must be a change from the johns," he added, stepping into the entrance.

Pauline suddenly remembered the woman hadn't a stitch of clothing on. She strode in front of Pedro, plucking the glass off his tray, and thanked him, specifying she'd take it to the guest herself.

"Okeydokey," he said, letting her. "Tell *Mrs. Miller* to have a nice day."

The way Pedro said "Mrs. Miller" made Pauline curious. She stared at him and in exchange, he gave her an exaggerated wink as he left. *What on earth did he mean?* she thought. Was he hinting at the fact that Mrs. Miller pranced around in the nude each morning? Was she an attention seeker? Or worse? She felt her cheeks flare up again. Well, she was going to put her foot down. She wasn't having any of this.

When Pauline went back into the living room, the woman was on the phone, twisting the cord around her finger.

"I'm not ready," she was saying in a childlike voice. "I just woke up. Don't come now, Paula. Give me more time."

Pauline set the Bloody Mary on the low table, wondering who "Paula" was, trying to drag her eyes away from the pubic fuzz that appeared to have been bleached the same yellow color as her hair.

The woman hung up and reached out for the drink. She had lovely slender hands, Pauline noticed.

"Thanks," said the guest. She also had an appealing smile: perfect little teeth. It was the inflamed red eyes, shriveled hair, and exceedingly white skin that made her seem unwell. Perhaps she was doing poorly, after all.

Pauline took a deep breath.

"P-p-please, Mrs. M-Miller...Would you mind..."

"Yes, honey?"

Pauline was even more unsettled by the "honey," pronounced in the nicest possible way, as if she and Mrs. Miller were friends.

"...just putting on your bathrobe, please. I-I can get it for you."

Mrs. Miller stared back at her. The seconds ticked by. Pauline felt she was inwardly shrinking. She was aghast. What had she done? She had asked a guest to get dressed. This was the end. She was going to be fired. Fired from the Mapes Hotel. It was over. She could see herself crawling back to Washington Street, head hanging in shame. How would she ever get another job?

Blankly, Mrs. Miller looked down at herself, then back at Pauline. It seemed like she hadn't realized she wasn't wearing anything.

"Oh," she said. "Of course. Could you bring it to me?"

Relieved, Pauline went to fetch the robe from the bathroom. She helped Mrs. Miller into it.

"Thank you, Mrs. M-Miller."

The woman smiled at her again.

"You have a little stutter, don't you? I get one too. Started when I was a kid."

Plainly, the conversation was taking a personal turn Pauline could not have anticipated. Never had she brought up her stutter in front of anyone, let alone one of the guests. "Yes, it began when I was small," she admitted.

"How old are you?"

"I'm twenty-one, ma'am."

"So young, still. And it happens when you get emotional or nervous, right?"

True empathy rang out through that faint tiny voice, and it felt heartwarming to Pauline.

"Yes, ma'am."

"You don't have to worry if it happens with me. You know, I stammer, even at my age. It's a nuisance, at times."

Pauline had no clue what age Mrs. Miller could be. In her thirties, most likely? But her features were blurred with fatigue; perhaps she was older.

"Pardon me, but I need to go on cleaning your room," said Pauline, checking the time. "I haven't finished."

The telephone began to ring yet again, and Mrs. Miller answered it with listlessness. Pauline went back to work. In broad daylight, the room appeared to be in complete disarray, more garments lying around but, strangely enough, no underclothes; goblets smeared with lipstick; dozens of empty mini bottles of Piper-Heidsieck Champagne; magazines; newspapers; and a cemetery of pumps from an Italian brand and slingbacks stretching all the way under the bed. A large vanity table faced the window, its surface cluttered entirely with makeup products. Cleaning all this was going to be no picnic.

The room was spacious, boasting a king-size bed, a jade satin headboard, and pale green curtains. A big TV on its stand was rolled into a corner. Intrigued, Pauline also spotted some men's clothing—three wrinkled shirts, a pair of socks, some chinos. On the lefthand bedside table, she discovered a large stack of medications, a sleeping mask, and a moisturizing cream; on the righthand one, which was neater, she found a pile of books, a pen, a pipe, an ashtray, and a pair of horn-rimmed glasses. So a Mr. Miller was indeed in the vicinity.

Pauline had been faced with "a total shambles," the term her colleagues used, before, and she knew a mess meant twice the slog, but this particular one took top prize. The sheets were dirty. (Did those stains come from food? From blood? She didn't want to know.) Whatever it was, they needed to be changed. *Snap to it.* She could almost hear Mildred bossing her around.

As she toiled away, Mrs. Miller's voice came floating to her, echoing with the sweet tinkle of her childlike laughter. While she repositioned the numerous pill bottles—Benzedrine, Dexamyl, Seconal, Nembutal—all prescribed to Mrs. Miller, Pauline realized she had never seen so many. She wondered what illness Mrs. Miller suffered from. Then she corrected herself. It wasn't her business.

Once Pauline finished cleaning the room, she was faced with the disagreeable sensation of sweat trickling down her back. It was boiling. She closed the windows and switched on the air-conditioning. Now, she only had the bathroom to do. Yes, she was going to make it on time. She'd quench her thirst discreetly at the washbasin tap.

"What's your name?"

The soft tones startled Pauline as she was scrubbing the bath-tub clean.

Mrs. Miller was leaning against the doorframe, watching her. Her expression seemed a little livelier, her eyes less red.

"Pauline, ma'am."

"Pretty name. Are you from around here?"

"I live in Reno, but I was born in France. In Paris."

"In Paris?" repeated Mrs. Miller, feverishly clasping her slender hands to her collarbone.

And her whole face lit up, as if Pauline had pronounced a magic word.

1946

—≫≫≫—

Paris, France

"Pauline! *Pauline?* I want you to meet someone!"

Her mother was using her special voice, that slightly lower, throatier one she turned on, Pauline knew, when she wanted to make a good impression.

The sturdy man standing in the living room had on a distinctive olive-brown uniform: field jacket, wool trousers, tan leather boots, and rescue belt. Even at only seven years old, Pauline was aware he was one of those American GIs often seen in Paris since the liberation. The second thing she noticed was his smile. It was one of the kindest, nicest she had ever seen. He had light blue eyes that gazed right into hers.

He reached out his hand to her and said her name. He pronounced it "Pauly."

"This is Doug Hammond," said her mother, her voice quavering.

There was a silence, but to the child, it didn't appear awkward;

44

Doug Hammond seemed to fill up the space with his quiet, reassuring presence.

He barely spoke French; Marcelle Bazelet's English was terrible, but to Pauline's amusement, they were still able to keep up a conversation in both languages, using their hands and mimicry, and punctuating nearly every sentence with a burst of laughter.

Pauline had no memories of her father, Jacques, who died when she was a baby. His features only had any sort of familiarity to her because his framed portrait sat on the mantelpiece: a young mustachioed man with an angular, solemn face. He had succumbed to liver cancer when he was barely twenty-eight years old. Her mother had been widowed at twenty-five. Pauline wasn't used to seeing men in their home, apart from her uncles or cousins. There had been the rare, occasional male visitor for her mother, but none she had been formally introduced to, like today. This man was different from all the others; he appeared at ease with himself, with the world. He sat there, quite naturally, cigarette hanging from his lip. He winked at "Pauly" from time to time. She rather liked it. And the way he gazed at her mother was also new to Pauline. Marcelle, with her tiny waist and her dimples, had always drawn admiring glances from men but this young American seemed besotted. He couldn't take his eyes off her.

That evening, her mother was wearing a new turquoise draped dress with a cinched waistband that revealed her slim figure. Marcelle was so dainty and elegant, with coordinated shoes and purse, and, of course, her dark brown hair done up in a flawless coil atop her head—but that was her job, after all. She ran a successful hair salon on rue Bréa, a couple of minutes away from their apartment on Square Delambre in the heart of Montparnasse.

One of her mother's friends, Brigitte, turned up with more Champagne. There were so many reasons to rejoice since the war was over. Paris had turned into one big, boisterous party that didn't seem likely to end anytime soon. Brigitte spoke a smattering of English, which helped. She was able to translate Doug's sentences. He was from Nevada, she told Pauline, who had never heard a name quite like that. *Ne-va-da*, she repeated. Where was *Ne-va-da*? And what did the word *Nevada* mean? Pauline asked Brigitte, who in turn, asked Doug. It meant "covered in snow" in Spanish, she learned, because those high mountains were white all year long.

Doug asked for a piece of paper and a pencil, and he drew a map for the little girl. There was France, which seemed to her so small, and on the other side of the ocean, there was vast America. On the very left of that enormous country, Doug swiftly sketched a long, lopsided diamond shape with a pointy base. This was Nevada, he said, and then he penciled in a black dot toward the top left of the outline.

"And this is Reno."

He wrote those four letters in block capitals, and Pauline, who knew how to read, was able to make them out.

She later understood that her mother and Doug had met a month or so earlier, at a street fair at the Place d'Alésia. Brigitte had been there, and a couple of other girlfriends. Doug was with buddies from his regiment. What Pauline didn't know was that her mother and Doug had been seeing each other regularly since then.

Pauline led the quiet life of a happy little girl born just before the war started and who was so relieved it was, at last, over, like most children caught up in the grown-ups' elation. She did not have precise memories of the conflict, as she was barely born when it all began, but she did remember sirens howling like enraged wolves and having to go down into the cellar in the middle of night. She remembered food rationing, queuing for ages in front of the baker's and the butcher's, and the anxious expression on her mother's face when she listened to the news. The word "German" made Pauline quake, but she did not quite know why. The "Germans" were France's worst enemy, that's all she understood. It was over now. France had won. The Allies had won.

Pauline went to school on the rue Delambre, where she was a good pupil, with her best friends Chantal and Marie-Charlotte. After class, one of her mother's trainees came to pick her up to take her to the salon on rue Bréa where she'd stay and do her homework until Marcelle closed up. She was too small to tackle the tricky traffic lights of the rue Vavin intersection by herself.

Pauline loved spending time in her mother's salon, where all the beaming ladies welcomed her as she walked in with her *pain au chocolat* in her hand. Some of them were having their hair set, sitting under a helmet dryer; others were in the middle of a dye, a rinse, or a manicure, and Marcelle reigned over all with her customary poise and style. Wasn't she blessed, having such a pretty mother, the ladies cooed. When she grew up, she'd be just as lovely, they said, just as elegant as Marcelle. Her mother would coo as well and stroke the top of Pauline's head.

"I just pray she won't be too tall," she always said. "Her poor papa was six foot five, like General de Gaulle!"

The ladies twittered: Oh, Lord—that was far too tall! Oh, no, Pauline shouldn't grow that much, should she?

As a result, Pauline became anguished at the idea of turning into a gawky beanpole, the opposite of her swanlike mother. She was already a head taller than her friends Marie-Charlotte and Chantal, and she began to stoop, sticking her chin to her chest and bringing up her shoulders.

Doug Hammond spent more and more time at Square Delambre, often having dinner with them, arriving with flowers, chocolates, and small presents for "Pauly." He was gentle, kind, and witty and, though perhaps not handsome in the classical sense of the word, he definitely had charisma. Everyone in the building was aware that Madame Bazelet, the young widow, was dating a GI from America. And everyone approved. After all, that exquisite little lady who slaved away in her shop, diligently raising her daughter, deserved to enjoy herself. How plucky she was! And pretty as a picture, on top of it.

Doug did his best to speak French, resorting to a bilingual dictionary. His accent was comical, making Marcelle and Pauline roar with laughter, but he kept at it, undaunted.

Between her mother and Doug, it appeared to be the real deal. And on Marcelle's thirty-first birthday, Pauline at last understood how serious things were when her misty-eyed mother revealed an engagement ring. Marcelle was to become Mrs. Doug Hammond.

—≫≫·—

Pauline hadn't quite grasped to just what extent her life as well as her mother's were going to be turned upside down. She thought they'd go on living on Square Delambre in the humble flat that looked out onto a shaded courtyard and that Doug would move in with them. She thought she'd go on attending class each morning with her friends at the rue Delambre school, that she'd see her grandparents and cousins at Talloires, at the family chalet by Lake Annecy, during the holidays.

Ne-va-da. The name echoed, again and again. They were going to live with Doug in Nevada. The three syllables reverberated within her in a combination of excitement and anguish: They were going to leave Paris, the school, the hair salon, their home, their friends, their family; they were going to leave everything behind. It was from that moment on that Pauline developed a slight stutter, which went unnoticed in the beginning and became increasingly pronounced when she felt nervous or confused.

Never had Pauline seen her mother happier than on her wedding day at the fourteenth arrondissement town hall. Dressed in a crushed raspberry–pink ensemble that enhanced her porcelain complexion, Marcelle looked radiant. Doug, all smiles, was wearing a dark suit and a tie.

The grandiose place resembled a castle, and Pauline was impressed by the marriage room's coffered ceiling decorated with frescoes. But later on, after the merry get-together held in the apartment on Square Delambre, she thought back to the conversation she overheard in spite of herself between her aunt (Marcelle's sister) and her grandmother.

Her Aunt Irène was making a face, saying, "I certainly hope she knows what she's doing, poor thing."

Pauline's granny had nodded.

"Marcelle deserves to be happy. The American looks like a nice man, though."

Irène had frowned. She had spoken in a whisper, but Pauline could still hear what she said: a preposterous idea, running away to the other side of the planet with some fellow she barely knew and with whom she couldn't even speak the language.

Irène went on dryly, "Marcelle told me he went down on bended knee and gave her that ring on the Champs-Élysées, and everyone clapped and cheered. But how do they even communicate, seriously? I guess it all happens between the sheets. You get my gist. It will never last."

"Shush, the little one is listening."

Was her mother making a terrible mistake? fretted Pauline. What did her aunt mean by "between the sheets"? She felt chills. Whenever she proudly announced to her friends, her teachers, her neighbors that she was soon moving to America, explaining her stepdad came from *Ne-va-da,* no one seemed overly enthusiastic. She was even told with guffaws she could have done without: They were going to end up in the Far West with cowboys and Indians. Not quite Marcelle's cup of tea.

And then there was that astonishing moment at the beauty parlor when nosy Madame Berthier said Reno was known for being the Divorce Capital of the World. Everyone rushed there for a quick divorce, she announced with a sneer. That didn't bode well for a young bride, did it? And what about those casinos, nightclubs, hookers, and strippers? Wasn't Marcelle worried her daughter might be exposed to gangs of partygoers and scoundrels?

Pauline listened, fascinated, pen hovering over her writing practice book. *What was a hooker, or a stripper?* she wondered. Her mother's cheeks flushed red, and her dark eyes turned fiery.

When Marcelle looked that way it spelled trouble, as Madame Berthier was shortly going to find out. Her mother, still wielding a comb, came to stand over Madame Berthier, whose head lay in the neck rest of the shampoo bowl. How dare she? Her Doug was a good man, an honest man, a valiant soldier who had fought to end the war. He was a Reno car mechanic, for God's sake, he had nothing to do with any seedy underbelly. He came from a good, down-to-earth family, all hardworking people with values. Marcelle kept going, seriously worked up now, and Pauline secretly enjoyed watching Madame Berthier squirm. Did Madame Berthier really think Marcelle had been bamboozled by some big-time gambler, some cheap pimp who was going to play away her meager fortune while the mob got their hooks into Pauline? All the ladies in the salon gasped and Madame Berthier cringed, mumbled she was sorry, she had gone too far, she had repeated some hearsay, that was all.

Marcelle stood in the middle of the boutique, still clutching her comb as if it were a sword, raising it to the ceiling, and said in a thunderous, almost threatening tone, that she had never been happier than now, after all she'd gone through, losing her Jacques the same year their baby was born, and the war and its colossal burden, and now she had so much to look forward to, so much excitement in her life. She was headed for a new land of opportunity, where everything was possible. And she had faith in tomorrow.

Her mother's voice became quieter now, Pauline noticed, and she stopped pointing with the comb. Yes, she was still young and she could have hope—at last—in her own future. Doug had described his homeland in such a genuine manner she felt she had already been there; he'd looked up each and every word in the dictionary to portray his corner of Nevada to her: the wild beauty of it, the nature, the mountains, and the house on Washington Street in Reno as well his kindhearted parents who couldn't wait to meet Marcelle and Pauline.

Pauline noticed some of the ladies shedding a tear. Could it be possible her mother was overdoing it, as she sometimes did?

In the weeks that ensued, the little girl often had the impression Marcelle was walking on air. Doug had left France with his regiment and was back in Nevada where he eagerly awaited his new bride and her daughter, preparing for their arrival. Marcelle told her friends and clients how brides' trips to join their husbands were entirely financed by the American government and the Red Cross. It was meticulously prepared, she kept on saying. Terrific.

Pauline didn't think it was in the least terrific. She was losing her bearings and didn't know who to confide in. Her mother had given her the smallest of suitcases, telling her they'd buy new things once they got there. Meanwhile, the apartment grew emptier each day, its furniture sold or given away, and Pauline, who had never known another home, couldn't help being disturbed by the stripped walls and floors.

—⫸—

The day of their departure finally arrived. They said their good-byes. Marcelle exuded such energy, such determination, that their entourage had chosen to smile along with her, to banish any despondency and misgivings. Pauline did her best to live up to it as well. Her mother wouldn't want a crybaby by her side.

Her cousin had given her a key ring adorned with a tiny Eiffel Tower, which she clasped in her pocket with all her might.

It was raining when they got to Saint-Lazare Station to board the Le Havre train. Marcelle had not been able to bear leaving her precious turbans and hats behind; never mind, she would take a cumbersome hatbox along. She had also packed her finest garments; her friends had gently teased her: Would she need all that regalia for cowboys?

What a commotion! Pauline was aware the trip was a long one, even if she hadn't quite fathomed just how it would unfold. Marcelle had warned her: She would have to be patient. Pauline had so many questions: If she didn't speak any English, how was she going to be able to attend school over there? Would she make new friends? Would she see her family again, and Marie-Charlotte and Chantal? Her mother always said yes, but was unable to comfort her.

Once they were sitting in the train, after watching family and friends disappear from sight at the end of the platform, Pauline realized they were surrounded by women. The only man around was the controller. Most of the women were young, French, and newly wedded to a GI. Some were pregnant, a few others carried babies in their arms, but there were no children Pauline's age.

As usual, her mother made herself noticed, but in an enchanting manner. Marcelle wanted to know the names of all the women in their compartment, where their husbands were from and where they were headed. The passengers were delighted to share their stories. Pauline was astounded at how loud their nattering became; she almost felt like covering her ears with her hands. Instead, she stared out the window at the drizzling Normandy countryside, holding her tiny Eiffel Tower so tightly it pricked her fingers.

The train ride felt fleeting to Pauline, only a couple of hours. When they arrived at Le Havre, all the war brides (that's what women like her mother were called, she learned) were greeted by a band of musicians playing a wedding march. All the women were smiling. So she smiled too. Then they had to file outside, two by two in school-like fashion, to a flock of waiting buses.

Were they going to take the boat to America now? she asked her mother.

No, no, they were going to a transit camp first.

On the way, Pauline spotted several bombed villages, charred ruins lying open to the rain. She hadn't seen anything like it. But the other women seemed not to notice; they were too busy chatting. Then, she saw the signs to the camp as the bus wheezed to reach the top of a hill: CAMP PHILIP MORRIS. LE HAVRE. PORT OF EMBARKATION.

The rain was still falling when they left the bus, and Pauline felt worn-out and famished. Her mother's countenance was upbeat, full of momentum, and it remained that way even when they were shown into one of the many wooden barracks clustered on the hilltop. Theirs was barracks number 12, and they had to share it with at least twenty other ladies. However, this still did not dampen her mother's high spirits, nor the other women's. Two passengers who had been in their train compartment, Valérie and Anne-Laure, were here with them. They remained at Camp Philip Morris for three long days.

But why weren't they sailing to New York? complained Pauline. Why were they stuck in this place?

Because of all the paperwork, explained her mother. It took time to study each case.

One morning, though, she understood they were at last to be on their way. The boat was to sail at noon, and excitement overtook her. Several hundred women were expected to board the SS *Santa Paula*, an American cargo ship specifically chartered to transfer war brides to New York City.

Crowds had gathered along the docks to wave good-bye to all the brides; photographers captured the scene while the ship's foghorn bellowed. As Marcelle and Pauline moved forward in line, loud voices could be heard: a group of scornful old men waving their pipes at them. Did these ladies really think they were going to live the high life in America? They'd soon be back home with their tails between their legs. It was not going to work out. Serves them right for becoming infatuated with Yankees!

"Don't listen to them," said Marcelle to her daughter, firmly.

"Old farts!" railed Valérie.

Pauline became riddled with doubt. What if those old fogies spoke the truth? What if all those hasty marriages were doomed to fail? But she had little time to get into a state about it. She had finally located a child her age on board. With Eric, she wandered through the ship from top to bottom, passing through the kitchens, nurseries, a reading room, being scolded by the staff as they did so, eluding their mothers' supervision. None of the crew spoke any French; nevertheless the children rapidly understood the meaning of "*Non!*"

Pauline and Marcelle shared a cabin with eight other women, including Valérie and Anne-Laure. As always, Marcelle governed this small group with her innate leadership, and she got on their good side with her beauty tips and hairdo ideas. Early in the morning, Red Cross teams and American government delegates knocked on each door to see if all was well and check on how the paperwork was progressing. Marcelle had taken Pauline only once to a conference about French wives adapting to their new country, which evoked American culture, but it was solely in English. Marcelle hadn't stuck around long. They also had to be vaccinated, with all the others. Against what? Serious diseases, they were told.

One of the waiters kept slices of cake and cheese for Pauline every time she went by the kitchen or restaurant. He was a tall man with dark skin. His name was River, and he made her feel like she was an important person. It was the way he saluted her, putting his hand to his temple, clicking his heels neatly, and uttering, "Miss Pauline!" with a show of respect. She managed to explain to him she was on her way to Nevada, and he, in return, was able to make her understand he was from Mississippi, another name she found captivating. River unearthed a small map of America for her and read out the names of all the states to her.

In the evenings, the war brides enjoyed movies and orchestra concerts, but Pauline was too small to attend. She had to remain in the nursery with the infants, and Eric was stuck there as well, so they were soon up to their usual mischief, pretending to be sound asleep when the nannies went nearby for a cup of cocoa, then sneaking out in their pajamas, up the stairs, hiding behind tables to spy on their mothers dancing.

"You mom is the prettiest one," said Eric, as they watched Marcelle twirl by in her sophisticated dress.

"I know," said Pauline with pride.

The day before they were to reach the port of New York, the weather suddenly changed and became stormy; the ship dipped and rolled in choppy waters, causing many passengers to be seasick. In their cabin, Marcelle heroically passed around a basin while Valérie and Anne-Laure threw up, moaning as they did so. But there was worse in store for Anne-Laure and Valérie, as they were soon to discover. They had been told their spouses were coming to New York to pick them up and take them to their new homes, but no husband ever turned up for either one. Pauline was heartbroken for them. Apparently, there were several other abandoned brides. Marcelle was just as distraught. *Was she worried because this might happen to her?* thought Pauline, feeling sheer dread.

She glimpsed the Statue of Liberty from afar in a daze. New York was the noisiest, busiest place she had ever seen, crammed full of cars, taxis, and people. They were all taken downtown to a special center for women. The next day, Red Cross staff were going to accompany Marcelle and Pauline to the train station. Before she finally fell asleep that night, Pauline couldn't help thinking about Anne-Laure, Valérie, and those women whose husbands had not shown up. She clenched the tiny Eiffel Tower in her hand and tried not to be frightened.

—≫≫.-

Ever since they had left Paris, her mother persevered with her morning makeup routine, spending time in front of her hand mirror, doing her hair expertly, then making sure Pauline looked impeccable as well. Their life had been turned topsy-turvy;

Pauline felt uprooted, disoriented, and the mere act of laying her eyes on her elegantly dressed mother struggling with her hatbox on the platform, gawked at by appreciative porters, sufficed to bolster her.

A Red Cross member was traveling with them to Chicago in a sleeper train, and the next morning Marcelle and Pauline were booked on a connecting train to Reno by themselves. The entire trip lasted three days and three nights. Pauline pored over River's map, tracking their journey with her finger: Leaving New York state, they were headed through Pennsylvania, Ohio, Indiana, Illinois, Iowa, Nebraska, Colorado, Utah, and, finally, Nevada. Her stepfather had sent a telegram to the New York City YWCA where they had been put up, to confirm he was expecting them at the Reno station in three days, and Pauline had seen the relief on her mother's face.

From Chicago onward they traveled alone, without an escort. Pauline discovered how considerate the other passengers were of her and her mother. It seemed to her, back in Paris, that Pauline was part of a rarely spoken to, invisible caste—children—whereas in this new land, where everything seemed so different, people were interested in her, in her story, her background. There was always a warm smile coming her way, a wink, a "Hi, Pauline!" Marcelle remained on edge, unaccustomed to signs of interest from complete strangers. They were trying to be nice, she whispered to her daughter but, truth be told, their attention made her feel a bit uncomfortable. And as for that nasal drawl, she didn't understand a thing. The lady from the Red Cross had left them a brochure with easy-to-learn English expressions; Pauline tried to decipher it, mumbling the sentences in a low voice. Her mother didn't glance at it once.

Evening meals in the dining car delighted Marcelle because they had to get dressed. When they appeared in front of their table, all eyes were on her mother. Her chicness caused a sensation. While Marcelle laid on her charm, Pauline admired the fine linen tablecloths, porcelain crockery, heavy silver cutlery. The attentive waiters wore white jackets with long aprons.

Never in her life had the little girl seen such dramatic landscapes; she felt blown away discovering them: endless, rolling golden cornfields, wide foaming rivers, enormous road bridges spanning even larger lakes, taller trees than she had ever imagined, rugged granite mountains that resembled cathedrals, lofty cliffs, tunnels carved deep into rock, thick, dark-green forests, and snow-capped peaks. Every day offered a new view, even more impressive than the previous one: reddish-orange buttes of the most outlandish shapes as well as miles and miles of sunbaked desert sand. She saw towns and villages streaming past, people tending to their gardens, church spires, cows in pastures, children playing in parks, and with a cry of wonder she even caught sight of deer.

"Look, *Maman*!" she'd say, trying to catch her mother's attention.

Surely Marcelle had not seen anything like this either. But her mother was busy writing her letters or doing her nails. On the last day of their trip, as they were about to reach Reno, an older lady sitting across from them began to speak to them in faltering French. Her idioms were old-fashioned, even rather quaint, but she managed to make herself understood. The woman told them Reno was called the "biggest little city in the world," which Pauline did not grasp. "Was Marcelle on her way there for a quick divorce?" asked the lady. Her mother's face fell.

"Certainly not, how rude!" she snapped. "I'm going to Reno with my daughter. My husband is expecting us."

And with that, she turned away from the old lady pointedly. The latter shrugged and smiled at Pauline.

Pauline's eye had been caught by something moving along the arid plains, a group of horses running madly, even faster than the train itself. There were five or six of them, of different coat colors—black, white, spotted, bay, and chestnut—and they ran so magnificently, manes and tails floating in the wind, with such flamboyance and liberty that Pauline was spellbound, face flattened to the windowpane.

"Those are mustangs," pointed the old lady.

"Mustangs?" repeated Pauline. She rather liked the sound of that word.

"The wild horses of Nevada."

"Do they belong to anyone?"

The old lady shook her head. She said no, they didn't, mustangs were free and untamed, and they had been roaming the hills in the region for a long time. They were the descendants of domestic horses brought to the Americas by Spanish explorers in the sixteenth century and had escaped. In fact, their name came from the Spanish words *mostrenco* and *mestengo*, which meant "wild" or "masterless" cattle in Spanish. Pauline watched them until they vanished from her sight in clouds of dust.

It was time at last to get off the train, to make sure nothing had been forgotten. Marcelle was beside herself with excitement, checking that her lipstick had been applied properly, that her perky beret sat on her head the way it should. Groups of travelers disembarked as well, but they all seemed to know where they were going, and it wasn't long before Marcelle and Pauline were alone on the platform, facing the smallish white brick building with its red-tiled roof.

A single rail track disappeared at either end into a measureless, sand-colored expanse. Above, the sky was a hard blue dotted with puffy white clouds. The breeze played with Pauline's hair. She couldn't help looking all around her, wondering if she'd see those mustangs again, breathing in the air which was full of a delightful smell—something earthy, green, yet sandy. She didn't know it yet, but it was the true scent of Nevada: sagebrush.

The minutes slipped by and Marcelle was beginning to fidget in her pretty blue suit, looking down at her watch incessantly. Pauline felt uneasy as well. What if Doug was not coming? They'd be like Marcelle's poor friends, dumped war brides having to go all the way back to France, alone.

After a while, a man wearing a cap and a whistle around his neck made his way over to them and asked them questions they did not understand. He wasn't unkind, but it was obvious he had not seen anyone dressed that way on his platform, and he ogled Marcelle. Pauline grabbed the Red Cross brochure and handed it to him; the man looked at it for a few moments, seemed to understand, then left them alone after casting a last incredulous look at Marcelle, her beret, and her hatbox.

Her mother, once again, checked her makeup in her small mirror. Her gloved hands were shaking; she kept glancing all around, rattled, as if she no longer understood what she was doing miles from anywhere. Pauline was puzzled. Where had her gutsy, chirpy mother gone—the one who cheered up everyone on the boat, the one who soothed those spurned wives once they landed in New York?

It was then that Pauline saw three people coming quickly to meet them, escorted by a bouncing white puppy. She didn't immediately recognize Doug, no longer wearing his soldier's uniform, but a mechanic's overalls smeared with grease and a funny-looking cap. He was followed by an older stooped couple, hatless, carrying a bouquet of flowers.

"Look, *Maman*," she said quietly as they approached. "It's them!"

Marcelle straightened up, observed them, then sniffed.

"No, darling. That's not them."

But Doug was calling them now, in a voice hoarsened by emotion, yelling, "Marcelle! Pauly!" at the top of his lungs, and Pauline, after the grueling trip, felt carried away by the intensity of the moment.

He had turned up. He had kept his word. He was there.

The little girl rushed to him, arms outstretched, crying, laughing, as the puppy barked and jumped all around her, and Doug lifted her off the ground as if she were a feather.

"I saw mustangs!" she squealed.

"Wonderful!" Doug shouted, imitating a horse's whinny. Then he told her, showing her, that the little white puppy was hers. Only hers. His name was Prince.

Pauline was filled with joy.

It wasn't until much later that she noticed the disconcerted expression that came over Marcelle when she glanced at Doug, his stained coveralls, then his kind, devoted parents, so humble, with their old-fashioned, patched clothes, heavy shoes, and coarse hands.

It seemed to her that her mother, voiceless, overwhelmed, was already looking behind her along the railway line toward the east, to France, to everything she had left behind.

Her life. Her friends.

Cafés, theaters, museums.

And Paris. Paris. Paris.

SUMMER 1960

─────≫─────

Reno, Nevada

"Oh, Paris.... Paris!" whispered Mrs. Miller again, closing her eyes rapturously. "So do you speak any French?"

"I do indeed," said Pauline. "I speak fluent French."

"But there's no accent when you speak English," marveled Mrs. Miller.

Pauline explained that she came to Reno as a seven-year-old child, when her mother, a Parisian widow, had married a GI from Nevada.

Had she ever been back to Paris, Mrs. Miller wanted to know. Yes, in 1955 when her grandmother died, said Pauline. That time, she had taken the plane to return to her homeland.

"I've never been to Paris," said Mrs. Miller. "I'm longing to."

"I'm sure you will go, Mrs. Miller," said Pauline, putting the dustpan away.

It was time to go, to leave Suite 614, to store the cart in its place and return to the main floor.

Mrs. Miller had followed her to the entrance, looking pensive. She kept nibbling at the skin around her index finger.

"Could you maybe help me...?" she started.

"Of course, ma'am. How could I be of use to you?"

"I would like to write a letter. In French."

"Certainly."

There was something almost impish in the way Mrs. Miller gazed at her. Pauline suddenly thought how pretty she looked in spite of her pasty skin.

"A love letter," she elaborated. "A special love letter."

Pauline managed to hide her surprise. She'd be happy to help.

Mrs. Miller stretched out her arms, and Pauline thought for a moment she was going to hug her.

"Let's get started! I'm thrilled!"

There was a knock at the door. Mrs. Miller froze like a child caught in some mischievous act.

"Who's there?" she asked through the panel.

Pauline caught a masculine voice.

"Is that you, Rafe?" asked Mrs. Miller.

"It's me," replied the voice.

Was this her husband, Mr. Miller?

Standing on the doorstep was a tall, muscular, black-haired man with a square face, wearing jeans and a striped shirt.

Mrs. Miller nestled against his chest like a child.

"Oh, I know you'll do me some good."

The tall guy put a tender hand on Mrs. Miller's shoulder and came in, nodding briefly to Pauline.

The phone began to ring once more.

"That must be Paula," sighed Mrs. Miller.

"She'll sit tight," said the man.

He strode right to the bedroom and after a minute or so called that he was ready and waiting for her.

Pauline, self-conscious, decided it was high time to slip away. She would not find out who "Rafe" was to Mrs. Miller, as she no doubt would not set foot in Suite 614 ever again. Tomorrow, Mildred was going to send up Linda, Kitty, or another cleaner. Not her.

Meanwhile, Mrs. Miller had disappeared into the bedroom and closed the door.

Pauline let herself out with the cart as fast and as noiselessly as she could, rushed to the storage room, put the cart away, and left the sixth floor. The elevator was full when she stepped into it, so she wasn't able to thank Casper again verbally, but she gave him a discreet thumbs-up, which he acknowledged with a smile.

Once back in the restrooms, there was some cleaning Pauline had to do, as everything had been left unattended while she was up on the sixth floor. She got to it straight away. Some kind soul had even dropped a tip for her. As she scrubbed and rinsed, she thought back to Mrs. Miller and her odd, rather romantic request. Hardly anyone spoke French in Reno. All these years later, her mother was still regarded as the "Parisienne." Marcelle had not lost her accent, unlike Pauline, who was quick to pick up her new language. Jimmy, her little brother, born in 1947, the year after Marcelle and Pauline arrived in Nevada, didn't speak French either.

A love letter in French, mused Pauline dreamily, still down on her knees, scouring away. Who was Mrs. Miller planning to write to behind her husband's back? Was it to the tall, dark-haired guy she called "Rafe"?

Pauline was busy pondering all this when a click of heels

announced a client. Hastily, she stood up, straightening her apron, a smile pasted to her face. Everyone who worked at the Mapes was told to smile at guests. It was an order. But her smile faded when she saw who it was.

Evaline Spencer, Kendall's wife, with a small child. This, Pauline knew, was their firstborn, Percy. *Why did Evaline continue to come down to these restrooms,* thought Pauline, *when she could use the ones on the second floor next to her husband's spacious offices?*

Every time they crossed paths, usually at the Mapes, Evaline did her best to be as unpleasant as possible to Pauline. She still had not gotten over Lily. *But did she know what her husband was really up to?* wondered Pauline. Everyone at the Mapes was aware he considered Pauline his property, but there were a couple of other girls, usually scullery maids or young phone operators, who came to his office secretly at his beck and call.

With a supercilious glare aimed at Pauline, and not a word of greeting, Evaline propelled her child into one of the stalls and tended to him.

"Good day, Mrs. Spencer," said Pauline politely, polishing a faucet.

Evaline didn't answer. She never did. She flounced out again once her child had done his business and after she had washed his hands. They had left the toilet a real mess.

Pauline hardly had time to digest this latest affront when Mildred scurried in again, just as jittery as she had been earlier that morning. She plied Pauline with questions, barely taking time to draw breath. So Mrs. Miller had been there, after all? How had it gone? How had Pauline dealt with that? Had there been a problem with Mrs. Miller of any sort? Because if there had been one, Mildred needed to know about it right away. Did

Mrs. Miller seem satisfied? Had Pauline managed to clean up everything?

Pauline listened, befuddled. She couldn't get a word in edgewise, dreading that her stammering was going to be worse than ever. As Mildred went on with her unremitting interrogation, now was the time to invoke Commander and his august powers. The images of the black stallion's smooth gallop took over Mildred's hamster-like jowls, instilled calm in her turmoil. Yes, Mrs. Miller had been there, asleep in the bedroom. The vacuuming had woken her up. It had been fine. Pauline had done the job as best as she could. No, there had been no problem at all. Mrs. Miller had asked for a Bloody Mary. Pauline had ordered one for her. Mrs. Miller gave the impression she was happy with Pauline's work. Yes, Pauline was able to clean up the entire suite.

"Was Mr. Miller there?"

Pauline hesitated; she didn't wish to sound indiscreet or put Mrs. Miller into a tight spot.

"A man arrived at one point, but I don't know if it was Mr. Miller."

"What did he look like?"

Pauline couldn't help stuttering as she described the jet-black hair, the muscular build.

"Was this man wearing glasses? Smoking a pipe?"

"N-no."

"Well, that's not Mr. Miller. This must be Mrs. Miller's masseur. He comes morning and evening. Mr. Roberts."

Pauline kept silent.

Mildred leaned forward. Her bulbous nose was shiny and pink.

"Pauline, I hope you've gathered who Mrs. Miller is? Please reassure me: You're not a total nincompoop, are you?"

Pauline lied. There was nothing much else she could do. She said that yes, yes, of course, she knew. But she didn't know anything at all.

Who was the woman in Suite 614, that lost and languid creature with a wisp of a voice? And why was it so important to Mildred?

When she went down to the staff canteen on the lower floor for her lunch break, Kitty waved to her. She was already sitting with two other cleaners, Harper and Maud. Pauline installed herself with her tray and was greeted with enthusiasm. They all seemed to know about her morning experience on the sixth floor and wanted to hear the details. According to Pedro and Casper, Pauline had apparently done more than all right, and even Mildred, for once, had agreed.

"Was she in the nude?" giggled Maud.

"Who?" asked Pauline, digging into her hot dog.

"Duh, Mrs. Miller!" quipped Maud.

"Yes," said Pauline with a grimace. "And I asked her to put on her bathrobe and she did!"

"Way to go!" snickered Harper. "She's stark naked in the mornings. Pilar didn't dare say anything."

"So did you clean up the mess? The empty bottles, the shoes, the clothes?"

"I did. What a tip..."

"And did she say anything special to you?"

Pauline kept the letter in French to herself. She added, "She was nice. But she seemed worn out."

"She's been like that since she got here," said Maud. "There's something fishy going on in the Miller suite. They haven't stopped bickering."

"If Mildred is pleased with you, then she'll have you back doing the rooms."

"You really deserve it, Pauline! What's going on here is so unfair."

Pauline felt buoyed by the sincerity of her coworkers' support. They were fully aware of her situation.

Kitty slung an affectionate arm around her shoulders. "We got you, Frenchie. Remember that."

The cleaning ladies had only a brief slot for their meal; Maud and Harper were already on their way out. Kitty waited until Pauline finished her dessert.

Drowned in the cafeteria's ruckus, they sat face-to-face. The entire Mapes workforce, apart from the general managers, came down here, to the long low-ceilinged room, for meals. It was a loud and busy place, where the elevator repairman could be seen sitting cheek-by-jowl with the bellman, the operators, or the Sky Room musical director.

Kitty said, "Are you planning to tell your mother? I can already picture her face."

Pauline put her spoon down. "K-Kitty," she stammered.

Her friend, noting the stutter, felt concerned. She asked her what was wrong. Pauline pulled herself together; she said she didn't dare talk about it, and only Kitty could help. She took the plunge. "I don't get all the fuss around Mrs. Miller."

Kitty was silent for a couple of seconds and Pauline began to wonder what was going on. What hadn't she seen or guessed? What was the big deal? Pauline knew Kitty was a loyal colleague, not the type to poke fun at her, nor shame her.

Kitty whispered, "You have no idea who she is?"

"No," Pauline whispered back ashamed. "And I feel so dumb. I saw a dog-tired, scruffy lady with too many Champagne bottles by her bed, that's all!"

Kitty patted her hand.

"It's okay. We all heard from Pilar and the room service guys that the woman is unrecognizable without makeup first thing in the morning, even if old Jones has forbidden us from talking about it. It's hard to believe, but when she's hanging around in her bathrobe, no one knows who she is. Apparently, it takes a couple of hours before she can be seen." Kitty tittered.

"Right, but who *is* she?"

"Now, I get it! You were away for two weeks on your Lake Tahoe vacation! You missed out on it all. But I'm surprised your mother didn't mention anything. She's so into that kind of stuff."

Pauline was starting to get annoyed now; she felt left out. She frowned and stopped smiling. "Yeah, sure. My mother spent most of her time complaining and getting sozzled. It was hell."

Kitty patted her hand again. "Don't get angry, Frenchie!"

"Just tell me who that woman is. I'm going to go crazy if you don't."

"Okay, keep your hair on." Kitty leaned forward to murmur in her ear. "Mrs. Miller from Suite 614 is Marilyn Monroe."

And the deafening canteen suddenly seemed totally silent to Pauline.

In the living room of the white clapboard house, Marcelle stowed all her precious magazines on a shelf, the ones her sister, Irène, sent her from France each month: *Paris Match, Jours de France,* and *Point de Vue: Images du Monde.* She also purchased American periodicals devoted to Hollywood celebrities, such as *Movieland, Screenland,* and *Movie Life.* This was her passion. Doug, Pauline, and Jimmy had become accustomed to the sight of Marcelle settled on the sofa, hair in curlers, an ultra light menthol Capri between her fingers, a glass of bourbon resting on the table, and her gazettes. She should not be disturbed.

When Pauline got home from the Mapes that afternoon, she provided snacks to her daughter and to her brother, Jimmy, as usual, and feverishly consulted the publications. She could do this quietly as her mother was not due back from the salon until later.

She didn't have to search long. Marilyn Monroe's new movies and problematic love life often graced the covers of the latest issues. Pauline thus learned she had been married to playwright Arthur Miller for the past four years, but there was trouble in paradise. Of course, Pauline had heard of Marilyn Monroe. She was the blonde in *Gentlemen Prefer Blondes,* which she saw at the Majestic Theater in Reno for her fourteenth birthday. But apart from what she had gleaned over the years here and there, listening to her mother, or hearing news on TV and radio, she didn't know much about the actress and her life, other than she had had an unsuccessful marriage with a great baseball player, and her real name was Norma Jeane.

No matter how long Pauline pored over the famous perfectly made-up face, half-open crimson lips, and platinum locks, what she saw on those glossy pages bore little likeness to Mrs. Miller, as if these were two different women. But she was fully aware Mrs. Miller was indeed Marilyn Monroe.

"Pretty lady!" commented Jimmy, coming to look over her shoulder and munching a cookie a little too close to his sister's ear. He was now a teenager and sometimes acted like one, although he was never difficult or sulky.

Pauline pushed him away gently, on the verge of telling him what happened this morning.

"Do you know who she is?" she asked him.

He lifted his eyebrows, with the full scorn of his thirteen years.

"Everyone knows who Marilyn Monroe is, Pauly! And everyone knows she's in Reno for the movie. Staying at the Mapes."

Everyone except your dumb sister, she nearly added.

Later, before Marcelle got home, she telephoned Billie-Pearl and gave her the whole story. At first, Billie-Pearl hooted with laughter, but then she quickly cheered her friend, reminding her they were both obsessed with horses, not film stars; they never went to the movies, they couldn't care less about Tinseltown. They got their kicks in the company of mustangs, that was their thing, spending hours in the blazing desert sun riding them and caring for them. In all honesty, she wouldn't have recognized Monroe either. And speaking of riding, when was Pauline next coming to Wadsworth?

Pauline caught the noise of Marcelle's Dodge coming up the driveway. It was time to hang up. Her mother did not approve of their friendship. She promised her friend she'd in be touch soon.

"Hang in there, Mademoiselle," whispered Billie-Pearl.

Tossing her car keys and purse on the table with a sigh, Marcelle entered the house. She overdramatically mopped her brow, adjusting the air-conditioning. Heaven above, this blasted heat! It would soon be fifteen years since she moved to Nevada, and every summer she sang the same tune: complaining about the stifling, dry, burning hotness, the fine dust that seeped everywhere, into her eyes, her throat, her nose, but also inside the house, into wardrobes and drawers. And what about those Reno winters? The snow, the ice, the blizzards. She had not been able to acclimate to the freezing temperatures. Pauline and Jimmy listened to her laments without interrupting. They were used to it.

At forty-five, Marcelle Hammond had kept her lissome figure and dressed with the same care as though she were still back in Paris, despite the severe Nevadan weather variations. In her Winter Street hair salon, *Marcelle from Paris*, she had managed to recreate a Parisian atmosphere down to the last detail. On the pastel-pink walls, she had hung posters of the Eiffel Tower, Notre Dame, Sacré Cœur, and Brigitte Bardot, Simone Signoret, Alain Delon, and others. Tunes by Dalida, Gilbert Bécaud, Édith Piaf, Yves Montand, and Charles Aznavour were heard on the gramophone throughout the day—records also sent by her sister, Irène. Customers raved about the French décor, and the shop did well; the only downside being the extra glass Marcelle poured herself more and more frequently, starting at lunch break. Marcelle was perfectly miserable in Reno, and everyone knew it. And Pauline didn't know how to deal with it.

When Doug came home a little later, he pecked his wife on the lips, as he always did. She was already busy cooking, her apron sitting nicely on her slim hips, the glass of bourbon never far. He looked at her with such love and pride. *But how*, wondered Pauline yet again, *was he so blind to the unhappiness gnawing at her?* Perhaps he did not want to see it. Perhaps that was his way of dealing with it. So Pauline did the exact same thing: not seeing it. Closing her eyes to her mother's despair. Just like she didn't want to see the way she was treated by Kendall. And she hated herself for not being able to stand up for herself. For her spinelessness.

During the meal, Pauline did not mention what had happened in Suite 614. She was already thinking about tomorrow morning, fearing Kitty might be tempted to tell the staff she had not recognized Marilyn Monroe. If that were the case, how could she ever bear the taunts? The Mapes seemed such a big place but, sooner or later, everyone found out the latest gossip and it spread like wildfire. She knew that all too well.

But it was Marcelle who brought up the subject. According to her clients, the two-week holiday in Lake Tahoe had prevented them from keeping up with the events linked to the filming of *The Misfits*, she complained. Had Pauline caught a glimpse of any of the actors on her first day back at the Mapes? Monroe, in particular? Could she get an autograph, did she think? That would be priceless.

Pauline smiled at her mother. Then, she said lightly, "*Maman*, do you really think Marilyn Monroe is going to use the main floor ladies' room?"

After dinner, Jimmy was allowed to watch *Dennis the Menace* on TV, his favorite show. Marcelle never missed an episode of the *I Love Lucy* reruns on CBS, while Doug preferred *Alfred Hitchcock Presents*. Pauline watched along with them. It was her way of keeping them company while little Lily was already tucked up in bed.

She slept badly that night and woke the next day with a lump in her stomach. But when she showed up at the Mapes, on time that morning, no one looked at her askance or sniggered as she walked by. Maybe Kitty hadn't said anything after all. Pauline set to work, concentrating on what she had to do.

"Hey, Frenchie!" It was Marty's voice, one of the front desk bellboys, a skinny ginger-haired young man. He came to tell her Mildred wanted to see her pronto in the housekeepers' office.

Pauline froze, then dropped her broom.

"Are you in a pickle?" he queried.

She hoped not, she stammered. He gave her a warm pat on the shoulder. It was going to be fine! Chin up.

Pauline went along to the housekeepers' office on the first floor. Hands on her hips, Mildred was standing in the room waiting for her. Oddly enough, she didn't look annoyed, merely puzzled. She cut to the chase: What happened yesterday morning in Suite 614? Pauline had to be precise, and no beating around the bush, please.

Pauline thought she might faint. It was because of that darned bathrobe. She knew it. Mrs. Miller must have complained. No one asked Marilyn Monroe to get dressed. Who would ever dare do such a thing? What an idiot she had been. What a twit. A good-for-nothing. A ninny. A perfect fool. She began to shake.

Mildred was still waiting. For a brief moment, Pauline closed her eyes, time enough for the powerful black stallion to materialize at her side. Commander was right there, dominating them both with his bulk: He kept Mildred at a distance and he shielded Pauline. Then, at last, she could speak without stuttering. Commander's warm breath enveloping the top of her head and gliding down her neck, she went over the course of the cleaning carried out in the suite, Mrs. Miller's requests (except the letter), and Mr. Roberts's entrance.

Mildred listened, then checked her watch.

"Fine, now back you go. Hurry."

"Very well, Mrs. Jones. I'll go back down."

"Down? Don't you get it? You're going up."

Pauline gazed back at Mildred. What did she mean?

"Wait a minute. You need the right uniform. Yours won't do."

Mildred disappeared into the next room. Pauline could hear her rummaging around. She darted back holding a hanger with a costume like those worn by Kitty, Maud, and Harper: navy blue with a V neckline, short sleeves with cuffs, a white collar, and breast pockets embroidered with the letter M. Mildred handed her the garment, telling her she could change quickly next door, no one was around.

Pauline stood there, flummoxed.

"Mrs. Miller's secretary called this morning. She said Mrs. Miller wants you to clean the suite from now on. Yes, you. You must have made a good impression, Pauline. And you need to go on being as low-key as possible. Whatever you might see, whatever you might hear, you keep it to yourself. No chitchat with all those cafeteria blabbermouths about what goes in the Miller suite. It that crystal clear? Good. Now make it snappy. I haven't got all day."

The young woman's heart pounded as she changed into the other uniform, fingers fumbling over buttonholes. Once Pauline was dressed, Mildred handed her the key again.

"Up you go," she ordered. Then, "Stop."

Mildred's pudgy fingers raked over her hair, putting it into place, then she adjusted her collar.

"Don't you ever wear makeup?" asked Mildred.

"Rarely, Mrs. Jones. Only on special occasions."

"Well, isn't working for Marilyn Monroe at the Mapes Hotel a special occasion?"

"Yes, it is."

"Think about it. And do something about your hair. Ask your mother. She'd know."

"Yes, Mrs. Jones."

"You're a pretty girl. You should make the most of yourself. Now scoot along. And do as well as you did yesterday. When you're done with 614, clean the standard rooms on the sixth floor until you get to the end of your shift—and don't forget to fill out the chart."

In a daze, Pauline left the housekeeping office to go to the sixth floor. Mrs. Miller had asked for her to come back. *Her*. Pauline Bazelet. It was mind-boggling. As she headed for the elevator, she realized how euphoric she felt, but how nervous too. Would she be up to it? Would she do as well as her colleagues?

As she mulled this over, a figure appeared in her line of sight, at the end of the long corridor, advancing toward her. A trim man wearing a suit. It was her daughter's father. She hadn't seen Kendall Spencer in some time.

"Well, well," he murmured, standing close to her, close enough for her to smell the minty scent of his cologne.

He checked that they were alone, then pinned her against the wall; his hand slinking between Pauline's legs, his mouth glued to her neck. Oh, but his favorite little French girl had a new out-fit, didn't she, how pretty she was, so adorable, it was a far better fit than the horrible burgundy thing. So she was going up in the world, it seemed? Did she have old Mildred in her pocket? What a young hussy she was. He had missed her so much. Could she step into his office now, briefly, so he might prove how happy he was that she was back from her holiday?

Pauline couldn't escape; she was stuck, she knew it and he knew it. He paid for Lily's nanny, he had found her this job at the Mapes, and he gave her extra money every month. He had kept his promise. But in return, Pauline had become his creature for the past three years. The fact that he had gotten married and had a child made no difference. She had to bow to this bargain. She had to endure it. And he made the most of it with full impunity, telling her over and over how much he worshipped her, how crazy he was about her. Nothing had happened with his wife since she gave birth to their son. They even slept in different beds, he said. They didn't have sex. The only woman he made love to was Pauline.

For a long time, she had believed him. So young, so naïve. For a long time, she had trusted him, she even had feelings for him. Not anymore.

She managed to break free, telling him Mrs. Jones had ordered her to replace Pilar, who was on sick leave, up on the sixth floor. She had to go there at once or she might be late. He kept on kissing her in the hollow of her neck, pushing her toward the staircase that led to the second floor, where his offices were.

"Mr. Spencer," she said, at last. "Please."

"You can use my first name when we're alone, angel. You know that."

"I really have to go now."

"Why the heck are you in such a hurry? After all the stuff I do for you, the way I bend over backwards for you?"

He tweaked his tie, ran a hand through his slicked hair. He was no longer smiling.

Pauline suddenly knew what to say. "Kendall, Marilyn Monroe cannot be kept waiting."

He let out a wolf whistle. Now wasn't his little Frenchie dandy? So Mildred had assigned her to Suite 614. That was ace. Then, yes indeed, Pauline had to dash up there. The idea of Mrs. Miller hanging around all morning was unthinkable.

He caught her by the wrist as she was walking away—she mustn't forget to check on him later, before she left for the day, in his office, as usual, right? He'd be waiting. He was counting on her. And he stole another kiss from her as the clang of the elevator bell rang out.

Pauline stood in front of Suite 614, one hand on the cleaning cart, the other on her thumping heart. Her nervousness had gotten the best of her, and she couldn't breathe properly. Little black dots swirled in front of her eyes, running up and down the numbers etched on the door. How was she going to summon enough courage to go in there? When she hadn't known who Mrs. Miller was, it had been easy. Now she knew, and she had never felt more scared in her life: Marilyn Monroe was behind that door. Waiting for her.

She swallowed, took a deep breath, closed her eyes. But Commander didn't appear. She remained all on her own.

"Housekeeping!" Pauline said in a quavering voice, raising her fist to knock.

Before she did so, the door flew open and a tall gangly man with a dour expression rushed out of the room, nearly colliding with her. He muttered something she didn't catch and hurried off. Pauline recognized this bespectacled guest from Marcelle's magazines: Arthur Miller.

She watched him bolt down the passageway, then she rolled the cart into the suite, closing the door behind her. The place seemed to be in less of a state this morning.

The soft murmur of voices floated to her from the bedroom.

"Housekeeping," she said again with a firmer tone.

The dark man she knew as "Rafe" came out of the room and smiled at her.

"Hi, there. You're from around here, right?"

"Yes, sir."

"Does it always get this hot?" he asked.

"Yes, it does, sir. And worse."

"I'm from North Carolina. It's a lot cooler over there. What the Mapes Hotel needs is a swimming pool," he grinned, picking up his jacket. He left.

Pauline started with the living room and the dining room. As she worked, she caught Mrs. Miller's voice on the phone: giggles and whispers. She had to forget who Mrs. Miller was. There was no other way. Mrs. Miller had to be considered a guest like any other, that was all, not one of the most famous women on the planet. But that was tough to do.

She focused on a stubborn stain embedded in the honey-colored carpet, jam, it seemed. As she scrubbed briskly, she thought of Kendall. She had for once managed to put him off. But she knew with a heavy heart that, later on, he would have his wicked way with her, using condoms, and he would smile at her gently and say they didn't want to make another mistake, did they? He was her cursed lover, the one she gave in to over and over because she didn't know how to disentangle herself from his grip.

"Hi, Pauline."

Mrs. Miller was there, wrapped in a bathrobe, a cup of coffee in hand. Her gaze was spry this morning, her eyes less red. She wore no trace of makeup, her hair was still in a fuzzy tangle, but Pauline saw it in her smile, that inimitable smile. There was no longer any doubt, she was indeed in the presence of the famous, the unique Marilyn Monroe.

Moored to her sponge and carpet cleaner, she couldn't utter a single word.

Mrs. Miller acted as if nothing had happened. How glad she was to see her! Pauline hadn't forgotten, had she? That love letter, in French. And Pauline was the only one who could help her.

Like a child, Mrs. Miller pranced about, humming a little tune, fishing paper and a pen out of the desk, and Pauline couldn't help noticing how sprightly each gesture was. Where had yesterday's lethargic creature vanished to?

"There," said Mrs. Miller. "Let's sit at the table so you can write."

Pauline hoped this wasn't going to take too long as she did have all the cleaning to do. As if she read into her thoughts, Mrs. Miller told her not to worry about the dishes: She'd do them herself in a jiffy. Pauline would never guess how many dishes she had cleaned as a child—she used to be a downright champion. In fact, she'd do them now, while Pauline got started, so they'd waste no time.

Incredulously, Pauline watched Mrs. Miller rustle out rubber gloves from the cart, skip into the kitchen, and fill the sink with soapy water. She felt like pinching herself. Nobody would ever believe her if she described what she was looking at now.

"You ready, honey?"

"Yes, Mrs. Miller," said Pauline, her pen poised above the paper.

The telephone began to ring with its usual strident insistence.

"Oh, no!" groaned Mrs. Miller over the clatter of plates and glasses. "That's Paula. If I pick up, she'll keep me on the phone for hours. We won't ever get the letter done."

Pauline wondered again who Paula was.

"Mrs. Miller, what if I answered and told her you were in the bathroom?"

"You clever girl! Do just that!"

Pauline got up to pick up the receiver.

"Hello?" she answered.

"Who's this?" asked a nasal female voice.

"This is the cleaning lady, ma'am."

"Put Mrs. Miller on, please."

"Mrs. Miller is in the bathroom."

"Well, at least she's up. A miracle! Have her call me, will you?"

"Yes, ma'am. And you are?"

"Paula Strasberg."

The lady hung up.

"Yes, that was indeed 'Paula,'" Pauline told Mrs. Miller, who had finished the dishes. So they had a full half hour, at least, ahead of them, Mrs. Miller said.

They sat close to each other, close enough for their elbows to brush against each other. Mrs. Miller's milky skin seemed to glow, and now that she was near, Pauline could make out the delicate pale down covering the actress's face, especially her cheeks, like the fuzz on a peach.

"I'd like to start by saying how much I miss him," said Mrs. Miller, with that breathless tone Pauline was starting to get used to. "How I miss him day and night. How I can't stop thinking about him. . . . About his hands all over me . . . his kisses . . . his smell . . . his gorgeous voice . . ."

"Wait. . . . Can you slow down a little?" interrupted Pauline, scribbling away.

Mrs. Miller said she was sorry. The only things she knew how to say in French were, "I love you," "friendship," and "love." When Pauline was done, she'd copy out the letter, so he'd recognize her handwriting.

"Shall we go on? Where were we?"

"His gorgeous voice."

Mrs. Miller got up and went over to the kitchen refrigerator. She grabbed two small bottles of Champagne, popped them open, and set them on the table, placing one in front of Pauline. She took a few swigs and went on talking as Pauline wrote down every word: Yes, she missed her magnificent lover dreadfully; she was bored to tears in this godforsaken place, shooting a rotten movie in this ghastly heat. How she longed for their cozy bungalow, their delicious privacy, their sensual lovemaking. And his mouth, those full lips: That mouth drove her crazy as well as everything that mouth was capable of doing . . . slowly . . . feverishly . . .

"Say, you don't want a drop of Champagne, do you? You can count on me to say nothing to that terrifying Mrs. Jones."

Pauline was thirsty. She nearly said she preferred water, getting up to fetch it herself, but she didn't dare. She was alone in the suite with Mrs. Miller, who was looking her way with a naughty expression. There was no one to supervise her, no one to lecture her. She gulped down a few sips and the icy bubbles burst against her palate.

"Isn't it irresistible?" gushed Mrs. Miller.

They got back to the letter. Mrs. Miller opened more small bottles. Pauline began to feel warm all over; the whispered, spellbinding sentences and the Champagne bubbles were gently going to her head. The beige walls of Suite 614 seemed to undulate as if under the influence of a playful breeze. A wooziness overtook Pauline, and it wasn't unpleasant. She couldn't fight it; she didn't want to fight it. She could see all the things Mrs. Miller wanted this mysterious man to do to her; she was right there in the room with them, in that love-scented bedroom, and not a single devouring kiss nor sigh of pleasure eluded her. The pen between her shaking fingers felt damp.

"Could you read it in French, honey?"

Pauline complied. The sentences seemed even more smoldering, racy, in her native language. She felt her cheeks burn but, oddly, she didn't stammer once.

"I don't understand a single word, but I can tell this hits the mark because of the way you're blushing."

The doorbell rang. Mrs. Miller started. That was probably Paula. Quick now, Pauline had to get back to work. Mrs. Miller took the letter, folded it, and slipped it into her pocket.

"I can't possibly thank you enough."

"It's my pleasure, Mrs. Miller."

As she took up the vacuum, Pauline still felt lightheaded. Mrs. Miller opened the door to a small, dark-haired sixty-something woman with a slight build.

"Oh, it's you, May! I was expecting Paula, coming over to make sure I'm really up."

May was holding a stack of letters, which she handed over to the actress. This was, no doubt, her personal assistant, thought Pauline. She left them both in the living room as she set off to tidy the bedroom. While she made up the bed, she wondered about the couple who slept in it. Did Arthur Miller have any inkling his wife was writing love letters behind his back? Was that why he looked so hard-faced when she saw him earlier?

Scraps of conversation drifted over to her, and she couldn't help but listen as she dusted. Mrs. Miller's secretary seemed to be cautioning her: The articles were going to be released this week, worldwide. There was nothing to be done, they were going to have to prepare for it and hunker down. Mrs. Miller was going to have to face it. Obviously, this meant vast publicity for the upcoming movie with Montand, May continued, which was slated for release in September, and the studios were already rubbing their hands in glee. As ever, the uproar would last for a while, then the headlines would move on to something else. Pauline could no longer hear Mrs. Miller. She remained silent, as if in shock. Then, she at last heard her mutter that this was going to make matters even worse with her husband—in fact, it was going to get ugly, it would be sheer hell.

—⟫—

The next morning, when Pauline arrived at Suite 614, the DO NOT DISTURB card was dangling from the handle. That was a golden rule, she knew: Do not knock or go in when that card was displayed. She went off to clean the other standard rooms on the sixth floor and returned to the suite later. The sign was still there. While she hesitated, the door opened and the tall, dark masseur appeared. His real name, she had learned, was Ralph. He saw her and gave her a smile. Then he whispered, "Best to come back at another moment."

"Sure," she said.

He added, still whispering, that this wasn't a good day for Mrs. Miller. Pauline said she was sorry to hear that, and took the cart back, wondering what had happened, and why Mrs. Miller needed to rest. The girls on the afternoon shift, probably Shirlee or Debra, would clean the suite.

Pauline had the next day off. On those days, she looked after her daughter and helped out with housework and grocery shopping. She sincerely enjoyed doing all those things, which she didn't consider chores. It seemed natural to lend her mother a hand and to care for her daughter. But sometimes, she couldn't help comparing her week to Kitty's, and she wondered how it must feel to have a husband, a home, and to bring up children together. *Would this happen to her?* she wondered. Would she fall in love, get married? Or would she remain pinned down by Kendall's power forever? It felt at times like her life had been stolen from her, that her dreams had been shattered. What was there to look forward to?

While she set out coloring pencils and sheets of paper on the kitchen table for Lily, she realized that meeting Mrs. Miller was an extraordinary event, lighting up her summer. She still had not told her mother about Marilyn Monroe; this felt like her secret, one she could keep to herself, something to cherish.

At the end of the day, she was playing treasure hunt with Lily in the garden in the shade, when Marcelle arrived from the hair salon in an unusual state of excitement.

"Look!" she squealed, throwing two magazines at her daughter. "Unbelievable. Everyone is taking about it."

Paris Match and *Life* both displayed the same cover: the close-up of a dark-haired man embracing a blonde; eyes closed, lips half-open, seemingly ablaze with lust. Astounded, Pauline recognized Marilyn Monroe and Yves Montand in a still from their next film, *Let's Make Love.* Silky-voiced, tall, dark, and handsome, Montand was her mother's favorite French actor and singer. Marcelle told her daughter that during the filming, only this last spring in Hollywood, the two actors had a secret sizzling affair. Montand's wife, actress Simone Signoret, had left to shoot in Italy, and Arthur Miller, Monroe's husband, was on location near Reno scouting for *The Misfits.* (Clearly, her mother knew the story like the back of her hand.) Housed in adjoining bungalows at the Beverly Hills Hotel in Los Angeles, Monroe and Montand had found themselves alone. And what was bound to happen did happen. And now the whole world knew. The pain poor Signoret was going through, gasped Marcelle. And what a public humiliation for Miller! The mood in their Mapes suite must be terrible; Marcelle was sure Pauline's cleaner friends would fill her in on all the juicy gossip and details.

"You must tell me everything. I'm dying to know."

The beige, sand-colored walls of Suite 614 came back to Pauline as she listened vaguely to her mother's prattle, as well as the small, icy Champagne bottles, and that blue gaze, both knowing and cheeky.

A love letter, Mrs. Miller had said. A special love letter. In French.

1952

Reno, Nevada

Every Saturday, Doug took Pauline, Jimmy, and Prince, the dog, out for a long ride in his old stake truck. He worked in a garage in nearby Sparks, and Saturday was his day off. However, that was Marcelle's busiest day at the salon as many ladies would come in for a perm or a dye. Doug packed peanut butter and jelly sandwiches he made himself and lots of water (it got so hot from June onward), clapped hats on the children's heads, and they took off for the entire day. Pauline loved these road trips and looked forward to them. She noticed her mother did not seem to mind missing out—all that heat and dust were not to her taste, not to mention the risk of running into a rattlesnake or a mountain lion. She also began to notice that her mother was always helping herself to another sip of bourbon. It seemed to happen more and more often. Marcelle begged Doug to be careful. Pauline was thirteen, but Jimmy only five, still a little boy. Doug laughed, it sounded like she was convinced he was driving the children into the most dangerous place in the world. Why didn't she come along, on a Sunday when she was free, so she could see for herself how beautiful Nevada really was? But Marcelle preferred to rest on Sundays, and as she worked hard, and everybody knew it, Doug didn't insist. He did look wistful, Pauline could tell, when the children later told their mother all about the thrills of the day, and Marcelle paid scarce attention.

Pauline understood her mother still pined for France and for Paris; she hadn't settled down happily in Reno, even after Jimmy's birth. Despite the hair salon doing well, Marcelle felt left out, different; she was convinced the local folks, and even her in-laws, made fun of the French accent she seemed unable to tone down. Doug's parents even ended up moving out of the Washington Street home to Carson City, as cohabiting with their daughter-in-law proved to be strenuous. Another unfortunate issue was those tiresome ladies who persistently made it clear they thought French women were floozies while their bad-mannered husbands acted like downright oafs, pawing Marcelle behind their wives' backs just because she was French. Pauline was aware Marcelle had not embraced the American way of life, the convenience of it, the well-equipped kitchens and bathrooms; she was not impressed with the astonishing amount of food in the grocery stores, those plentiful displays of fish, meat, cheese, and fruit, which made France seem like a poor country, especially after the adversity of the war years; and the banana splits and hot fudge sundaes her children craved left her cold. She despised the fact that people here did everything by car, that nobody walked a couple of blocks to run an errand or pay a visit to a neighboring friend. The only place where Marcelle seemed at home was in her pastel-pink shop listening to French songs on a continuous loop.

Doug had taken it upon himself to do everything in his power to make Pauline and Jimmy fall in love with Nevada—and he succeeded. They couldn't get enough of the state. On those Saturdays, when they drove along the uninterrupted dead-straight roads, through immense gray and taupe landscapes encircled with mighty mountains, with the windows wide open letting the tangy morning air in, he told them about his childhood, how the clapboard house on Washington Street used to stand on an unpaved dirt road lit by flickering gaslights. In those days, he could look right over the picket fence and his mother's sweet peas to the fields of scrub stretching to the west, all the way to the foothills of the Sierras standing tall. It was a vast open land, with miles and miles of silvery hill peaks and ochre-tinted knolls, of ashen desert scattered with sagebrush.

Sometimes, during these long trips, Jimmy would fall asleep at her side, and Pauline then felt she had Doug all to herself. There was some peace and quiet to be enjoyed as Jimmy was such a chatterbox. She had never felt jealous of her little brother. From the start, Doug treated her like she was his own daughter; he cared for her, asking questions about school and her friends, her teachers, congratulating her on her good grades and the gold stars on her report card. He was the one who bought her the Mickey Mouse lunchbox she treasured. She now spoke English fluently, without the trace of an accent. It had been difficult, in the beginning. What an ordeal that first day of school was, back in 1946, all those curious eyes on her, and all those words flung at her she simply didn't understand.

Each morning, before class, all the children had to stand up, palm flat on their chests, and recite what seemed to be a poem. Pauline didn't dare ask what it was all about, but she tried to learn the words by heart before she even knew their meaning. She learned later, from Doug, that the speech beginning with "I pledge allegiance to the flag of the United States of America" was a sort of promise, a way of honoring the country, of showing respect. And Doug reminded her that soon she would be getting her American passport.

One of Pauline and Jimmy's favorite places was the spectacularly blue Pyramid Lake and its rock formations, about thirty-five miles north of Reno. When they drove there, Doug told them how the land used to belong to the Indigenous American Paiute Tribe, and that some members of the tribe still lived there today. He described the old Paiute legend of the Stone Mother, who wept so abundantly for her children that her tears filled the lake. She sat there for such a long time, said Doug, that she turned to stone, and she still sits there today, with her basket by her side. Whenever they went to the lake, Doug pointed to the stone shape resembling a sitting woman looking out to the blue waters. Jimmy always asked Doug why the Stone Mother seemed so sad; Doug answered it was because her children had disappeared.

Every Saturday was a new adventure and Pauline was filled with anticipation each time. The excursion usually started out with a quick stop at the five-and-dime store around the corner where Pauline chose a strand of red licorice, her guilty pleasure, and Jimmy got a pack of M&M's, his favorite, then they drove along Virginia Street under the historical arch that proudly read RENO: THE BIGGEST LITTLE CITY IN THE WORLD. That was the signal: Doug went back to the past for them. Pauline could listen to his voice for hours; he was such a good storyteller. "The Silver State," Nevada's nickname, Doug told them, dated back to when silver was first discovered during the nineteenth-century mining. Nevada's population boomed because everyone wanted to come and live here, he said, lured by the silver mines' potential. A bunch of brand-new towns were built quickly to make homes for all these people, but when business slowly dried up and miners moved away, most of the desert towns that had popped up during the silver and gold rushes were abandoned, and buildings remained empty. These became ghost towns, and Nevada still had plenty of them, Doug said. They had enigmatic names: Weepah, Belmont, Delamar, Rhyolite, and they were part of Pauline and Jimmy's preferred places, dried up and forgotten, gripped in inexorable decay, yet still standing after all those years. Families had lived here, once, marveled Pauline. Children had played in these parched gardens, life had gone on, then it had all stopped. Overcome, they wandered through derelict schools, roofless houses, crumbling post offices, shops, saloons, barns, and mines, all empty. It was fascinating, but eerie, and sometimes Pauline had to hold Doug's reassuring hand.

Doug's road trips lasted all day long, and often they weren't home until dinnertime. Marcelle would be waiting for them, the meal heating in the oven, while she watched TV, smoked, and sipped her drink. More and more, there had been a little too much of the bourbon, but Doug never said anything, Pauline noticed. *Why did he say nothing?* she wondered. Once, he presented his wife with a bouquet of yellow and white wildflowers they had picked for her by the side of the road, and somehow he wasn't able to see Marcelle had been crying. Why could nobody help her mother? What was wrong? Pauline felt useless and too young to understand.

One day in early summer, when the heat was blasting down on them, creating strange mirages on the asphalt ahead, shapes like a mountain, a lake, or even a train, Pauline glimpsed a herd of mustangs galloping in the rangelands on their right. Doug managed to steer his truck so they could catch up with them. They had often seen wild horses during their day trips, but this was the first time Pauline found herself so close to the animals, and her sheer delight made Doug smile. She could not take her eyes off them.

Later, he told her he knew a lady who cared for mustangs, who fought for their well-being and preservation—an exceptional person, according to him. He had known her since they were kids because her parents, the Bronns, had a home a stone's throw from the Hammonds' place on Washington Street. Her name was Velma, and she lived near Wadsworth with her husband, Charlie Johnston, not far from Pyramid Lake. In a couple days' time, he was going to drive over to their ranch to fix one of their cars. Would Pauline care to come along? Did this lady have any mustangs on her ranch? Pauline wanted to know. She sure did, Doug replied, and more than a few—a whole herd. Velma tended to them, as some were wounded, and when they recovered, she turned them loose.

Doug drove her to the Double Lazy Heart Ranch for the first time directly after school, leaving Jimmy with a school friend. On their way to Wadsworth, Doug revealed that Velma looked a bit peculiar, and he wanted to explain why so Pauline wasn't startled. When she was a girl, about Pauline's age, Velma caught polio, and the virus left her with a distorted appearance, as Pauline would soon discover. She was the nicest, bravest person ever. Her husband was charming as well. Velma grew up in Washoe County, like Doug had, and her dad was a drover, a man who cared for animals, who respected them, and who passed on those values to his daughter. Pauline asked why Velma came to care for mustangs, and Doug described how, a couple years ago, on the road to Reno while she was driving to her job (she worked as a secretary), Velma noticed a dark liquid pouring from an old stock trailer in front of her. It was blood. She thought at first it was coming from wounded sheep or steer, but the blood trailing away seemed too thick for a single injured animal. She wanted to warn the driver, so she followed him to a stockyard in Sparks, just outside Reno. And there, said Doug, Velma made a horrible discovery.

"What was it?" asked Pauline, holding her breath.

There were no sheep, no steer, inside the truck, but rather a dozen hideously maimed wild horses herded together tightly, wading in pools of blood. They were in the most terrible state: some had lost parts of their legs, a stallion's eyes had been torn out, and a trampled foal lay dead. Appalled, Velma learned the mustangs had been rounded up, captured, mutilated, thrown into the truck, and were on their way to be slaughtered for pet food. It was that day, said Doug, faced with that intolerable brutality, that Velma Johnston decided she was going to fight to save the wild horses. Hunting mustangs was an atrocity and it had to stop. Little by little, Velma rallied people to her cause; she was going to go a long way, Doug asserted. With her team, they were already freeing penned mustangs, taking them to safety. Her first victory was recent, only last month, when she managed to get a new resolution voted in Virginia City Courthouse prohibiting the use of planes or helicopters as a means of chasing or rounding up wild horses.

The Johnston ranch nestled in the hilly grounds sprawling along the Truckee River, which seemed oddly green to Pauline because they were covered in grass, a rare sight in Nevada. The area was coveted by ranchers due to the bountiful water supply, Doug explained. But when they got out of the truck, the fierce summer heat still found its way to them, as well as a burning nagging wind, and Pauline was glad she was wearing a straw hat and a pair of her mother's sunglasses. The Johnston ranch house was a low, L-shaped building with a shingled roof. As they walked up to it, Doug told her the owners had built everything themselves from scratch, six years ago. Children were merrily playing in front of the entrance, where a knocker with two hearts graced the door.

"They don't have any kids," said Doug. "But this place is full of them."

They walked up through the porch and veranda into a living room with a large chimney and an old piano in a corner. The slender dark-haired woman in her forties who came to meet them wore a fringed buckskin jacket and jeans. It was good that Doug had warned Pauline beforehand: Velma's face was indeed completely lopsided, the left side had collapsed, and when she smiled, one side of her mouth turned down while the other side went up revealing her gums; one eye remained half-closed. Her chin seemed to have disappeared and one shoulder rode higher than the other; her torso leaned forward as if she were about to take a tumble. When she greeted Doug, it was with a low smoker's voice and a lovely twinkle in her eyes. Then she saw Pauline and stretched out her hands. Ah, so this was Doug's delightful stepdaughter! she exclaimed. Doug puffed up with pride and said yes, this was Pauline, and she was here to see the horses.

"A horse lover, eh?" grinned Velma, with her wonky yet charismatic smile. "Always welcome here. Let's go outside and meet them."

Pauline felt her heart pump with joy as they drew nearer to the corral, and she at last saw the horses. She asked Velma if they were all mustangs and Velma said yes, straight from Nevada's wild herds. Her father, Joe, knew how to take the wild out of a mustang, she said, and he liked to do it in a softer manner than most ranchers. He used to tell her mustangs were born in the wind and that breaking them in needed to be done without brutality or haste.

A young boy was driving a horse around the pen as they watched on, using a lariat and a long whip. After a light flick of the whip, the animal changed direction. This took time, explained Velma to Pauline, teaching a mustang to adapt its pace, to get it to canter, trot, and halt. Some wild horses became scared and hostile, lashing out with their hooves. Patience was key.

"Good job!" shouted Velma and the boy nodded his head under the wide Stetson.

Pauline took this all in, forgetting the heat, the wind, her dry mouth; she watched the young boy break in the horse as Doug went to work on Velma's car. A tall, burly man, Velma's husband, Charlie, said hello, and Pauline answered politely, not taking her eyes off the palomino colt in the pen.

"That's Tundra," said Charlie, as he left. "Last week, you couldn't even get close to her."

When the young boy finished working with Tundra, he came over to Pauline and, as he took off his hat to wipe his brow, Pauline saw that she had it all wrong; this was no boy, but a freckle-faced girl her age with a head of curly hair.

"Hi," she said to Pauline, "I'm Billie-Pearl."

Pauline said hi in return, taken aback.

"Fancy a ride?" said Billie-Pearl. "Not on Tundra, who'd throw you off big time, but on an older, gentler horse."

Pauline admitted she had never done any horseback riding.

Billie-Pearl whistled, but not in a rude way. "Not ever been on a horse and you're from Nevada?"

"I'm not from Nevada. I'm from Paris, France."

Another admiring whistle.

"Son of a gun, I've never met someone born in Paris, France!" she hooted. "Gee, hello, Mademoiselle! I'll go fetch Rocket. Are you ready for your first lesson?"

Billie-Pearl vanished before Pauline could protest. A few minutes later, she was back with a blonde-maned chestnut mare. Rocket was a sweetheart, Billie-Pearl told her to reassure her, because Pauline must have looked worried stiff. They were going to take it easy, there was no rush, but first they had to get to know each other, right? Rocket needed to be introduced to Pauline, and it was as easy as saying hello.

"Watch. Move nearer. By the way, Mademoiselle, what's your name?"

"Pauline."

"She's not going to bite you; you can come closer. Do you see those quivering nostrils? That means she can smell you. Smell is like a language to them. You can stroke her, like this. On her neck. Go ahead. Yes, good."

Billie-Pearl was knee high to a grasshopper, but her fearless banter impressed Pauline. She felt like a simpleton in comparison. As if she had sensed Pauline's discomfort, Billie-Pearl asked her not to pay attention to her, to address the horse as if Billie-Pearl was not there. Pauline could try talking to Rocket in French, while she was at it! Rocket would surely find that most intriguing.

While Billie-Pearl, whistling between her teeth, busied herself placing a saddle on the mare's back, Pauline spoke to Rocket in French, gently stroking her neck and shoulder. The sensation of the rough yet velvety hide under her fingers was extraordinary. How beautiful Rocket was, with her large, dark eyes and her golden mane.

"What are you telling her? I'm just curious." Billie-Pearl was now adjusting the stirrups.

"That she is gorgeous and how honored I am to meet her."

"She seems to like it! Gosh, you are tall, aren't you? I'm going to have to lower those stirrups some more."

As Pauline was wondering how on earth she was going to haul herself up on top of the horse, Billie-Pearl led Rocket to a mounting block, which would help Pauline up and into the saddle. Billie-Pearl was saying that later, when Pauline became a regular rider, she wouldn't need the mounting block—she'd heave herself up like the rest of them, one foot in the stirrup.

"Up you go, Mademoiselle!"

Pauline climbed the three steps, hitched one leg over the

saddle, and cautiously sat down. The mare shifted, and Pauline lurched sideways. There was nothing to hold on to, but she maintained her balance naturally as Billie-Pearl pushed both her feet into the stirrups.

"Good! Now pick up the reins, like this. And sit up straight, put your shoulders down."

Pauline felt high up, dominating Billie-Pearl and everything else. It didn't feel too bad.

"I'm going to lead her, but next time, you'll start her off yourself. Are you ready?"

Pauline nodded, and Billie-Pearl led Rocket slowly out of the pen, toward a larger paddock on the other side of the terrain. Pauline looked out ahead between Rocket's ears, her hands held rigidly in front of her; the horse's rolling motion made her seem even stiffer.

"Hey," called out Billie-Pearl. "Relax, Mademoiselle. You need to go with the flow. You'll get the hang of it."

It wasn't easy, but Pauline clung on. She wanted to show this unusual girl she could do it and, above all, she wished to become one with the mare: to share this unprecedented moment with her. They circled around several times, and Pauline began to feel better on Rocket's back, to finally thaw out.

"You're coming along," said Billie-Pearl. "I told you!"

Pauline blushed with joy. She didn't want to get off the horse; she wanted to stick to it, doggedly, and this surprised her.

"What's so special about mustangs?" Pauline asked her new friend, as they walked around some more.

"I'm no expert, you know!" the latter said, amused. "You should ask Velma."

"But you must know why you love them so much?" insisted Pauline.

Billie-Pearl stroked Rocket's beautiful head and ran her palm along her nostrils, which Pauline dreamed of doing, but didn't dare just yet. Billie-Pearl said she'd always loved them. Her father was a neighboring rancher who often collaborated with the Johnstons, but he raised cattle. She had grown to love and respect the wild horses; they were a part of the Old West legend, and the idea that they could be harmed made her sick.

"And they are harmed," she muttered. "You should see what we see here, how the mustangers treat them, the scumbags who hunt them down with their lassos, trucks, and planes to sell them for dog food. They should all go to hell!"

She spat on the ground, cursing. Pauline was both impressed and somewhat shocked—she would not be allowed to use such language.

"I'd like to come back here," said Pauline timidly. "But how?"

Billie-Pearl shrugged.

"Easy peasy. Velma drives to Reno and back every day. And to me, it looks like your daddy wouldn't mind."

"My father died a long time ago. Doug's my stepfather, but I love him just as much."

"Looks like that goes both ways."

"And how about you? How do you get here?"

"Well, what do you reckon, Mademoiselle?"

"I get it! On a horse!"

"You bet!"

—>>>>·—

Never would Pauline forget that first time at the Double Lazy Heart Ranch: the beginning of her friendship with Billie-Pearl, a profound and sincere bond that would withstand the years sweeping by and all sorts of hardships thrown their way. They became inseparable in that summer of 1952. During the holidays, Velma and Doug liaised to bring Pauline to and from Reno, so she could spend time with Billie-Pearl and the horses. Everyone understood just how important their friendship was, except Marcelle.

Pauline just couldn't get enough of the atmosphere of the ranch: the smell of hay and dung in the barn, the horses she was soon able to recognize by name, and week after week she made progress riding Rocket, even though she knew she'd never be as good as Billie-Pearl. It seemed that girl was born on a mustang. She became familiar with Velma's team, a bunch of different people of all ages, from all over Nevada and even California, united in their quest to preserve mustangs. Pauline had a soft spot for Doctor O'Brian, the veterinarian who regularly drove over, bringing his big black satchel. He had a melodious Irish accent, and she loved watching him work, the way he spoke reassuringly to the wounded horses as he tended to them.

After that first summer, Pauline became one of the ranch's regular visitors, coming to see her new friend and the Johnstons, as well as the horses she had learned to love. Marcelle was the only one to remain unenthusiastic; according to her, riding a horse and hanging out with ranchers were unfeminine activities, unworthy of a young Parisienne from a good family. Pauline was going to end up looking like that tomboy Billie-Pearl, whom she found coarse and ill-mannered. Doug took Pauline's defense and that of her friend, but even if Pauline was sorry to see how often the quarrels between Doug and Marcelle turned sour, that didn't stop her from going back to Wadsworth and becoming a skilled rider. It seemed to her there was nothing more important than going to the ranch whenever she could and being near the mustangs. Little by little, she felt more confident, sure of herself. Even if she knew she still had a long way to go.

—⟫⟫⟫—

Three years slipped by, marked by the rhythm of Pauline and Billie-Pearl's cavalcades, by the arrival of new mustangs cared for and safeguarded by the Johnstons. Velma was an exceptional leader, revered by them all. In 1955, she even earned herself a new nickname: "Wild Horse Annie," thrown at her in a heated debate by a disgruntled officer of the Bureau of Land Management. It made headlines. In 1955, two other significant events left their mark: Marcelle's mother passed away, and Pauline accompanied her to Paris to attend the funeral. They flew for the first time. It had been almost ten years since they had left France. Marcelle, overwhelmed with grief, broke down in tears when she saw family and friends again. She had missed Paris so much.

It was a different story for Pauline. In spite of the happiness of being reunited with her kin, she no longer felt at home, and that was instantly obvious to her. Her native city seemed gray, grimy, teeming with tiny cars and frenzied pedestrians rushing around like ants. The air reeked of pollution. She missed Doug. She missed Billie-Pearl. And Rocket and Tundra. She craved the immensity of the desolate, wild landscapes she had learned to love, the ever-changing glow of the sky; Lake Tahoe's startlingly cool waters (even in the heat of summer) where she swam with Jim and Doug each holiday. She missed their neighbors, their friends, Daisy from the five-and-dime store, her classmates, her teachers. She missed Reno with all her heart. While her mother sobbed at the thought of leaving Paris, Pauline had only one goal in mind: getting back to Nevada.

The same year, near Christmas, after a cataclysmic storm, the Truckee River burst its banks, swamping Reno and its surroundings; the damage was extensive throughout the region, and recovery took weeks. For several days, Charlie and Velma's partly waterlogged ranch remained unreachable. But the Johnstons were fine, the mustangs were all safe, and Pauline was soon reassured.

––––⟫⟫⟫––

One Saturday in February 1956, fresh powdery snow fell during the night, and as Pauline was dropped off at the ranch by Doug, she straight away sensed agitation. A gang of unscrupulous mustangers had snapped up an entire herd, she learned, wounding some in the process. Velma's team, including the brazen Billie-Pearl, had managed to free a good amount right under the assailants' noses—a dozen mares, a couple of foals, and a very angry young stallion.

Pauline could hear earsplitting screams coming from the barn, which sent shivers down her spine. Those noises weren't human, that she could tell.

"That's the young stallion," said Velma. She looked shattered. "He lost his family. He's inconsolable."

Pauline would not forget the moment she saw him for the

first time. She could only make out a large, inky black mass, and the whites of his eyes and teeth, which he bared as he screamed. Ears flattened, he was backed up against the barn wall, head low, pawing the ground again and again, letting out that awful, shrill noise. Nothing or no one could calm him down.

"He's been badly hurt," said Velma, "look at his leg and his ear. They're bleeding and torn. But even our good Doc O'Brian can't get near him."

Pauline felt near tears. She could tell how upset Velma was; she didn't know how to comfort her.

Later Pauline found Billie-Pearl straddling the wooden fence in front of the barn, looking in, where a large black shadow lurked in a corner. His feet were splayed, and his neck hung so low that his muzzle grazed the ground. The young stallion had gone silent; he hadn't eaten or drunk anything; every time someone tried to approach him, he became incredibly threatening. Doc O'Brian told Velma there wasn't much he could do, and he seemed most sorry about it. The bleeding had stopped, but the stallion needed stitches to his leg and ear.

Pauline went to sit next to her friend on the fence. Billie-Pearl's face was grim under the wide Stetson; she seemed older and wiser than her sixteen years. There was immense determination in the way she set her mouth.

"He hates humans because they killed his family," Billie-Pearl said at last. "I was there. I saw it all."

Pauline slid her arm around her friend's shoulders as the snow fell softly around them.

"I'm going to save that horse," Billie-Pearl muttered. "I'm going to save his life. I swear."

"I believe you," said Pauline.

"He won't let anyone near him. Not even Doc O'Brian. But I'll find a way. I don't care how long it takes. Did you see him?"

"I did, but not for long. He was too angry."

"He's a lord. The lord of the desert."

Billie-Pearl jumped off the fence, zipping up her padded jacket against the cold. She raised her chin and grinned.

"I found him a name, Mademoiselle. Want to hear it?"

"Sure."

"His name is Commander."

SUMMER 1960

Reno, Nevada

Each day, murmurs of gossip rustled over the cafeteria. All to do with the movie; no one talked about anything else. Montgomery Clift wallowing in the Sky Room, stone drunk; John Huston gambling away all his cash in the Mapes Casino; and the Millers, up on the sixth floor, flinging plates at each other and making such a racket that other hotel patrons complained to the manager. Not to mention stoic Clark Gable, who despite his courtesy and good manners, became fed up with waiting around in the blazing heat. Marilyn Monroe let him down daily, failed the entire crew, and Pauline caught on to that, even without the canteen natter. Mrs. Miller was no longer able to get up and, when she finally did, it was already past noon and she was a complete wreck.

"So, Frenchie, tell us, what's Monroe like when she finally crawls out of bed?"

"Already wasted and stark naked?"

"Linda let it slip she wears no underwear. There isn't a single bra or pair of panties in the cupboard."

Crude guffaws echoed around Pauline.

"Is she nice, at least?"

"Yes," said Pauline, unfazed, chewing on her burger. "Very nice."

"Meg over at the post department says she gets over five hundred fan letters a week. They're swamped!"

Pauline had learned to grow wary of the moments she spent at the canteen and decided to reveal as little as possible to Casper, Lincoln, Ernesto, Addie, Dan, and Pedro, or to any of the other cleaning ladies, telling them that when she started her shift Mrs. Miller was still asleep. That was her line and she stuck to it. She told them she hardly saw Mrs. Miller, and when she did she was with her coach, her personal assistant, or her masseur.

"That coach is a real sourpuss," seethed Fern.

"The guys on the set call her Black Bart," chortled Lincoln. "One of the drivers told me."

More sniggers.

"Montgomery Clift orders cocktails through room service all night long," said Pedro. "One after the other."

"After guzzling dozens of them in the Sky Room," added Dan.

"He and Huston make a beeline to the bar as soon as they get back to the Mapes after filming."

"And what about the king of cuckolds, Arthur Miller, does he ever smile? Never leaves a frigging tip either."

"Hey, keep it down, Marty, will you? Old Jones is staring at us."

"That movie sounds like a disaster. How are they able to shoot it with all that stuff going on?"

"They're running really late, right?"

"And what's it about, by the way?"

"Frenchie, do you know?"

"No idea," said Pauline.

That was a lie, because she had read in her mother's magazines that the film was written by Arthur Miller himself, centering on one woman and three men: four lost, damaged souls finding each other within Nevada's vast, dead emptiness and its ghost towns. That was all she knew.

She listened to them, smiled when necessary, laughed along with them, but gave nothing away. When her mother, bemused, had heard from an indiscreet client it was indeed Pauline, her own daughter, who cleaned the Miller suite, she found a way to tell Marcelle she rarely crossed paths with the movie star. Marcelle was crushed. She had insisted, hadn't Pauline had a single chat with her? Apart from good morning and good-bye, nothing else, Pauline replied. And besides, Mildred Jones forbade her to tell anyone about her work in the suite. Pauline had no intention of going back to the main floor restrooms, so she followed those instructions to the letter.

But things were different indeed, all those things that went on in the privacy of Suite 614 when Pauline was alone with Mrs. Miller. Things she kept to herself.

First, there had been that dreadful morning when she found Mrs. Miller seated in the living room, stonelike, staring out at the Sierras, a glass of Champagne in her hand. Her tearful, glazed eyes redder than ever, and her pallor almost grayish, making her seem ill. She hadn't even glanced up when Pauline came in, and she didn't say a word the whole time.

What did Pauline expect, seriously? That Mrs. Miller was going to become her best friend just because she had asked her to write a letter in French to her lover, Yves Montand? How could Pauline have fallen for that, thinking she'd build an intimate connection with one of the most famous women in the world? How could she have been so stupid, so vain? Thank God she had not breathed a word of this.

To Mrs. Miller, Pauline was a nobody. She was invisible. She was nothing. She was the faceless maid who cleaned up the mess every morning. Nothing more.

During the night, Pauline thought back to the frozen figure on the couch, clutching her drink. Was it going to be like that from now on? She dreaded going back there in the morning.

The next day, when Pauline let herself in to the suite, she heard loud voices. Horror-struck, she realized she was walking straight into an argument—a man was shouting, and he sounded angry. A door slammed, making her jump.

Arthur Miller stood in front of her, taking up all the space with his lanky frame, his face twitching with fury. He glared at Pauline, no doubt trying to figure out who she was and what the hell she was doing there, then stormed past without a word, grazing her shoulder as he rushed ahead, banging the door behind him.

"There goes old Grouchy Grumps," came the soft, girlish voice. "Don't take it personally, Pauline."

Mrs. Miller was there, wearing her bathrobe, with her tangled hair and drowsy, pink eyes. Pauline was happy to see her smile, but even happier hearing Mrs. Miller pronounce her name. She got to work on her chores, while Mrs. Miller answered the phone. She seemed to love doing that, unburdening herself to all those successive callers as if these people were in the same room, and Pauline's presence clearly didn't bother her. Out it all came: her exasperating husband who persisted in rewriting the script overnight and handing the new edits to her in the morning when she had already learned her lines with Paula; the stifling heat; the skirmishes between her coach and Huston, who couldn't stand each other, while "Arturo" (Pauline understood that was her nickname for her husband) took Huston's defense, which made the atmosphere, already unpleasant on set, even worse; the lack of sleep; the canker sores eating away the inside of her mouth; her period, which seemed ever more agonizing; the tenacious skin rash; and the devastating, uncontrollable yearning for Montand, who hadn't answered any of the calls or messages she had left for him at the Beverly Hills Hotel. How she had laughed with Montand, laughed so deeply, so delightfully, and today, there was no more laughter, none at all. In order to write that damned screenplay, her abhorrent husband tapped into their private life. Mortified, she had discovered he used her own sentences, her inner fragility, her most intimate misgivings, and she couldn't bear it any longer. She felt like he was plundering her, ransacking her very soul. And how could she ever trust him, after what she read in his diary four years ago in England? No, she hadn't forgotten. He had written he found her disappointing, that he was embarrassed by her in front of his intellectual friends. How could she possibly put that aside?

Pauline did her best to remain as discreet and noiseless as possible, pretending to ignore the unbroken monologue. When she plugged in the vacuum cleaner, Mrs. Miller disappeared into her room and continued her conversation there. Just as she was about to leave, Mrs. Miller came out, holding a periodical.

Pauline recognized it right away, *Paris Match*, the French magazine, with the cover she had already seen at home.

"Can you translate this article for me?"

Mrs. Miller handed her the spread about Montand and herself. Pauline looked down at the photos of the two movie stars; she had already read the piece, which Marcelle had commented on as well: It went into the details of how a room service waiter at the Beverly Hills Hotel had tattled to a journalist; how Simone Signoret had heard the scandalous news, which blazed all the way to Italy where she was shooting a movie; how Montand and Marilyn cozied up every morning over breakfast and every evening after they left the set, having dinner in one of the bungalows or in a small, romantic restaurant on the outer rim of Hollywood. After all, the movie they were shooting was called *Let's Make Love.* Was anybody really surprised?

Pauline did as she was told, quickly. When she got to the end of the article, Mrs. Miller remained silent. Pauline watched her walk to the refrigerator to fetch some Champagne, which she set on the table, then she went back to her room. She returned holding a flask of pills and a single needle. She sat down, seized a hard-shelled capsule, pricked it with the needle, emptied the powder into the champagne glass, and gulped it down.

"They work faster that way," she said. "Monty showed me. My actor buddy. He's as messed up as I am."

Thanks to the canteen chatter, Pauline had found out that Montgomery Clift had not recovered from his car accident four years ago; the young actor had just left Elizabeth Taylor's place in Beverly Hills when he fell asleep at the wheel and crashed into a telephone pole. He came out of it disfigured, depressed, and addicted to the bottle.

Paris Match was still open on the table, and Mrs. Miller flicked though it almost absentmindedly as she sipped her Champagne.

"I guess you're familiar with this French magazine?" she asked.

"I am. It's my mother's favorite. She reads it every week."

Mrs. Miller got up, cradling her drink; she went to stand in front of the large bay window, facing the glare of the sun. She stopped talking, but her silence didn't seem offensive. The phone rang, and she went to answer it. She told the person on the other end of the line she was far from ready, that she was expecting "Rafe," and couldn't do a thing without her morning massage, nor her nightly one, for that matter. With a dry little laugh, she said she was expecting another nightmarish day on the set from hell. She deeply begrudged her tormentor of a husband; he had written that script out of love, allegedly, so she could at last play a part that had nothing to do with a dumb blonde, but in the end, he was holding a callous mirror to her face: the depiction of a vulnerable, high-strung being, incapable of reaching inner harmony, of finding true happiness.

Pauline was in the bathroom scouring the tub, but she picked up the entire conversation, and Mrs. Miller's overburdened weary voice made her feel sad; how lonely, how fragile she seemed, with no one to watch over her.

"Are you married, honey?"

Pauline glanced up to the figure standing in front of her. She didn't dare say that in her case, there was no husband, but there was a three-year-old daughter.

"N-no, Mrs. Miller, I'm not."

The smile on Mrs. Miller's face was more like a grimace and it pained Pauline to look at it.

"No rush. Take your time. I know now I should have known

better. I thought the third time 'round, I'd find the one. I was wrong."

Mrs. Miller said her marriage had been marked by dreadful tragedy. Pauline remained by the tub, and Mrs. Miller leaned against the door frame, her glass still in her hand. She washed down another pill, Pauline noticed. She seemed drained, and Pauline nearly interrupted her, feeling she should get her to sit down, to have some water, or a bite to eat, but Mrs. Miller couldn't stop talking. She was on a roll.

Yes, she should have known, she went on, in such a low voice Pauline had to strain to hear. It was back in 1956, the day they got married, June 29. How could she ever forget that date after what had happened? She knew right then and there the marriage was doomed. He did too. But they never talked about it, they had tried to forget, she said, tried to push it all away, the hideous memory that marred that day forever.

Mrs. Miller rubbed her eyes, which looked very red all of a sudden; Pauline kept on listening attentively, the sponge still in the palm of her hand.

"Why am I telling you all this?"

Pauline, at a loss, felt unexpected pity. Would she dare comfort Mrs. Miller the way she consoled Lily when she hurt herself or was scared? She decided to risk it. "Sometimes it's easier to confide in somebody you don't know."

There was silence. Pauline held her breath.

"You're right. It is easier," Mrs. Miller said at last. "Thank you. You're so kind."

The phone rang again, but Mrs. Miller didn't budge. She went on talking as if her life depended in it. It had happened just before the press conference concerning their upcoming marriage, she went on, the one given by her and her fiancé in Roxbury, where he had a country home. They were being tailed by journalists as they headed for Old Tophet Road, but they were familiar with those narrow, twisting, treacherous lanes, and those journalists weren't.

They were all speeding, going too fast no doubt, and the reporters' car missed a hairpin bend, crashing into a maple tree with an awful smash of glass and metal that still echoed in her ears. They halted, retraced their steps. She had not been able to erase the sickening sight before them: a green Oldsmobile flattened against the tree trunk, and a woman, who had been thrown through the shattered windshield, lying on the ground. Her young driver, safe and sound, had collapsed in tears.

Mrs. Miller was looking at Pauline intently as if seeking some form of comfort from her. Pauline stuttered, saying how sorry she was, the whole thing was dreadful, and it must have been such an ordeal to undergo. Mrs. Miller seemed to muster up the rest of her courage to go on. In spite of her future husband begging her to keep her distance, striving to shield her from the atrocity of the scene, she had drawn nearer; she couldn't help herself, she felt she had to see it all.

Mrs. Miller's voice was barely a whisper now. The woman had been stretched out, with a broken neck and a bloody face, and she could see the big brown eyes blinking up at her confused, and she felt like crying because it was horrible and unfair. She got down on her knees, while her fiancé shouted at her to get back, and somehow the woman's blood got on her white blouse. She was pulled away, through a row of photographers and onlookers, and they drove to Old Tophet Road in stunned silence while she wept, haunted by the stain on her clothes and the frantic blink of those big eyes. She barely had time to change before the press conference began, but she was aware the marriage didn't stand a chance even before they pronounced their vows later that afternoon; it was as dead as a stillborn baby. The woman lying on the side of the road with her pearl earrings, her elegant pencil skirt, her high-heeled shoes absurdly still wedged on her feet, had been killed because of them.

"She died in the ambulance. Her name was Mara Scherbatoff. She was the New York correspondent for that French magazine, the one your mother reads every week. *Paris Match*."

There was such sorrow in Mrs. Miller's expression that Pauline was at a loss for words. Someone knocked at the door, startling them both.

"That'll be Paula," said Mrs. Miller. "Do you mind opening?"

Mrs. Strasberg was in her fifties, short and squat, and attired in an unflattering black sack dress. She wore large glasses that ate up most of her face and a black scarf tied over her graying hair. Pauline noticed she was wearing three different watches and she couldn't quite think why. Later, she learned it was because Mrs. Strasberg needed to know the time in London, Sydney, and Tokyo. During her lunch breaks, Pauline hadn't heard anyone put in a good word about her; she was considered standoffish. But Pauline had to admit she showed great tenderness toward Mrs. Miller, in an almost motherly way—asking her how she slept, if she'd had a good breakfast, how she felt.

"He changed the script again, you know," sighed Mrs. Miller. "I'm not going to make it."

Her coach placed an encouraging hand on her arm. "I know, dear. But you are going to make it. We'll go over the whole thing together. Remember, you are an extraordinary actress. You are the best."

"Are you sure?" came the childlike voice.

"The best, just like I said. Now, let's get back to it. Page one forty three. Are you ready?"

"Yes. You're doing Clark's lines?"

"Let's go."

Captivated, Pauline listened as she got on with the bedroom. She could see and hear everything from there. Mrs. Strasberg took on a gruffer, deeper tone, a man's voice.

"Where are you at? I don't know where you're at."

"I'm here, Gay, I'm with you. But...what if one day you turn around and suddenly you don't like me anymore?"

A silence.

"That was great, go on."

"I'm going blank."

"No worries, I'll take on your part with the attitude you'll need for all that bit. Remember Roslyn doesn't want to offend Gay, but she needs to speak her truth. Okay?"

"Okay, Paula."

"Have a sip of water. Breathe. That's it. Did you take a Benzedrine this morning? Do you want another?"

Mrs. Strasberg rummaged around in her bag and handed a tablet to Mrs. Miller, who swallowed it right away. Pauline wondered how many she had had since she woke up.

"Okay, I'm doing your part: *I know that look, and it scares me, Gay. Because I could never stay with a stranger.*"

It was time for Pauline to go, and she took her leave reluctantly; she would have liked to stay, listening to snatches of the mysterious movie that was being rewritten each evening to Mrs. Miller's despair.

As she gently closed the door of Suite 614, she heard the actress say in a beseeching, heartbreaking manner: *"Oh, love me, Gay! Love me!"*

And with that, Mrs. Miller burst into tears.

———⋙———

Pauline hadn't noticed anything in the beginning, but now, she could no longer ignore what was going on. Her coworkers obviously had a grudge against her, giving her the cold shoulder. Kitty was the only one to address her in a normal way. She was no longer welcome at the cleaning ladies' table, no one kept her a seat, and she had to eat elsewhere, with the operators, or the boiler room team. She hadn't yet grasped why they were acting this way, nor what she had done to deserve it, but it soon became apparent: Her colleagues were envious. They had found out Mrs. Miller had ordered Mildred Jones to assign Pauline to Suite 614 and to them, it was unfair. Why Pauline, and not them? Moreover, Pauline had less experience than they did, she was younger and only looked after the restrooms. And there was also the fact that Pauline was now in Mildred's good graces, the latter acting as her new protector, which was unprecedented—as well as unfathomable. So she did everything in her power to go unnoticed, lowering her head, remaining silent, hugging the walls. It was only when she found herself with her daughter, so adorable and comical, or when she was with Billie-Pearl and the mustangs on her days off, that the smile was back on her face.

From time to time, Mrs. Miller left her notes when she went

off to shoot on location. It was mostly quick hellos scribbled on Mapes stationery, but occasionally, there was a specific request concerning clothes, a dress, or some laundry. Pauline became familiar with the odd, winding handwriting that curved down along each side of the paper. Once, she found all the furniture in the living room pushed back against the partitions. The note left that day said, *I'm sorry for the mess, Pauline. I just needed some space.* Pauline kept all the notes, preciously.

Mrs. Miller often ate and drank in bed, which Pauline came to understand quickly due to the state of the sheets. The actress favored steaks, even first thing in the morning, and they had to be rare, with blood running out of them, otherwise she sent them back, which Pedro from room service had discovered. Each day, Pauline refreshed the bed. When Mildred wanted to know why she was doing this, Pauline showed her the dirty laundry still in the basket. The sheets looked like they'd endured a bloodbath and even the undaunted housekeeping director blanched when she saw them.

"You're not to tell anyone about this," she said.

"Of course, Mrs. Jones."

But there were many things Pauline did not mention, like the fact that Mrs. Miller was often naked and that it was deeply embarrassing, or the amount of empty prescription bottles she found every day in the bedroom trash; the quantity of medicine the actress was consuming daily was shocking. *What were all these pills for?* she wondered. Pauline knew Mrs. Miller was drained by the endless drives back and forth to the film locations, which were outside of Reno, made even more trying by the heat, glare, and dryness of the desert.

When the film crew returned in the evenings, Pauline was no

longer at the Mapes, but all she had to do was listen to Ernesto and Lincoln describe the limousines driving up and the passengers getting out of them, as stiff as zombies, and Mrs. Miller, prostrate, held up by her coach and her masseur who never left her side; apparently, he massaged her between takes during the day.

Ernesto and Lincoln had told her about the joint surprise birthday party thrown a couple of weeks ago on the mezzanine at the Mapes for John Huston and Kay Gable, Clark Gable's wife. Mr. and Mrs. Miller had attended, but they hardly spoke to each other. Mrs. Miller had seemed pleased enough to be seated next to Clark Gable, but she left early, going up to her suite right after dessert. The others stayed on to party, and Lincoln noticed Gable looked beat. That movie was sure taking its toll, he said, shaking his head. And was Mrs. Miller nice to her? Ernesto asked. It was funny, the amount of people who wanted to know this. She said Mrs. Miller was very nice. But she didn't add anything else, and Ernesto looked disappointed, just like Marcelle, day after day, eager for tidbits, snippets of information she never got from her daughter when Pauline got home.

When Pauline turned up one morning, a burly man in his late forties was standing in front of Suite 614, getting ready to knock. He sported a grizzled crew cut, khaki trousers, and a patterned shirt and looked like a simple tourist. Perhaps this commonplace man was a friend of Mrs. Miller? There was nothing glamorous about him, however. Nothing to do with Hollywood, surely.

"Good morning, may I help you, sir?" she said, pleasantly.

He smiled in return. He seemed gentle and caring.

"Hi. I don't think my knocks are being heard. I tried the doorbell as well, but that's not working either."

"I can let you in, sir, I have a pass," she said, and then turned bright red. She had no clue who this man might be and for all she knew he could be one of those adoring fans skulking in front of the Mapes all day hoping to catch a glimpse of the movie stars staying there. Lincoln, Ernesto, and the bellboys knew how to keep them out of the hotel, but maybe this one had escaped their surveillance.

The man gazed at her kindly.

"Oh, don't worry," he said. "Mrs. Miller is expecting me."

He read her name tag.

"So you're the Pauline she's mentioned. From Paris, France, right?"

Pauline blushed even redder, clutching on to her cart. She couldn't get over the fact Mrs. Miller spoke to other people about her.

"I'm Allan," he added, "but she calls me Whitey."

Doing her best to pull herself together, Pauline opened the door with her key and let him through. She was now used to the perpetual clutter in the suite. But she didn't let it get her down; after all, that was her job, cleaning up other people's mess. Right away, Whitey knocked on the bedroom door, which was ajar. He must be close to her if he was able to do that, thought Pauline. She wondered what his occupation was while she got to work in the untidy kitchen. Personal trainer?

The telephone began to ring ceaselessly, like it did every morning, but after a while, Whitey's voice could be heard; he was saying "she" was awake but under the weather. He'd start working on her while she was still lying down, he'd already done that. Yes, Ralph had been and gone, and Agnes was going to show up any minute. They were all going to do their best. They had no choice.

What was he going to do to her while she was still in bed? pondered Pauline, while she put away the champagne glasses in the kitchen. Some sort of workout? It was most mysterious. She went on to the living room and plugged in the vacuum cleaner, closing the connecting door so as to not disturb them. Even if she let her thoughts wander, she did her best to do her job properly, and she wasn't driven by the fear of Mildred Jones, but by the desire to make sure Mrs. Miller felt cozy and comfortable in the suite where she was spending most of her time. The Miller couple did not go out at night, as the front desk team had told her: He was busy in another room tweaking his screenplay, and she closed herself up in her suite with her inner circle. Neither of them went anywhere. Apparently, Arthur Miller sometimes joined John Huston at the casino, but that was it.

Somebody knocked on the door, and Pauline went to open it. It was a person from the film crew who handed her a garment bag with a smile.

"Outfit of the day!" he said and left.

Pauline peeked through the plastic and glimpsed a white sleeveless cotton dress with a low-cut neckline and a pattern featuring red cherries, green stems, and leaves. She hung it up carefully in the entrance, admiring it, and went back to tidying the living room. She couldn't hear any noise from the bedroom. Had Mrs. Miller gone back to sleep?

As she wiped down surfaces here and there, she thought about the conversation she had had last night with her mother.

A tearful and tipsy Marcelle had told her daughter she couldn't stand Reno any longer, she hated it, and she knew everyone here hated her. She'd had it up to here about being the *Parisienne* with the accent, she felt buried alive in this godforsaken dump, she had no friends, and for the past fifteen years she'd been petering out and no one saw it. She missed Paris so badly she felt she was going to die; she hungered to go back there, back to her old life, back to it all. What madness to have followed a man who was so different, to believe she might adapt to the hugeness of this country, to think for one moment she could be happy here. Day after day, she felt herself wilting away and no one gave a damn. Soon, she'd be fifty, no longer young, with no future, no drive. Those old men on the dock at Le Havre had been spot-on: It wouldn't ever work out with the Yankees. She should have listened to them. Wasn't Reno where everything ground to a halt, Marcelle had laughed, bitterly, especially marriages, and all that cash ending up in the casino sinkholes.

Pauline was used to her mother's meltdowns and knew how to calm her, but last night, she had found herself helpless faced with such woe; she hadn't been able to find the right words to soothe her and felt bad about it. Before going to bed, silently so as not to wake Lily, she had gazed at the small Eiffel Tower her cousin had given her and that she had carefully kept; she didn't miss Paris in the least, but her life here, right now, weighed heavily upon her because she was still under Kendall Spencer's yoke. She had not been able to pursue the veterinary training she dreamed of; everything had come to a stop when Lily was born. At times, for other reasons, she felt just as plagued as her mother. It was impossible to start a new relationship with a man because Kendall acted like he owned her, even if he was married to that insufferable Evaline; furthermore, whenever a potential boyfriend discovered Pauline had a daughter and was a single mother living with her parents, he backed off. Pauline felt as though Kendall had branded her, like she was his possession. She was stuck in a rut and had no inkling how to get out of it.

She was thinking about all this, energetically dusting, when the doorbell rang yet again. A white-haired woman in her sixties stood there, holding a large square box. She was small, stout, with a benign smile, a dowdy dress, and flat shoes. She looked like someone's charming granny, thought Pauline.

"Hello there. I'm Agnes."

Pauline remembered Whitey mentioning that name. She racked her brain trying to imagine what Agnes had to do with him and with Mrs. Miller. And what was in that big box?

"Is Whitey here, dear?"

"Yes, ma'am. He got here a while ago."

"Oh, good, so he's probably made progress. And is Paula here?"

"No, not yet."

"I'll get myself some coffee. I know where it is. Say, you're that nice Pauline from France, I believe?"

Pauline from France. She couldn't help grinning.

Agnes made some coffee, going on with her mild banter. The box sat on the table. Drat! Wasn't it horribly hot in Nevada, she exclaimed. She came from New Jersey and couldn't handle heat waves. How did they all manage out here?

Whitey's voice was heard.

"Agnes? She's all yours."

Pauline watched her put down her cup, grab the box, and rush to the room while Whitey came out of it, composed and beaming. Who was this attentive, considerate couple? Two people who cared deeply for Mrs. Miller, obviously.

Mrs. Strasberg turned up, donned in her black garb, sporting an outlandish colonial helmet. She settled in the living room, her large handbag at her feet, and began to talk sotto voce with Whitey while Pauline finished up in the bathroom. But Pauline had a sharp ear. Mrs. Strasberg was dead set against Arthur Miller, that was clear. According to her, he was taking matters too far, constantly altering that infernal screenplay, and they were all going to blow a fuse. Those Magnum photographers covering the production had fully grasped the ill-tempered mood on set. From now on, two opposite camps were formed, she grumbled—theirs, which included Marilyn, Ralph, May, Whitey, Monty, Agnes, and herself, and the director's camp, which had the producer, Frank Taylor, his assistant, and the continuity girl. Of course, Miller had sided with Huston's clique, she railed, locked up in two fully soundproofed suites at the Mapes, equipped with a projection booth, where Huston worked with his film editor. This was their war room where they watched the dailies without summoning anyone except Gable, who did not belong to either camp.

Pauline listened, without missing a beat. Mrs. Strasberg went on: What about the fact the movie was being filmed in black and white, for crying out loud? What an old-fashioned idea! Courteously, Whitey inserted it was probably best that way because of Marilyn's bloodshot eyes, and Mrs. Strasberg had to admit that, in that respect, he was right.

The clock was ticking. All smiles, Agnes finally joined them.

"She's coming," she announced.

"Great," answered Mrs. Strasberg, "for once, we are only *two* hours late."

She picked up the phone and ordered reception to send the cars along. And please could they make sure not to forget the bottles of water like last time, she sighed.

Now Pauline caught a floral, powdery perfume she had learned to identify, since it often lingered in the suite in a subtle manner—today, it flourished in full bloom. On the threshold, a woman came to a standstill, wearing a tight white dress with a cherry print and high-heeled white pumps that lengthened her slim calves. Her face was exquisitely made up: doe-like eyes, scarlet mouth; her blonde hair, thick and lustrous, tumbling in delicate waves against her shoulders. Under Pauline's stunned gaze, she undulated into the room, her body swaying in a new way, full of sensuality and poise; and when she spoke to the others, even the way she moved her lips differed from Mrs. Miller.

Pauline felt like the wind had been knocked out of her. Yes, it was her. The one she had failed to recognize, because in real life, first thing in the morning, without a hint of makeup, Mrs. Miller had nothing to do with who she was now—that dazzling blonde in the low-cut dress holding herself in a different manner, talking in a different manner; she had simply turned into someone else: the movie star.

The small group was getting ready to leave.

The actress slowed in front of the young woman, giving her a flash of the famous smile.

"Hi there, Pauline," said Marilyn Monroe.

1956

Reno, Nevada

Pauline had gotten her driver's license the previous year when she
turned sixteen. Marcelle thought sixteen was far too young, too
risky, and she wouldn't listen to Doug when he explained it was
a milestone in the lives of young people in this country, something of a tradition. He had lent her an old Buick Roadmaster,
a secondhand convertible he had mended himself, and whenever
Pauline set off to Wadsworth to spend time with Billie-Pearl and
the mustangs, sheer joy consumed her: She felt such freedom,
her hair flying in the wind, singing at the top of her lungs as she
drove along tracks bordered by wilderness where she only ever
passed a car or two.

Sometimes, on her way, she'd stop at the only place to get gas,
as Doug always told her to make sure the Buick was not going
to run out of fuel in the middle of a dirt road. The gas station
was on a higher spot surrounded by thickets of wild herbs and
tall yellowing pine trees letting out a sweet gummy smell. The

man running the service station knew Doug, and he looked as gaunt and yellowed as the pine trees circling the premises. Pauline liked him. His name was Parker and apparently he'd been running his business there forever. He knew the Johnstons too. Whenever anyone in the area needed a refuel, they were bound to go by Parker's. He sold homemade milk shakes, which were surprisingly tasty, and there was a phone. At each refill, Pauline enjoyed spending time there, sipping her strawberry milk shake, watching the clouds being chased by the breeze.

"You goin' up to see Velma and the mustangs?" Parker would always ask.

"That's right," she'd say.

"Good people," came the invariable answer.

Sometimes a woman was there, cleaning up the kitchen area, and Pauline figured this had to be Parker's sister, as she was as tall, as lean, and as yellow-skinned as he was. She was pleasant too. During summer, when it got so hot, she'd put extra ice in Pauline's soda.

"You like it out here?" Parker asked one Saturday. He was busy fixing the tarpaulin on the roof.

"I do," said Pauline.

"You don't mind all that emptiness? Drives my kids crazy. They get bored. They prefer the casinos."

"No, I like it. I'm never bored of it."

Parker seemed surprised.

"Just miles and miles of dust, rocks, and horses. Nevada's nothin' like Paris."

She had to laugh. How could she explain to Parker that Paris was another existence now, one she never wanted to go back to? She could try to describe her enthrallment with the landscape, the way the sun drew patterns on the wind-whipped wilderness, but she knew he wouldn't understand this was her world now—those rocky, arid plains stretching far away and out of sight; that waterless territory she had come to love, reveling in the pure air, the scent of snow and sand she only ever picked up here.

———

There was excitement at the ranch. In the past few weeks, a new stable boy had come to lend a hand with Velma's team. He was from Montana and his name was Gus. Pauline liked him, and she soon discovered the feeling went both ways. He was seventeen, the same age as Pauline, tall and slender, with a timid smile and twinkling eyes, and he was a magnificent horseman; even Billie-Pearl had to bow to his supremacy. Pauline had garnered a few clumsy kisses from boys in her class, but the clandestine ones she shared with Gus behind the stables ignited her from head to toe. When she reappeared, she felt tipsy, all pink and limp, having to deal with Billie-Pearl's grins and gentle teasing. When she got home, all she could think about was Gus and his kisses, and once, Marcelle asked her suspiciously why her mouth was such a dark red. She did not want to tell Marcelle she had a boyfriend. Her first! She couldn't wait to get back to the ranch, to spend time with him. Doug picked up on this.

"You like that young fella, don't you?" he asked one evening. "The one from Montana."

Pauline flushed, but managed to say that, yes, she did like him, very much.

"I won't tell your mother," said Doug, winking.

But despite the thrill of being with Gus, Pauline's major concern was to do with Commander. One month after his arrival at the ranch, the horse still refused to be tended to, ate little, and seemed to wither away before their very eyes. Pauline spent many an hour by her friend's side, just watching the black mustang. They hardly drew near him, but Billie-Pearl was convinced he knew they were there, that they were safeguarding him in their own way. She often spoke to him, and she told Pauline he'd get used to her voice that way.

"If he keeps this up, he's not going to be around much longer," declared Doc O'Brian one morning.

Listening to him, they were filled with dread. Velma also had a bad feeling. She told them some mustangs never got over being separated from their kin. Pauline asked whether freeing him now would be a good idea? But Billie-Pearl already knew the answer to that: Commander was still doing too poorly to confront the wilderness. There was no way he could fend for himself.

Gus and the other stable boys had been able to confine Commander to a smaller, ring-shaped, dappled paddock, but he quickly felt isolated in there, showing signs of impatience whenever he spotted the other horses together in the nearby larger corral. Doc O'Brian feared he might injure those mares and foals who weren't from his original herd. Billie-Pearl disagreed, insisting he could do with some company. Velma was undecided.

One day, Commander hadn't stopped bucking, pounding against the wooden fence, snorting, quickly finding himself covered with foam. Pauline asked her friend what was wrong with him.

"He wants to beat it, is all," hissed Billie-Pearl.

Again and again, the stallion threw himself against the poles walling the corral, making them quake under his weight. Doc

O'Brian wasn't there that day, and neither were Velma and Charlie. Nobody knew what to do.

One of the bars gave way after minutes of hefty battering, and then another. The stable boys, Gus included, tried not to panic, doing their best to mend the fence, while Billie-Pearl yelled at them, shoving them away. They had to let him go, she screamed.

Commander was losing his mind, and it seemed to Pauline the cramped enclosure was smothering him, he had to get out of it at any cost, demolishing anything standing in his way, and as if to reinforce her thoughts, he began to gallop faster and faster, gaining momentum; he seemed beside himself, eyes wild with rage, white foam gathering at the corners of his mouth.

"He's going to jump!" shouted Gus.

But Commander didn't have enough space to clear the fence, which was over seven feet high, so he reared up on his hind legs and began to hammer away at the wood with furious hooves until the whole thing crumbled apart. Billie-Pearl tried to calm him as if she were talking to a troubled child, but Pauline sensed her dismay, could tell how powerless she felt.

The stallion suddenly shoved his head into the opening created by his own blows, heaving himself through the shattered planks. Pauline was horrified by the sight of him trapped by the splintered wood lacerating the hide of his neck, creating an agonizingly gruesome choker. Commander whinnied in pain, trying in vain to break away, and he at last retreated, toppled over, and came crashing down heavily on his back where he lay, dazed and hemorrhaging. Aghast, Pauline saw one of his eyes had been affected.

After a fleeting moment of silence, Billie-Pearl shrieked, "For Pete's sake, go call the Doc! Move it! Get cracking!"

Gus rushed off to the ranch, but nobody needed the Doc at the present minute to see how critically Commander had been hurt. He lay there, panting, knocked out from his fall, his neck full of deep gashes with blood pumping from them, and Pauline listened to the unbearable wheezing that sounded so human, like a wail for help.

"Do you think he's broken something?" Pauline asked Billie-Pearl, whose face had gone completely white.

Her friend did not respond, eyes glued to the horse flat on the ground. She came nearer to the gate, slowly, reaching out with her hand to open the latch.

"Don't go in there!" bellowed Gus, who was now back. "The Doc is on his way. He said to leave him be. He'll be here in half an hour."

"Come back, Billie!" pleaded another stable boy. "You know how powerful he is, don't be such a hothead."

The young girl entered the paddock, levelheaded and sure of herself, coming closer, step by step, watched by the others, who remained dumbfounded. Nobody spoke. A coy spring sun shone down mildly, birds chirped, and everything seemed peaceful, apart from the blood flowing thickly and the stallion's unremitting rale.

She squatted by Commander's side, speaking to him. His left ear, the injured one, hardly moved, but the right one seemed to have a life of its own, twitching, like the horse's eyes, which darted up and down. One of them had been horribly scratched by the splintering wood. Pauline clenched her fists as tight as she could; she dreaded the horse might buck, sending a vicious kick toward Billie-Pearl, but Commander did not budge, he seemed to have given up. Giving up wasn't in his nature, however. Billie-Pearl, at last, laid a hand on him, after an endless moment, right down on his mane, then she quickly lifted it off. But Pauline would not forget the sight of the small pale hand on the black horsehair, as if Billie-Pearl had branded him with her respect, admiration, and adoration. Gus came to stand by Pauline and, for the first time, hugged her in front of all the others, kissing her cheek. Everyone noticed, but no one said anything; it was a special day.

The Doc turned up in a rush, with his big satchel. He didn't tell Billie-Pearl off for not following his instructions; he simply asked her to describe exactly what had happened, then he swiveled, saw Pauline at the fence, and called out to her, motioning her to come.

"I could do with your help, as usual. But this is going to be a bit more daunting. Ready? You, Billie, go on talking to him. Seems to like it. Don't stop."

Pauline had often assisted the Doc during his rounds with the mustangs, but she had not been involved before to such an extent. A sedative needed to be administered by means of an injection in the neck with a long syringe, which made Billie-Pearl shudder. Commander didn't appreciate it at all, and the Doc had to sit on top of him to press the plunger and empty the entire product.

"Come on, man," said the Doc. "This is for your own good."

Billie-Pearl went on speaking to Commander in a low voice, never far from his trembling ears. It had taken a while for the horse to finally calm down, and then the Doc, with Pauline's help, cleaned, bandaged, and stitched up the numerous wounds. The one around the eye was ugly, but mercifully not serious.

"You're an ace at this, Pauline!" said the Doc. "You'd make a good vet."

"I agree," added Billie-Pearl.

Embarrassed, Pauline pulled a face. She didn't like drawing attention to herself.

"I'm serious, Pauline. How old are you now?"

"Seventeen."

"Well, you'll be finishing school soon. Think about it. You're good with horses. Calm and precise. And you love them. Don't you?"

Pauline nodded. She had seldom envisioned her future because she felt she was too young to do that. It seemed to her she had many things yet to discover and learn. But maybe the Doc was right. Maybe she should give it a thought.

"I already know I want to devote myself to mustangs, just like Velma," said Billie-Pearl, proudly.

Nobody doubted it.

Commander was aware of what was going on; he remained groggy, no longer putting up a fight, but that didn't mean much, warned the Doc. When he was healed, he'd go back to his natural wildness. Some mustangs couldn't be tamed, nor mounted, and that's the way it was. While he said that, the Doc looked right at Billie-Pearl. She had to understand Commander might not turn out to be what she longed for: a trained animal who'd obey her.

Billie-Pearl spoke in turn to the Doc, and Pauline noticed her possessive hand was back on the stallion's mane. She answered she had no intention of turning Commander into a circus horse; she had too much consideration and awe for him to lower him to that, and after all, he was the lord of the desert, she said twice, and that's what she wanted to protect and preserve, his status as a leader, his liberty on this land and everything that stood for. She wanted to give his independence back to him, so he could start his tribe, find his mares, breed foals, defend them in turn. The life he had had before was what she wanted to offer.

"The good news," said the Doc, "is that our big rascal hasn't broken anything. But this fall sets him way back as he was already weak. He's going to be with us a while longer."

As spring crept into summer and the almighty Nevadan heat returned, Commander took a long while to heal. He was in a larger paddock, but still by himself and, according to Velma, as soon as he was better he'd be set free. He went on limping for a bit, which worried Doc O'Brian, but then he seemed to get better. His wounds were drying out, leaving a web of scars forming an ornate choker around his neck that wouldn't go away. Now that he was recovering, it became difficult to get close to him again: Every time the Doc tried to do so, out came a low rumble, like a warning. Pauline couldn't believe she had actually been able to touch him when he was sedated. There was no way she would dare do that again.

But, one unforgettable day, she came close to him again. Billie-Pearl was in town that morning for a visit to the dentist and, as usual, Pauline took up most of her friend's tasks at the ranch. She felt at home here. This was where she could concentrate on her efforts with the horses and derive keen pleasure from it. Yes, she was part of the team now and she set her heart to it. Sometimes she grinned to herself, thinking of her mother's expression when she got home, reeking of manure. She was unable to explain to Marcelle how being near the mustangs made her feel alive; how tending to them put meaningful joy in her life. How could Marcelle understand? All day long, her mother dealt with hairdos and perms, nail varnish and perfume—a form of futility Pauline did not relate to. They were worlds apart.

Pauline started out by caring for Tundra and Rocket, her favorites. She could hear Gus whistling as he went about his own work in a nearby pen. Velma was firm with routine. They had to stick to it: adding grain, cleaning and refilling water buckets, mucking out stalls, replenishing fresh hay. This could take a good half hour for each stall. Rocket was getting on now, she was slower, but she retained her graceful beauty, and Tundra had certainly calmed down since she'd given birth to a couple of foals.

"You lovely ladies can now get on with your day," Pauline murmured as she finished up, stroking the mares affectionately.

Commander was in his own stall, where he'd remain until Billie-Pearl came to fetch him to lead him to his paddock. She was the one who looked after him, with the Doc. No one else dared. As she passed in front, Pauline looked in, just to check, then drew back, startled. The stallion was standing right by the entrance, inches away from her. Her first instinct was to back off, but somehow she remained there, facing him.

And after a short while she realized her initial fear was fading. Oddly, she felt both soothed and empowered by his presence. And later on, whenever she thought of him, that feeling of quiet calm would overtake her once more. It became her little secret. No one else had to know.

———⟫———

Day after day, after her work with the other mustangs, Billie-Pearl came to sit on the fence to watch over Commander, even under a downpour or in a heat wave. She didn't come near him nor try to brush against him when she fed him or changed his water, but she always spoke to him, murmuring words no one could hear. And no one made fun of her either. Whatever it was she was doing with Commander was taken seriously. And Velma approved.

Pauline discovered the stallion seemed to keep an eye out for Billie-Pearl. While she was in the corral next door, busy breaking in a mare, he kept pricking up his ears every time he heard her voice. Whenever she looked after the foals, Commander popped his head over the fence to see what she was up to. One day, he even neighed loudly. It sounded so much like a plea that everyone who heard it grinned. Velma finally gave in to Billie-Pearl's request: The stallion was allowed to mingle with the yearlings.

Commander circled each youngster with panache, showing them who was boss, but he didn't overdo it, nor take advantage of his authority. One long-legged two-year-old colt with a pale gray hide and surprising blue eyes followed him around adoringly, not leaving his side. Sometimes Commander shunted him away with his muzzle, not aggressively, but the colt came back eagerly. And after a while, Commander gave in to the pleasure of frolicking, which he had been deprived of for so long, playfully engaging with the colt, pretending to fight him, then taking off, all the better to start over again. The stallion was careful not to harm the little one, as he was so much heavier and larger.

"What's that little gray's name?" asked Gus, entertained by their frolicking. "He's not spooked, is he?"

"He hasn't got a name," said Pauline. "Any ideas?"

"I know!" said Gus. "Dustin."

—⋙—

For the next couple of days, Commander and Dustin became inseparable and their antics were a joy to watch. But the morning came when Commander was to be turned loose. He was now back to his magnificent self, apart from the torn left ear and the scars on his neck. Billie-Pearl knew in her heart of hearts the young stallion could not stay at the ranch. According to her, the good thing was that Commander now knew humans weren't all bad, not like the bastards who had decimated his family.

"He won't remember me, anyway, will he?" she asked.

The Doc shook his head. He said he didn't think so, but there was something special about Commander. They had all felt it. He was different.

The gate was opened, and the stallion sensed straight away he could take off; for a short moment, he lifted his nose to the wind, smelling it, pawing the ground. He tossed his head like a haughty lord, snorting loudly, flicking his tangled tail, then he dashed out, a streak of ebony, building up his gallop in a couple of seconds, then he was gone, escorted by the quick thud of his hooves. The other mustangs neighed, especially Dustin, while Commander, now a mere black spot, sped across the distant hills, disappearing at last from sight. Billie-Pearl remained silent, her face turned down.

"You did a great job with him," said Velma, consolingly. "You can be proud, Billie."

"And you'll look after Dustin now," added Pauline. "He'll need support too."

Billie-Pearl managed a rueful smirk. During the next couple of days, Pauline racked her brains trying to figure out how to bring a smile back to her friend's face. She finally had an idea: next Wednesday was July Fourth. Over the course of the past ten years of her life in Reno, Pauline had seen that that date was one Doug liked to spend with his family, like Thanksgiving; he even said to Marcelle that this was like her Bastille Day for Americans, and it was just as important. They usually celebrated Independence Day with Doug's parents, at Lake Tahoe, to watch the fireworks, but this year, Doug wanted to try something else. He had booked a dinner table for them all at the Sky Room in the Mapes Hotel on Virginia Street, where they'd be able to see the fireworks in the distance and enjoy a refined meal with all those French wines his wife loved. Marcelle was over the moon. This meant she could dress up, rub shoulders with the elegant hotel clients, which could also be useful for luring them to her hair parlor. Pauline had never been inside the Mapes Hotel, and she was looking forward to it. When she asked to bring Billie-Pearl along, Doug said yes immediately.

Billie-Pearl went into a panic—she had nothing to wear! Pauline reassured her she'd lend her a dress.

"Oh, come on, Mademoiselle, you're twice as tall as me!"

Pauline managed to convince Marcelle to give Billie-Pearl a dress she no longer wore, as they were both more or less the same height, Marcelle being a little taller. And when they all saw her wearing it, a pretty sleeveless one in blue georgette with a sash waist, even Marcelle had to admit Billie-Pearl cleaned up real nice.

"Wow," breathed nine-year-old Jimmy, wearing a tie for the first time in his life. "We should go to the Mapes more often."

Her brother looked so handsome and grown-up all of a sudden, with his carefully combed hair, new white shirt, and shiny shoes.

Pauline wore a green silk dress her mother had picked out for her last year, with rounded shoulders, a cinched waistline, and full skirt. The color brought out her eyes, Billie-Pearl said. Marcelle liked to make everyone wait while she got ready. They were all getting impatient in the living room, with Doug hollering they would be late, and they could lose the table, which would be a real pity, when she appeared in all her finery, every inch the Parisienne with an ivory lace evening dress, slender ankle-strapped shoes, and a white pearl clutch.

"Oh, my," mumbled Doug, starstruck. He admired Marcelle as if, at that moment, he was rediscovering the woman he had fallen in love with in 1946. For him, she had not changed, and he chose not to see the sadness that gnawed at her today. *For how much longer?* Pauline wondered, as they piled into Doug's station wagon.

On the way, Marcelle told them that she knew the Mapes quite well, because her flushest customers visited it and often invited her for drinks at the bar, or in the famous Sky Room. She'd even done the boss's sister's hair once or twice. The Mapes was indeed the "chicest" place in Reno, she insisted, and thank heavens it existed, bringing a touch of class to a city that lacked so much of it. Doug listened to her chatter without flinching. He seemed so cheerful nothing could touch him. He added that the name of the hotel came from a notable Reno family, cattle ranchers from the previous century. They had done well.

A valet came to pick up the Ford, while Pauline followed her family up a couple of steps. A porter wearing a red morning jacket opened the large glass doors for them. His name was Ernesto and he was happy to welcome them to the Mapes Hotel.

Everything was impressive here, and even Jimmy, usually

exuberant, had fallen silent. Several shops opened directly into the hall: a barber, a beauty salon, a florist, and even Turkish baths. A stylish crowd thronged there; men wore suits and ties, and the women pretty dresses. Cigarette smoke swirled blue above the fray, while background music playing over loudspeakers drowned out the murmur of voices.

"We're so much better off here than at the Riverside across the street," said a made-up lady to her husband, squeezed into his dinner jacket.

"I also prefer the Mapes casino to the Riverside one," replied the latter, lighting a cigar.

A scrawny, red-haired young man dressed in a uniform came up to meet them, greeting them politely. Pauline deciphered the first name on the badge: *Marty*. In an affected voice, Marcelle replied they had a table for five in the Sky Room, in the name of Hammond. He asked them to follow him, led them to the front desk, where a man named Lincoln checked their reservation. Everything was in order. Marty showed them the way to the elevators.

"Is this your first time at the Mapes?"

Marcelle smiled at him benevolently, like a queen confronted with a humble subject.

"For them, yes. Me, no. I come here often."

Her mother's French accent was even more pronounced tonight, Pauline noticed. They rode up with a liftboy called Casper.

"How many elevators does the Mapes have?" Jimmy asked him.

"Four," Casper replied. "But this one is the only one that goes directly to the twelfth floor, to the Sky Room."

"So you go up and down all day?"

"That's right. Like a yo-yo."

Everyone laughed.

"And you don't get bored?"

"Not at all. There's so much to see here!"

Billie-Pearl whispered in her friend's ear, "Say, Mademoiselle, you certainly caught that dude's eye!"

Indeed, Casper kept staring at her, but they had reached the top floor, and they got out of the lift. Marcelle led the way, holding herself straight, like an empress. Pauline looked around them, impressed by the size of the bay windows, by the gorgeous deep red of the lush drapes and carpets. They drew closer to the windows facing southwest, from which the view was breathtaking, even for Reno natives like Doug, who had never seen his hometown from so high up, observing the blue surge of the Truckee River weaving all the way to Pyramid Lake.

They were installed in a booth with upholstered leather benches in the same dark red. The room was crowded. On the stage, a pianist in a white jacket played fashionable tunes. Pauline recognized "Melodie d'Amour" by the Ames Brothers, which Marcelle liked. When he struck up Elvis Presley's latest hit, "Heartbreak Hotel," Billie-Pearl swung her shoulders in rhythm, imitating the crooner's pout while Jimmy looked on, spellbound.

Marcelle glanced right and left, patting her chignon to make sure no loose locks escaped, checking to see whether she recognized other diners, then, with trepidation, she mumbled that Casey Smith was here, with her family. Pauline knew this was one of her most important clients, the wife of the wealthy owner of the Harold's Club casino, located a stone's throw away. Father and son owned a thriving casino but no hotel, she pointed out, so they often came to the Mapes. Pauline noticed how her mother did her best to catch Casey Smith's eye, a red-haired lady, dripping in jewelry, who was talking loudly.

"I'm just going to go over and say hello."

Doug's hand came down on his wife's.

"You're staying right there. With us. Please."

Marcelle acquiesced, unenthusiastically. Doug gestured to the waiter and asked for the wine list and menu. She cheered herself up by reading aloud the list of wines from France.

The fireworks weren't set to start until it got dark, after nine, so they decided to order. Doug and Jimmy shared the Mapes farmhouse steak for two, Pauline and Billie-Pearl went for the spring chicken with julienne potatoes, and Marcelle chose fillet of trout, with a Sauternes from France to wash it down. While Marcelle continued to scrutinize the room for any familiar faces, Doug asked Billie-Pearl all sorts of questions about mustangs: what they ate, if they were easy to break in, and how Velma was doing with the Bureau of Land Management and, although Pauline was sure he already knew most of the answers, she could tell this was doing her friend a lot of good, drawing her out of her grief concerning Commander. Billie-Pearl became quite chatty, giving Doug all kinds of details, which he listened to with all his attention, as did Jimmy, while Marcelle toyed with her food, tried not to look bored, and downed the wine. When Billie-Pearl mentioned Velma's team, the stable boys, and Gus in particular, Pauline couldn't help blushing, which her eagle-eyed mother detected on the spot.

"A stable boy? Really?" said Marcelle, with a sneer.

Pauline remembered her mother's remarks about the dark color of her lips after Gus's kisses and she blushed even more.

"He's awfully nice," said Billie-Pearl, rising to defend her friend.

Marcelle glanced at her daughter, and Pauline knew exactly what her mother was thinking, as if she had spoken out loud: *You can do better than a stable boy, my dear.*

They were ordering dessert when a young man in his late twenties, with slicked-back hair, wearing a smart suit, came to stand by their table. A big golden M was pinned to his lapel.

He welcomed them to the Mapes, saying he hoped they were having a nice time. Then he introduced himself as the assistant manager. "My name is Kendall Spencer. I'm delighted to meet you."

He had light-colored eyes and a piercing gaze. Marcelle beamed at him, enchanted. Well, now, she seemed to say to her daughter, a young man of that ilk was what Pauline should be looking for. Not some stable boy.

SUMMER 1960

Reno, Nevada

"Pauly! You need to wake up. There's someone on the phone for you. From the Mapes."

Pauline opened her eyes. In the dark bedroom, Doug was standing in front of her bed, wearing his dressing gown. He was holding a flashlight. She remembered the power was out all over Reno.

"What time is it?" she whispered, glancing over to the small cot where Lily slept.

"Just before midnight."

Pauline got out of bed, rubbing her eyes.

"The Mapes?" she said. "At this hour? Who is it?"

"I only caught she was phoning from the hotel. The call didn't wake your mother. Luckily."

Pauline followed him to the phone in the living room. Who from the Mapes could be calling at such a time? It must be serious. Ever since the forest fires in the Sierras had started two days ago, shutting down all electricity in some areas of Nevada and eastern California, there had been panic at the Mapes. The chef was worried the food would spoil, the air-conditioning was no longer working, neither were the elevators. The fire started on a building site up on Donner Ridge, California, when a spark came off a bulldozer working on the new interstate road above Truckee, the small mountain town. This was thirty-five miles west of Reno, but the fire spread quickly, out of control, stoked by powerful winds. Other less serious bush fires had taken up as well, and Reno was soon ringed with a semicircle of blazing timber. Firefighters were working around the clock. The sky was thick with billowing black smoke, and like many other businesses, Marcelle had to close her shop as she couldn't use her hair dryers. On the radio and in the newspapers, people were told to eat canned food and to throw out any perishables that no longer seemed fresh.

Doug shone the light toward the phone and Pauline took the receiver, expecting to hear the grating tones of Mildred Jones; instead, she made out the strumming of a guitar and people chattering.

"Hello?" she said, puzzled.

"Is that you, Pauline?" came the unmistakable murmur.

"Yes, Mrs. Miller. It's me."

Doug's eyes widened when he heard the name.

"I'm having a little get-together with my Happy People," said Mrs. Miller. "And as you are part of my Happy People, I'd love it if you could pop over."

She sounded deliciously tipsy.

"You want me to come now?" asked Pauline, incredulous.

Mrs. Miller laughed. Well, yes, right now! They were up in the costume department on the ninth floor. Just the gang—Whitey, Agnes, May, Rafe, and Paula, all of whom Pauline knew, and her stand-in, Evelyn. A cute young musician from the Sky Room was playing the guitar for them. He had a lovely voice! They were having such fun! They were all waiting for her. And with that, the line went dead.

Pauline stared at Doug.

"What do you think I should do?" she asked, dumbfounded.

Doug went to fetch the car keys lying on the table. Well, for one thing, he said with a grin, she could start by wiping that scared expression off her face real quick. Did he have to repeat *who* was inviting her to a private party? He handed her the keys to the Dodge.

"Get dressed. Take your mother's car, it's less noisy than the old Buick. Enjoy yourself, Pauly. You deserve it."

Silently, with Doug's flashlight, Pauline picked out clothes drying in the laundry room. He'd gone back to bed. She quickly slipped into a white cotton skirt and a sleeveless green blouse, and grabbed her ballet flats on the way out.

Outside, even in the middle of the night, the air was still oppressively hot, laden with the acrid stench of the raging fire. The outage had also affected the streetlights, but there was little traffic at this hour. The headlights of Marcelle's Dodge lit the quiet, drowsy streets. Police with torches were guiding traffic when Pauline reached downtown. She felt like shouting out to them, *Hey guys, I'm on my way to meet Marilyn Monroe at the Mapes!* but she kept her elation to herself, not without some struggle.

It was strange seeing entire neighborhoods immersed in darkness. Stripped of garish neon lights and the flurry outside casinos, Reno seemed oddly unfamiliar, looking like those ghost towns Pauline used to visit with Jimmy and Doug on their Saturday excursions.

In front of the Mapes, a big truck engine rumbled. Pauline's eyes followed a never-ending cable running from the truck all the way up the façade to the sixth floor, where the lights of a suite were on, shining brightly in the darkness.

"Hey, Frenchie," came Aubrey's voice. He was the night porter. She rarely saw him, since they didn't share the same schedule, but she appreciated him, because he always had a kind word for her.

She asked him what the long wire connected to the truck was for. He let out a scathing snort: Well, that was Sir Arthur Miller's installation. While all Reno was in pitch-black, the playwright had a private generator installed so he could work in his suite at night.

"And meanwhile, poor Ed has been stuck in the elevator for hours. It appears John Huston has been serving him whiskey through a small opening. He must be pickled by now."

Ed was the hotel's elevator repairman.

"Are you working tonight, Frenchie?"

"Mrs. Jones asked me to come and check something in the housekeeping room," Pauline lied. "A stock issue."

"Don't mess with old Jones," Aubrey said. "You'll have to walk up. Ask for a penlight at the front desk. With the heat and air-conditioning failure, it'll be no pleasure cruise. Good luck!"

Pauline quickly understood what he meant. She slowly climbed the stairs, passing a few customers who held flashlights like she did. The higher she went, the hotter she became. She finally made it to the ninth floor. It was the twanging of a guitar and voices that guided her to the costume workshop, installed across several adjoining suites.

Soft candlelight flickered through the open door as Pauline drew nearer. She felt edgy, not quite knowing how to mingle once she found herself on the threshold. They were singing "I'm Sorry," the summer hit by that young singer Brenda Lee, only fifteen years old, Pauline had learned. She picked out Rafe's deep tones, booming along with Whitey's more nasal ones, as well as Mrs. Strasberg's wobbly falsetto; identified Agnes, dreadfully out of tune, making everyone giggle; then May, who sang quite nicely; and lastly, Mrs. Miller's sweet and sultry vibrato, rising high above everyone else.

Pauline was able to see them before they caught sight of her. Mrs. Miller sat perched on a trunk, champagne glass in hand, barefoot, dressed in one of the black slacks and white blouses Pauline found crumpled on the floor of Suite 614. She was not wearing the wig from Max Factor studios that Pauline now knew was fitted to her head every day by Agnes. This she did tell her mother, who had not been surprised. It was tough to style hair daily in the desert, with the heat, wind, and sand, Marcelle had pointed out with know-how, and the actress's hair had no doubt been damaged by constant dyeing and perming for so many years. Which was the case, but Pauline kept quiet. The wig was a good idea, according to Marcelle. Did Pauline know that Marilyn Monroe had her own colorist who flew in to bleach her hair every three weeks? Pauline didn't, and she had listened to her mother. Pearl Porterfield was a veteran hairdresser in her late sixties who had her own special secret blend for the perfect platinum blonde, as she had been Jean Harlow's personal hairdresser back in the thirties, giving her that signature white-blonde Monroe craved for her own locks.

"My guess is that because of the wig, Pearl Porterfield hasn't been to the Mapes," Marcelle had told her daughter. And she had been right.

Haloed by the opalescent candlelight, Mrs. Miller looked beautiful, wearing little makeup, Pauline noted. Her tousled hair had a hint of darker regrowth showing at the roots. She was laughing gaily, her head tilted far back. Next to her sat a young woman who resembled her, the same blonde hair and appearance. Pauline felt like rubbing her eyes—this must be her body double. She did not know what a body double was for, something to do with the lighting on set, she supposed.

Now Pauline could see most of the "Happy People" there, sitting on the floor, or on trunks, drinking, smoking, and singing. A young man wearing a white jacket played the guitar. It was hot in here as well. The candles flickered in the warm breeze coming in through the open windows.

"Oh, there you are, Pauline!" exclaimed Mrs. Miller.

And she felt all those eyes upon her, but smiles as well, and she heard warm voices greeting her. She went to sit between May and Whitey, and someone handed her a drink.

"Welcome, lovely to see you," May said in French, raising her glass.

Her accent was surprisingly good; Pauline thanked her, still using her native language, asking her if she spoke French fluently. Indeed, May spoke it well, with a slight accent.

"You're the one who helped her with the love letter, aren't you?" May asked.

Pauline blushed, recalling the episode.

"Nobody understands French here. Feel free to talk," whispered May.

"I wasn't aware then who the letter was for," Pauline whispered back.

May confessed to Pauline that she had read it: She dealt with all of Mrs. Miller's correspondence. But she had decided not to send it at the last minute, given all the tumult. The letter was still in her files. She would soon destroy it. That would be for the best. It should never fall into the hands of a malicious journalist.

"She still thinks of him, you know. Too much. A tricky situation to handle."

Pauline nodded. Yes, she suspected it must be indeed. She felt comfortable sitting there, feeling Whitey's bulky shoulder against her, and Agnes across them winking at her. Even the dour Mrs. Strasberg beamed at her. She was introduced to Evelyn, the body double. Nobody was judging her, she was much younger than the lot of them, but that didn't matter: on the contrary, she was part of the gang.

The Champagne was more than tepid.

"We need ice!" declared Mrs. Miller, at one point.

"No ice because of the fire, remember?" said Rafe.

"We do have ice!" giggled Mrs. Miller. "And I know where to get it. Don't you?"

Rafe got up from the floor, stretching out his frame. Yes, he knew where to go. Three floors below. To old Grouchy Grumps, added Mrs. Miller, pulling a comical face. Her husband was the only one around getting any use out of a fridge thanks to his generator, she added.

"Pauline, fancy coming along?" Rafe suggested. "I don't want to face Grouchy Grumps on my own."

"Sure," said Pauline, getting to her feet.

Rafe took one of the candles, and they headed down the dark, stuffy stairwell to the sixth floor. When they got to Suite 614, Rafe used Mrs. Miller's key. All the suite's lamps were lit up. They found Arthur Miller sprawled out on the sofa, eyes closed. They both said hello, and he looked up and nodded curtly. Rafe filled the bucket with ice cubes, and they swiftly went back up. The whole thing was over in a matter of minutes. Mrs. Miller asked them flippantly if her husband had growled at them. Meanwhile, the guitarist was playing and singing "The Twist" by Chubby Checker, a tune that was all the rage, with new dance moves that Pauline had mastered perfectly.

Everyone got up to dance, led by Mrs. Miller, who was highly skilled, expertly swinging her hips and thighs; Whitey, Agnes, and Mrs. Strasberg were mediocre dancers, but appeared to be having a ball. Rafe, towering over tiny May, was getting along fine, and Evelyn was nearly as nifty as Mrs. Miller.

Overcome with shyness, Pauline didn't dare join in, until the gentle Agnes came to fetch her with a maternal hand, and she got started, giving herself wholeheartedly to the music. Eyes closed, she let her hair down, surrendering to the dance steps with sheer pleasure. When she opened her eyes, she discovered them in a circle watching her admiringly, loudly cheering and clapping.

"Honey, those sure are killer moves!" squealed Mrs. Miller. "You're the queen of the twist!"

"Ah, to be young again…" exhaled Mrs. Strasberg, fanning herself.

A woman wearing a bathrobe, eyes puffy with sleep, appeared on the threshold.

"Hey, for mercy's sake, can you keep it down? Some folks are trying to sleep. I have half a mind to call the manager."

May took the situation in hand. She told the disgruntled guest the party was over, and that everyone was sorry. The woman had not recognized Marilyn Monroe, Pauline observed; her eyes had brushed right past her.

Mrs. Miller thought it was such a shame their gathering had to end. Darn, it wasn't even one o'clock! She felt happy in Reno only with this adored little group. The rest of the time was hell, she sighed.

Listening to her, Pauline thought back to the latest unappeasable canteen chatter. It was impossible not to overhear it, week after week. The atmosphere on the set was going downhill. Clark Gable got through gallons of whiskey a day and railed against Arthur Miller's perpetual script rewrites. He drank as heavily as Montgomery Clift and John Huston, and spiteful gossips hissed that everyone secretly hoped Marilyn Monroe would, once again, be late in the morning so they could all recover from their hangovers. Actor Eli Wallach, who played Guido, the film's third man, had found a way to fully alienate Mrs. Strasberg. Marilyn, for her part, was unable to remember her lines. They needed ten, fifteen takes for a single sentence. In the evening, she could be heard complaining in the suite, screaming at her husband, saying she would not make it, it was too hard, and she wanted to pull out. She yelled she would end up in a loony bin, like her mother.

At noon today, Pauline had learned that the world première of *Let's Make Love*, Yves Montand and Marilyn Monroe's latest film—which was to be held at Reno's Crest Theater in two days, without the lead actor present and including a panel of prestigious journalists—had quite simply been cancelled because of the power outage. Nobody was coming. Pauline told herself Mrs. Miller must have been secretly relieved. Marcelle, on the other hand, would be greatly disappointed.

The young guitarist was packing up his instrument, ready to leave. He thanked them for such a pleasant evening. He was supposed to play up in the Sky Room in front of three hundred guests with his pianist colleague, but tonight's dinner and concert had been called off due to the blackout.

"What's your name?" asked Mrs. Miller.

"Brandon, ma'am."

"Don't go," she pleaded. "Stay a little longer and play us more of those lovely tunes. You have such a gorgeous voice."

"Now, now, my dear," tutted May, "you saw that lady, you heard what she said. We all need to leave."

Mrs. Strasberg, Agnes, Evelyn, and Whitey were already on their way out, waving good-bye, and Pauline could tell Mrs. Miller had another idea in mind—she asked Brandon if he reckoned anyone was up in the Sky Room at that moment. He looked at her blankly and said he was pretty sure it was empty, there had been no dinner and no concert. Mrs. Miller had a rather enchanting way of gazing at people, with delicate, beseeching gestures, clutching her fists to her collarbone. What if they went up there, she said to him, and what if he called his pianist friend, who could pop over? That way they'd play piano and guitar, and she would sing. Up in the Sky Room. Wouldn't that be swell?

It was impossible to say no to her. May's lips twitched, but Pauline couldn't tell if it was due to exasperation or a fit of giggles. They ended up climbing the three flights of stairs, all together, carrying candles and Champagne, trying to keep quiet in the stairway. Brandon had called his teammate, who was on his way; he lived just next door.

Facing the inky, starless sky and the bulk of the Sierras, where the distant fire cut a ruddy streak like a bleeding wound, the enormous and silent Sky Room seemed to have nestled into darkness, its tables still laid and covered with white linen. Pauline felt like she had boarded an abandoned ship drifting on murky seas. The pianist turned up, moonfaced and in his forties, wheezing after climbing the twelve flights. His name was Jerry. Pauline, tickled, could see he hadn't recognized the famous actress. It wasn't until he sat down at the piano, accompanied by Brandon's guitar, and Mrs. Miller, glass in hand, started to belt out "River of No Return" that he jolted himself upright, nearly tumbling off his stool. May and Rafe were unable to hide their amusement.

Mrs. Miller was inebriated, but she merrily carried a tune, reaching out to her tiny audience with infectious joy. How beautiful she was, standing there on the dimly lit stage, with her glowing smile, her pale, pearly skin. Pauline thought about what Doug had said to her with fatherly affection: *Enjoy yourself, you deserve it.* She was indeed having fun. But she was aware it was much more than that, than mere entertainment: It was one of those key moments putting its mark on her life.

At the behest of Mrs. Miller, Jerry struck the first notes of a melody Pauline was familiar with, one of her mother's favorites, "Autumn Leaves." Brandon strummed along on the guitar. Yves Montand's greatest hit. Him, again. May and Rafe were no longer smiling. They seemed worried. All Mrs. Miller's euphoria had vanished, and she leaned against the piano as if to gather strength. Her voice had gone all reedy with woe. She sang in

English, but the lyrics had the same effect and Pauline's heart ached for her. Her words evoked time creeping by, broken relationships, the burden of being alone, regrets, and spadefuls of autumn leaves. She seemed disconsolate, and her apparent misery portrayed a very different picture than the glamorous photos in Marcelle's glossy magazines.

And Pauline realized, for the first time, that she was dealing with a person hardly anyone really knew. A person who wasn't the movie star, who was somebody else. A sleepy woman whose cheeks and forehead were caked in greasy cold cream first thing in the morning; a woman riddled with self-doubt (how many times had she heard her tell her coach she was a lousy actress?), the one who danced barefoot in a bathrobe in the living room of her suite listening to Ella Fitzgerald, the one who sobbed softly as Rafe or Whitey clasped her in their muscular embrace, the one who stood in front of the window for hours staring into space, twisting a strand of hair around her finger. Pauline was well aware that she herself was only an ordinary woman sucked into the orbit of an actress who was anything but ordinary, but nevertheless, she made that actress's bed each morning, she put away her clothes, her shoes, she touched all the everyday objects Marilyn Monroe touched as well—her comb, her toothbrush, her Chanel N°5 perfume bottle, her earrings, her tablet container— since that was what being a chambermaid was all about: unintentionally intruding into private lives, glimpsing the contents of wastepaper baskets, noticing the titles of books, reading the first sentences of cards, letters, and little notes lying around for all to see. An entire life, tucked away in a hotel room.

Indeed, just last week, a journalist had cornered her by the service elevator.

"Are you Pauline Bazelet?" he had asked, aggressively.

She had nodded yes.

"You're her maid, is that correct?"

How did this dreadful man know that? He had taken out a little notebook and a pencil. Well, what could she tell him about Monroe? Were the rumors true? All those pills and poppers and the brawls with her husband? Did she really drink Champagne first thing in the morning? Was she still trying to get hold of Yves Montand?

Pauline had tried to back away, but the man had followed her determinedly. This would take only a couple of minutes, he had said. He wouldn't even mention her name in the article. At that moment, Pauline had been relieved to see Mildred Jones appear. She had vigorously shooed the reporter away and went to reprimand the porters and bellboys for letting a journalist in. She then asked Pauline for details. Had the young woman given anything away?

"I don't talk about Mrs. Miller to anyone," Pauline had almost barked. "Not even to my mother. Just as you asked."

"I thought as much," Mildred Jones had answered self-righteously. "Mrs. Miller is very happy with your services. I was told by her personal secretary, Miss Reis. Keep up the good work, Pauline."

Up on the Sky Room dais, Mrs. Miller had stopped singing, and the musicians, bewildered, no longer knew what to do, confronted with this woman crying in the candlelight. May spoke to her gently, comforted her, while Rafe kneaded her neck, which, Pauline knew, worked miracles.

"I didn't want to be sad tonight," said Mrs. Miller, forlornly. "I'm fed up with being sad."

And she added she found the fire hair-raisingly beautiful but terrifying. She couldn't stop thinking about the hundreds of animals devoured by flames, the agony of nature. The fire was like what she was experiencing right now—a massive inner upheaval against which she could not fight. Pauline listened, struck by her fragility. How was it possible to be so famous, and yet so vulnerable and insecure?

"Don't you want to go to bed, my dear?" May asked. "It's late. We better get going."

Mrs. Miller protested. Bedtime? No way! She was looking at yet another restless night, waiting for sleep that never came despite the pills, having to put up with Grouchy Grumps snoring by her side. Unbearable. She craved Champagne, more music, and more dancing! Once again, they partied, sang, and laughed. Pauline kept an eye on her own glass, thinking about the ride back in her mother's Dodge. Betraying Doug's precious trust was out of the question.

It was coming up on two in the morning, and none of them, not even sensible May, was paying attention to the din: The Sky Room seemed above it all, inaccessible, a remote fortress where they cavorted, leaped, and bellowed at the top of their lungs, while Jerry and Brandon, sweating profusely, played as if they were possessed. They were hammering out a Ray Charles song, "What'd I Say," which made everyone go crazy, jigging around, belting out the lyrics as if they had to be heard all the way to Las Vegas, while Mrs. Miller laughed like a child, without drawing breath, holding her stomach.

Pauline felt the same way when she raced mustangs with Billie-Pearl: No one could catch them, no one could stop them;

they were young, wild, and free, and they rode like the wind for hours on end. Mrs. Miller was acting out the song, her lips miming the lyrics, daintily stretching out her arms, wiggling her hips with frenzy, summoning them to watch the girl with the diamond ring who sure knew how to shake that thing.

And suddenly the great double doors swung open and a group of uniformed men came marching in, bearing flashlights.

"What the hell is going on here?"

Pauline instantly recognized the furious voice. It was Kendall Spencer's.

May came forward. She was sorry; they had gotten a little carried away. They'd go now. Kendall glared down at her. In the dim candlelight, he could barely make out her face. The uniformed men shone their torches over the two quaking musicians, over Rafe, Pauline, and Mrs. Miller.

"Wait a minute!" came Kendall's thunderous tone.

He took a step toward Pauline, jerking his chin forward to stare at her.

"You? Are you out of your mind?"

"I'm sorry."

"You're *sorry*?" he mimicked her. Then he got a grip on himself. "Are you the one who brought these people up here?"

She said she wasn't. May came forward again, trying to explain that Pauline had nothing to do with all this, but Kendall wouldn't listen. He wanted the names of each person there that night. They weren't going to get away with this. As for those musicians, things weren't looking too good for them, and for the young cleaning lady either.

Rafe tried to intervene, but Kendall was too riled up to pay attention. Who did they think they were? Had they gone crazy? The Mapes was a top-notch, reputable, well-attended venue. Since when did employees throw noisy parties in the Sky Room?

Kendall grabbed Pauline's arm, rather roughly. He ordered the two musicians to follow them to his office. Time to quit fooling around.

The power came back, violently lighting up the enormous room with a blinding white glare. Kendall had probably dressed in haste; his tie was askew.

"Come on, let's go," he said, yanking Pauline's arm. "Party's over. Now the problems begin."

Was this how the evening was going to end? Pauline couldn't quite believe it. Might she lose her job? Would the musicians get fired as well? She stared down at the bloodred carpet helplessly. She was scared.

"If you wouldn't mind letting go of that young woman right away," said Mrs. Miller, composedly.

There was silence.

"Says who?" quipped Kendall, snidely.

"And you are?" she asked in return.

"Kendall Spencer, assistant manager of the Mapes Hotel."

"And I'm Marilyn Monroe, staying in Suite 614. Nice to meet you, Mr. Spencer."

It was the actress speaking, with her distinctive voice and body language, and even without her usual makeup and hairstyling, this was undeniably Marilyn Monroe herself standing there, looking him straight in the eye. The world's most famous blonde had popped up, marveled Pauline, as if Mrs. Miller had pressed a secret button.

Flabbergasted, the young man cleared his throat. All smiles, the actress then told him the last-minute party had been her idea; she was the one who had called Pauline at home—an obliging operator had given her Pauline's number—and she was the one who asked the musicians to play up in the Sky Room. Brandon and Jerry were awfully talented. Mr. Spencer must be so happy to have them on board. She wanted to thank the Mapes from the bottom of her heart. What a wonderful, unforgettable evening they had had!

"And as for Pauline, she's like morning sunshine."

Kendall Spencer nodded, embarrassed. Without a word, he at last let go of Pauline's arm.

"That's better," said the actress. "Good night, everybody."

She left the Sky Room, along with Rafe and May. How ingenious she had been, thought Pauline, and how considerate. The musicians were smiling as well. They too had had a lovely evening.

Kendall walked Pauline to the Dodge parked near the Mapes. He blurted out that he was sorry, grumbling that he had overreacted, and in the darkness, he hadn't figured out who he was dealing with. They must have all thought he was ridiculous. Pauline said she understood. He kissed her, promised he'd drop by to see Lily, one of these days. However, he didn't know when, his wife spied on him constantly. Evaline was insanely jealous. The situation wasn't easy for him, and Pauline must remember how sincere he was regarding his little Frenchie; he adored her, he was crazy about her, but he couldn't bear hurting his wife for the moment. Pauline listened absentmindedly; he hardly ever came to visit his daughter, put off by Marcelle's baleful glances and Doug's quiet dignity. He sent checks instead.

As she was getting ready to drive back to Washington Street,

Kendall stooped so he could talk to her through the open car window. He wanted to warn her: She shouldn't take Marilyn Monroe's friendship seriously. All this mustn't go to her head. Movie stars in that league weren't interested in humble folk.

"Don't ever forget that, in her eyes, you're just a cleaning lady. Nothing more."

The month of August dragged on, with its impossible heat, blistering sun, and Mrs. Miller's deteriorating condition. On some mornings, she couldn't get up at all, and Pauline didn't see her because she stuck to her room; on others, she left for the shoot like a stoned somnambulist propped up by Mrs. Strasberg, under Arthur's Miller desperate glare. A wreck lurking under the picture-perfect makeup.

One evening at home, a peeved Marcelle produced the autograph she had at long last obtained. What a letdown! Surrounded by other fans, she had waited for the actress to leave the Mapes one morning, and the latter hardly smiled as she autographed her photos. She could barely walk, so a lady dressed in black was holding her up. A total mess!

"Did you know she was in such a bad way?"

"No," lied Pauline. "I hardly ever see her, you know."

"But surely you hear all those things being said about her?"

"Mildred Jones keeps her eyes on me. There's no way I want to go back to the ladies' room. So I don't listen to the gossip, and I keep my mouth shut."

"Now that's a professional attitude," approved Doug.

Marcelle wanted to know how the Mapes was handling all those reporters cooling their heels in front of the hotel. Like a snarling Cerberus, Mrs. Jones kept them at bay, Pauline told her, but sometimes, they found their way up to the suite. Then they had to deal with muscleman Rafe.

"But she knows who you are, doesn't she?" Marcelle went on. "She knows your name?"

"I guess so," said Pauline. She borrowed Kendall's scathing terms: "I'm just the cleaning lady, *Maman*."

Pauline was painfully aware that Marcelle wanted so much more for her daughter—a well-off husband, numerous children, a pretty home. And now, Pauline wasn't even able to draw Marilyn Monroe's attention, to stand out from the rest, and she could see that too on her mother's countenance.

Doug was the only one to encourage and congratulate her. She had told him, in detail, about the night in the Sky Room and that magical moment when Mrs. Miller had said to Kendall, "Pauline, she's like morning sunshine." Doug understood she wanted to keep it all to herself, not even telling Billie-Pearl, and he was the only person to know. Perhaps he felt it was unfair, her keeping this from her mother, his wife, but he never mentioned it. He knew how complex their mother-daughter relationship was, and how harsh Marcelle could be with Pauline since Lily's birth.

That morning, when she fitted the key into the lock and opened the door, Pauline could tell right away things were very wrong in Suite 614. She heard screams and moans, awful ones, like an animal in pain. She froze, the key still in her hand. Maybe she should get out now, before anyone noticed she was there. Then she saw Mrs. Strasberg's hat and bag in the entrance.

The moans went on; they were horrible to listen to, and Pauline felt her blood curdling as they came like waves. More uncomfortable by the minute, she was about to beat a hasty retreat when she heard her name being whispered. She turned and saw Agnes, beckoning to her. Agnes looked troubled, her eyes tearful. She told Pauline that Mrs. Miller was in a bad way and it was difficult to get her back on track. Mrs. Strasberg had phoned a local doctor. At that point, there was a knock on the door. Pauline went to open it, and a young nervous man stood there, holding a black briefcase. He said he was the doctor Mrs. Strasberg had spoken to. Pauline stepped aside to let him enter, and he went into the bedroom. They heard a murmur of voices. After a while, the moaning stopped. Pauline hadn't even had time to start the cleaning. She knew she should be getting to it, but she felt rooted to the spot, sensing a forthcoming disaster.

The suite's door crashed open with a bang, making them jump, and Arthur Miller came running in like a crazed man.

"Is the doctor here?" he said to Agnes without greeting her.

She nodded. The screaming started again, but this time it sounded like Mrs. Miller was telling her husband to get the hell out, right now. She didn't want to see his face again, she hated him, she hated his guts. The screeches became unbearable; Pauline longed to put her hands over her ears; she could see nothing of what was going on in the bedroom, but she listened to it all.

Trying to make himself heard, Arthur Miller asked the young doctor what he was injecting into his wife's veins.

"Amytal," came the quavering answer. "A sedative to get her to calm down."

Arthur Miller snapped that he knew what Amytal was, thank you very much, but did the doctor have any idea how many barbiturates she had already taken? The young doctor admitted he didn't, but he was surprised she was still awake, as he had given her enough to knock her out. He added he had already been called in for Mrs. Miller at the Mapes, and other doctors had been as well, and there was something seriously wrong with this lady. He would not agree to any more shots of anything. Now he feared for her life.

"Get out! Get lost!" shrieked Mrs. Miller to her husband, and there was so much hatred and pain in her broken voice that Pauline winced.

There was another knock at the door, and Pauline ran to answer. It was Mildred Jones. She glanced behind Pauline at the bedroom door.

"What in the Lord's name is going on here?"

"Mrs. Miller is ill," said Pauline.

"What's wrong with her?"

"Get out! I *hate* you! ... I *hate* you!"

Mrs. Miller's tone was slurred now, full of sobs.

Pauline confessed she had no idea what was wrong with her. A doctor was in the bedroom, with Arthur Miller and Mrs. Strasberg, she told Mildred. Agnes, the hairdresser, was in the living room. Nobody quite knew what to do.

For a moment, Mildred seemed clueless, and Pauline figured she had never been confronted with a situation such as this before. She told Pauline to keep all this to herself.

"I sometimes wonder if you take me for a complete idiot," said Pauline before she could stop herself.

It was the first time she dared address her superior using that tone, holding herself straight, and without a single stammer. Mildred looked contrite, no longer meeting her eye.

The young doctor came out of the room, pale and perspiring, rushing away without a word. Behind him, Arthur Miller poured out his fury on Mrs. Strasberg in a low-pitched, terrifying tone, then slammed the suite door and took off.

"You'll do the cleaning at another time," declared Mildred. "It's time for you and me to go."

Pauline felt drained of all her energy. Those hideous screams were still ringing in her ears; her hands were trembling, and she felt sick and dizzy, as if someone had punched her. Mildred told her to pair up with Linda, on the fifth floor. She obeyed.

But at lunchtime, everyone was chattering about it; everyone wanted to know what Pauline knew. She stuck to her guns, telling them all that bossy Jones sent her to another floor. She kept repeating she hadn't heard or seen a thing. Then Lincoln breezed in, brimming with self-importance: Well, he certainly had news! Marilyn Monroe had been rushed off to the airport. Was she being sent to a hospital, someone asked? Lincoln said that judging by the way she looked, most probably. The film had ground to a halt. Nobody knew for how long. Huston must be tearing his hair out. Someone else added that, at this rate, he'd become a permanent fixture at the casino. Hoots of laughter rose across the tables.

"What is she so unhappy about?" Kitty asked Pauline.

What could Pauline reply without betraying the Mapes's most famous client? But she didn't need to answer, as Kitty and other chambermaids were busy blathering about what everyone already knew: the marriage was falling apart, the French lover, the movie being rewritten over and over again, the rivers of alcohol, the mountains of sleeping pills. To Pauline, it seemed like real life was catching up with the movie, that Marilyn Monroe had become Roslyn, the mournful, disturbed heroine of *The Misfits*, a vulnerable woman lost in a world she had no control over and that she could not understand, incapable of making her dreams come true. While they all chattered and ate, Pauline thought back to a couple of days ago, when a photographer from the Magnum Agency covering the shoot had turned up to take pictures of the Millers in Suite 614. Pauline had been busy cleaning the kitchen. Mrs. Miller, wearing a tight black dress, had refused to stand next to her husband. She had stepped away from him, as if in loathing. The photographer was a tall woman with curly dark hair. She had a German accent. While Arthur Miller, unflappable, puffed away on a cigarette, she had done her best to shoot them both together, but it had been impossible. Mrs. Miller kept spinning away, turning her back to them, looking out the window. That same week, Pauline heard that on set near Pyramid Lake, Mrs. Miller had slammed her limousine door in her husband's face, leaving him stranded there.

Mildred Jones asked Pauline to give Suite 614 a full cleanup the day after Mrs. Miller left—thorough dusting, shampooing the carpets, flipping the mattress. The works. They had to make the most of it as no one knew when Mrs. Miller was due back in Reno. Pauline asked about her husband. Had he gone with her? Mildred was unaware of his whereabouts; however, she had heard the production had booked him another room on a lower floor. She concluded he wouldn't be coming back to the suite for a while.

Pauline found herself alone in the sunlit string of rooms she had become accustomed to, but this morning, an empty feeling grabbed her. The floral perfume no longer floated in the air, nor did the smell of coffee, or Rafe's voice as he was usually the first one in. She wouldn't be seeing Whitey's and Agnes's smiles, nor Mrs. Strasberg's or May's black-clad silhouettes.

Mrs. Miller had clearly left in a rush. A tube of lipstick and dark glasses lay stranded on the unmade bed, and on the floor, shoes were scattered here and there, silk scarves and a couple of camisoles as well. Everything belonging to Arthur Miller was gone, and in the bathroom, his toiletries weren't there either. An abandoned, open suitcase cluttered the passageway. Mrs. Miller must have chosen a smaller one for her trip.

Unsettled by the odd, uninhabited ambiance, Pauline ended up turning on the record player in the living room, listening to the record already in place—a catchy blues tune sung by B.B. King, "Every Day I Have the Blues." She felt a little less lonesome, almost as if Mrs. Miller was on the phone in the next room. Flinging the windows wide open, she got to work, picked up what was on the floor, stripped the sheets from the bed, fetched the bathroom towels, and put the lot in the laundry basket. Not without an effort, she turned over the doubled-up twin mattresses, vacuumed the box spring. Under the bed, she discovered a stained negligee, fragments of a half-nibbled sandwich, Champagne bottles, and apple cores.

On Mrs. Miller's night table, she saw a well-thumbed book of poems, *Leaves of Grass* by Walt Whitman. *To Norma Jeane* was written on the flyleaf. She recalled that was the actress's real name. There were notes on nearly every page, and entire verses had been underlined. Pauline was only interested in books that had to do with horses, such as *My Friend Flicka* or *Black Beauty*. She knew nothing about poetry.

The large vanity table facing the window was still covered with makeup and beauty products. This was where Marilyn Monroe materialized every morning thanks to Whitey's expert hands; this was where Pauline had often seen Mrs. Miller sit for minutes on end, admiring herself, tilting her face from left to right, smiling at her reflection.

Was she coming back at all? wondered Pauline, as she cleaned the mirror, thinking that perhaps Mrs. Miller wouldn't want to set foot in the Mapes ever again, that she might well ditch the movie, her husband, and everything linking her to Reno.

On the desk in the living room lay a thick postal package. Inside were dozens of cards and letters, all fan mail, Pauline knew. Did Mrs. Miller ever read them, answer them? Next to them were piles of the black-and-white portrait Mrs. Miller autographed for her admirers. The credits on the back read *By Cecil Beaton, New York City, 1956.* The photograph showed the actress lying on a bed, her head resting against a pillow. She was clasping a flower to her chest, and her lips were half-open, revealing her front teeth. Her face had a dreamy, gentle expression.

Next to the fan mail were notes and cards lying around. Pauline was used to this mess and stacked them as best as she could. She shouldn't be looking at Mrs. Miller's private papers, but she couldn't help herself. The scrawled, irregular handwriting was sometimes hard to read. *"I feel the camera has got to look through Gay's eyes whenever he is in a scene and even when he is not, there has to be a sense of him. He is the center and the rest moves around him but I guess Huston will see to that."* Was Mrs. Miller writing to herself? Like a diary? "Gay" was short for Clark Gable's character in *The Misfits,* that she knew. Gaylord Langland.

She saw another card, sent to Mrs. Miller by Thelma Ritter, one of the other actresses in the movie. She was thanking her with warmth for a gift, calling her "Millie" Monroe.

Pauline told herself she should quit snooping around, right

now. But it was like a drug—once she started, she found she couldn't stop. She had not opened the address book with the initials MM engraved in the golden leather, but she did today. The first thing she came upon was a medicinal prescription from the office of Doctor Ralph Greenson, psychiatrist, in Beverly Hills, then she saw the postcard of a work of art, a sort of sculpture showing two inchoate figures emerging from a mighty hand. *The Hand of God*, by Auguste Rodin. Pauline knew nothing about art either, but she did know Rodin was a famous French sculptor. Once again, her native country seemed part of Mrs. Miller's world.

Somebody knocked on the door, and she promptly snapped the address book shut. It was Linda. Mildred had sent her to help with the carpet cleaning. Ever since Pauline had been assigned to Suite 614, Linda was among the cleaning ladies who still harbored resentment about it. She remained standoffish. They got to work together, and when they were done, they left the suite, as the carpet had to dry. In the service elevator, Linda asked if Pauline knew anything about where Mrs. Miller had gone and why. Pauline said she didn't know anything.

"Now, that's surprising," said Linda dryly.

Pauline asked what she meant.

They had reached the ground floor and were still in the elevator when Linda said with a sneer, "We all heard about the Sky Room, about you being part of the Happy People party and whatnot. And you being—what was it now? Ah, yes, *Pauline is like morning sunshine.*"

Pauline said nothing, stung by the bitterness in Linda's voice. How did she know all this? Jerry and Brandon must have blabbed in the cafeteria.

"Don't get bigheaded, Frenchie. Just remember who you are. A nobody."

Usually, Pauline would have kept silent, she would have let Linda walk away. But this time, she reached out and grabbed her colleague's arm.

"I know exactly who I am," she hissed, and then she put on a French accent. "I'm Pauline Bazelet, from Paris, France. Now get lost."

Breaking free, Linda hurried out of the elevator. Never had she seen Pauline so angry.

1956

———⟫⟫⟫⟫.———

Reno, Nevada

Doctor O'Brian thought she was coming along fine and kept telling her so. Had Pauline given some thought to next year? He reminded her she'd be eighteen then. She was good with horses; he'd been able to observe that in the past four years. The Doc was right, and Pauline knew it. The job appealed to her and she longed to devote herself to it. But that meant long years of studying, which were expensive, and her parents couldn't afford to pay. The Doc didn't seem too worried about the financial aspect, as he was convinced she'd land a scholarship, but she had to get started and she should also be thinking about a traineeship with an equine vet. He had an idea about that as well: Doctor Hicks, a fellow doctor in charge of a clinic near Mount Shasta, in Siskiyou County, Northern California, where many students wanted to work. He had already mentioned Pauline to Doctor Hicks.

Pauline felt elated by all these prospects. She spent more and more time at the Double Lazy Heart Ranch, turning up after school and staying there for most of her weekends. She kept her relationship with Gus away from her mother's inquisitive questions. He was a sweet, gentle boy, with whom she shared the same passion for horses; they went out riding together, usually on Dustin and Tundra, and sometimes Billie-Pearl came along. Billie-Pearl seemed broody since Commander's departure. She kept to herself and went about her chores in silence.

Velma was hardly there, busy at her office in Reno with her team, starting a national campaign to prevent aerial roundups of mustangs. Pauline noticed that her husband, Charlie, seemed to be ill—he had difficulty breathing and coughed all the time. This didn't stop him from keeping up his tasks at the ranch, but he tired more easily, it appeared.

One afternoon, as Pauline and Billie-Pearl were busy helping the ranch hands by cleaning out stalls and sheds, Charlie came to find them, wheezing away. He was coughing so hard they thought he might topple over, but he was able to tell them, between two fits, that he was pretty sure he had seen Commander during one of his horseback jaunts near the ranch, up in the hills, heading east. Billie-Pearl let go of the straw bale she was holding and paid attention. "Are you sure?" she asked Charlie. He gulped down a glass of water to catch his breath. He could spot that rogue a mile off with those scars around his neck and his half-eaten ear. Commander had a herd of mares and colts around him; he'd wasted no time founding a family, obviously.

"Do you think it's really him?" Billie-Pearl asked Pauline later. "I don't dare believe it."

She headed out east several times, riding Dustin or Tundra, but did not catch a glimpse of him.

Autumn drew closer, already blowing cooler winds on to

the dry lands. Pauline and Billie-Pearl were eating lunch on the porch with Gus and the stable boys. Charlie and Velma were in Reno. They were joking as usual, making quite a bit of noise.

Pauline enjoyed the camaraderie of those moments at the ranch, feeling at one with the gang. She was one of them now. These were the people she wanted to hang out with, not the fancy crowd her mother mooned about. Sometimes she'd sneak a look in Gus's direction and think how blessed she was. One day, he would go back to his hometown, but for the moment he was here, with her in Nevada, and she was officially his girlfriend, even if Marcelle had no inkling and would never see the appeal of his shy smile, the splendor of his horseback riding. Her mother wouldn't approve of his coarsened hands, his tousled hair, his sunburned neck.

Pauline went in to fetch some fruit and glanced out the kitchen window, which headed toward the road. Across the garden and the adjoining pasture, her eye caught a movement. There were horses roaming out there, near the main path. This sometimes happened. They were usually mustangs who had lost their way and had picked up the scent of other horses. They mostly left of their own accord, heading back into the hills. But these horses were sticking around, it seemed, circling the fence. Curious, Pauline stepped out through the kitchen door and walked closer to them. She could make out three mustangs, and as she drew near her heart pumped faster. The black stallion standing there, protecting his two mares, was unmistakably Commander, with the scars on his neckline, hardened into deep, dry grooves. In the past three months, he had gained in size and weight, he was mightier than ever. And she felt his quiet power soothe her, the way it did whenever she thought about him.

"Don't go away," she said in a low voice. "Just stay right there. Let me go get her."

Billie-Pearl was up to her usual antics, making the boys roar with laughter. It was tough plucking her away from them.

"What is it?" she said, irked. "What do you want to show me?"

Pauline said nothing, leading her around the back way, down to the outer fence bordering the main road. Commander was still there, waiting.

Billie-Pearl stopped in her tracks, thunderstruck.

"It's him!" she gasped.

Commander neighed while she ran toward him, leaping across the grass like crazy. Pauline feared he might take off, but he remained there, steadfastly, until Billie-Pearl got to the fence and stood on the other side, about six feet from him.

Pauline kept back, not wanting to interfere in this moment, which was taking a surprisingly intimate turn. Billie-Pearl was talking to Commander, and the horse, ears pricked, appeared to be listening intently. Pauline wondered what she was telling him. Gus and the other stable boys had approached in turn, captivated by this unusual get-together.

"Now how about that!" Gus exclaimed.

"He remembered her," said Pauline. "He came back for her."

"Maybe it's just a coincidence," Gus said.

But Pauline was convinced that the stallion had come back for her friend. When they heard the news from Billie-Pearl, beside herself with excitement, Doc O'Brian and Velma had no particular opinion on the matter. To them, Commander had returned, no one knew exactly why, and Billie-Pearl was over the moon. They all shared her happiness.

A few days later, Pauline, Gus, and Billie-Pearl rode off to the Sahwave range, northeast from Wadsworth. Equipped with water, they set out at dawn when the sky barely paled to the east, knowing Nevada sun should not be underestimated, even in September. Pauline rode the faithful Tundra; Billie-Pearl, Dustin; and Gus took Hook, a good-natured young horse he had just broken in. They left the strips of grass spreading out along the sides of the road behind them as they ascended the broad pathway heading north, where hill after hill rose to the highest point in a succession of sparsely vegetated pebbly slopes where at times rock pierced though like stone fangs. They climbed through groves of juniper, glens dotted with sagebrush and purple loosestrife, brightened by the last wildflowers of the dying summer, and unexpected babbling brooks. A crisp, musky aroma rose from the greasewood shrubs and their waxy leaves. From time to time, they spotted deer and sheep, but apart from the wind, the animals, a few bluebirds, robins, and lazy lizards, there was no human trace here, and that was what Pauline loved—the uninterrupted vastness.

The horses picked their way cautiously as they climbed the steep hills, hooves clicking against rocky soil, and Pauline felt profound joy as they ambled along, with Billie-Pearl ahead of her and Gus by her side. She was in the company of two of the people she felt happiest with: her closest confidante who knew everything about her, and her boyfriend, with whom she was just discovering her first amorous emotions; and she sat astride a beloved mustang, sensing Tundra move beneath her, at ease. She felt far from Marcelle, her outbursts of unhappiness, the drinking problem Doug never spoke of. One day, soon, her mother was going to reach a breaking point. She sometimes wondered if she shouldn't talk with her mother about it, but she was only seventeen and she feared Marcelle's sharp tongue. She knew how mercurial her mother could be, charming one moment, and nasty the next an extra bourbon later.

They reached an elongated, level terrain, flanked by thick bunches of juniper trees, and were able to pick up speed, breaking into an easy gallop, sending billows of dust all around them. Suddenly, Dustin began to whinny stridently, twisting his neck, making Billie-Pearl click her tongue in annoyance. She forced him to slow down, forcing Pauline and Gus, right behind her, to lessen their pace as well. Dustin seemed agitated, tossing his head, nickering in excitement or pain. Billie-Pearl couldn't understand what had gotten into him; Pauline suggested perhaps he had been bitten by a horsefly, and Gus got down to examine him while Pauline held Hook's reins.

"Can't see what the heck is wrong. Boy, is he jumpy!" said Gus after a while. "Or is it a problem with one of his hooves?"

As he bent over to check, Pauline spotted the black silhouette of a horse standing on the side of the wide flat stretch. It was Commander, and she knew Dustin had recognized him. With him were two mares and a colt.

"Billie-Pearl . . ." whispered Pauline. "Look."

Her friend glanced up and held her breath. Their three horses were restless now, reacting to the stallion's presence, beginning to snort and paw the ground. Pauline felt a flicker of fear.

"He won't harm us," whispered Billie-Pearl, as if she had guessed what her friend was thinking.

"How do you know?"

"I just know, is all."

"What is he doing?" asked Gus.

Billie-Pearl said he was showing them, once again, who was boss, but he wasn't being belligerent about it; and he knew exactly who they were, each of them, apart from Hook, the newcomer.

"Do you think he might come closer?" questioned Pauline.

"I hope he does. Let's just wait here and find out."

"Should we dismount?"

"Nope. We stay put."

Dustin, Tundra, and Hook had quieted down somewhat, while the warm wind played with their manes and tails, and Pauline's brown hair. Commander came forward, leisurely, taking his time, shielding his mares and foal, and the long sturdy legs and colossal neck gave him the stance of a scarred, indomitable warrior.

"I'm scared," mumbled Pauline, feeling Tundra shudder once again as the stallion drew nearer.

"You have no reason to be scared," Billie-Pearl said. "He's here to mark his territory, but we are no strangers to him."

And she spoke to Commander as he came forth, in a tone that was both self-possessed and respectful; she told him how glad she was to see him again, here on his own land, while the stallion rotated around them, retracing his steps over and over.

"What's he doing?" mumbled Gus. "He's creeping me out, spinning around like that."

"Don't lose it," said Billie-Pearl. "He's just herding us."

"Are you sure?" asked Pauline, still worried.

Billie-Pearl sighed. "What a bunch of scaredy-cats! He's guarding us, that's what he's doing."

Commander at last halted in front of Dustin, who was dancing with delight at the sight of his old playfellow, and Billie-Pearl had to rein him in tight and use the grip of her legs to prevent the younger horse from bucking with joy.

The stallion stood near Billie-Pearl, slanting his head to smell her thigh under her Levi's, and she held out her palm to him, which he snuffled carefully.

"Take it slow, my lord, my prince of the desert. Remember Mademoiselle back there, on Tundra? She also watched over you."

Commander was now so close to Pauline that she could sense his breath on her, as well as the pungent, wild odor emanating from his dusty hide. Tundra was shaking like a leaf, and Pauline wasn't far from shuddering either.

"Give him your hand," whispered Billie-Pearl. "He knows you. Trust him."

Pauline stretched out an unsteady hand, nearly closing her eyelids in fright. He brushed her skin with moist, dilated nostrils. Commander's eyes were a startling translucent gray-black, and she could clearly see two huge pupils staring right at her.

"What a magnificent horse!" said Gus, in awe. "Will you ever ride him, Billie, do you think?"

"No way. You don't ride Commander. No one will ever ride Commander."

They watched him leave with his family, heading down to the other side of the trail.

"Something tells me we'll be seeing him again soon," said Billie-Pearl.

———⟫⟫⟫⟩———

Ten days later, Commander was back, waiting at the gates of the ranch. This time, he was alone. Billie-Pearl went to him, standing in front of him, hands tucked into the pockets of her jeans as Pauline watched them from the porch, thinking they looked like old friends delighted to see each other.

"And do you think he'll come back?" Doug asked later, after Pauline had told him the whole story.

She said Commander already turned up, every now and then. He came out of the blue, with a part of his herd or alone. He'd wait until Billie-Pearl appeared, and they remained face-to-face. No one disturbed them. Billie-Pearl refrained from touching him and didn't try to. Sometimes the stallion sniffed at the top of her head and, once, he knocked off her Stetson. She picked it up, laughing.

"And doesn't your pal feel like riding him?"

Pauline repeated Billie-Pearl's own words: "You don't ride Commander. No one will ever ride Commander."

Doug understood. He loved sharing these moments with Pauline, listening to her describe what was going on at the ranch, gleaning every detail of her time there, everything she discovered and found exhilarating, and he took pride in the fact that he introduced her to the Johnstons. Marcelle was far less keen. A daughter who dreamed of being a vet? The prospect didn't blow her away, and she didn't hesitate to let it be known, often clumsily. According to her, Pauline had to move on to other social circles, to draw away from the ranchers and breeders. How else was she going to find a husband? She wanted only the best for her daughter: a serious, well-to-do suitor with a bright future. A string of flush ladies from Reno who had sons, grandsons, and nephews to marry off were regular customers at her hair salon. That was the coterie Pauline had to get into. She was about to turn eighteen; it was all happening now. Otherwise, she might be left on the sidelines, becoming an old maid nobody wanted. She had to do her hair properly, apply makeup more carefully, and there was surely more to life than riding mustangs!

Pauline found Marcelle's sermons infuriating. She felt like some sort of commodity yielded to the highest bidder. But she was too timid, too well-mannered to retaliate. Doug's caring presence was the only thing that cheered her up. From time to time, he asked his wife to change the subject, despite Marcelle protesting this was for her daughter's own good.

One night when the bourbon had flowed heavily, Marcelle unleashed herself, saying Kendall Spencer, managing director of the Mapes Hotel, was the type of man Pauline should be going for—handsome, well-groomed, ten years older, in a good position.

"Not some insignificant stable boy," she said, her lips curving with disdain.

"Now, that's enough, Marcelle!"

Doug hardly ever raised his voice, but when he did, it was effective. Marcelle kept quiet for the rest of the evening.

—————

A few weeks later, just after Thanksgiving, Doug happened to mention that on Sunday afternoon he was dropping off a car he had just mended to a client staying at the Mapes.

"Pauline can help you out," Marcelle said brightly.

Pauline guessed where this was going but remained silent.

"What for?" asked Doug. "I'm driving the guy's car straight from the garage to Virginia Street."

"Well, then Pauline can take you to Sparks in the Buick, follow you to the Mapes, wait for you there, and take you home."

Doug grinned. How clever his little wife was! He kissed the

top of her head. Pauline realized he was in the dark about what his "little wife" was plotting. On Sunday, Pauline was about to head out wearing ankle pants, loafers, and a knit pullover, but her mother called her back in, saying she was going to have to do better than that. Marcelle picked out a slim wool skirt only worn on grand occasions, an emerald green twinset, and high-heeled pumps.

"Why is Pauline all dolled up?" asked Jimmy.

"She's going to the Mapes," said Marcelle, combing her daughter's hair and pinning it up with dexterity. "You have to look smart when you go there."

Pauline balked at the pumps and Marcelle finally let her wear black ballet flats. During the drive, Doug said the business with the car at the Mapes would only take five minutes or so. She could wait in the lobby, and he'd be there in no time at all.

She found the Mapes as imposing as she did the first time, the summer before. Maybe it had something to do with the scent lingering there, the smell of money, elegant clothes, expensive luggage. It was the end of November, but a Christmas tree was already in full view, bedecked with glittering decorations. Inwardly cursing her mother for making her feel like a prize calf trussed for auction, with the bellboys checking her out, she felt self-conscious as she dawdled around. She walked by the florist and a nice bespectacled woman inquired whether she needed anything; the barber was busy giving a customer a shave, and the beauty salon was filled with a bunch of ladies getting their nails done.

"You don't need the beauty salon, you're pretty enough as it is."

She had picked up his minty aftershave even before she heard his voice. Kendall Spencer was not a tall man, but the intensity stemming from him made him seem bigger than he really was.

"Are you expecting someone, perhaps?"

"Yes, my stepdad. He has an appointment at the Mapes."

"It's wonderful to see you again after the Sky Room. You wore a green dress that night, I believe, which suited you very well."

He no longer spoke, observing her with a smile that was both cordial and greedy; she found him good-looking, with his fine features, clear eyes, and thin-lipped mouth. He was still young, barely thirty years old, and behind his neat appearance lurked a dark authority that unsettled her. He was both attractive and dangerous, and she had not met a man of his kind before. Her boyfriend was only seventeen, with little experience in any field, apart from his remarkable riding skills.

"Tell me your first name again?"

"Pauline."

"You're gorgeous, Pauline."

She wasn't used to such compliments.

"You're even prettier when you blush like that. How old are you?"

For an unfathomable reason, she told him she was turning twenty at the beginning of the following year. She couldn't bring herself to say that, at the present moment, she was still only seventeen.

"Would you like a private tour of the Mapes?" he asked. "I have a busy schedule, but I'd be proud to show you around. This place is quite something, as I'm sure you know."

Pauline found herself nodding, saying she'd love to, while an inner voice kept asking her what the heck she was doing.

Doug turned up and immediately assessed the situation. A

tour of the Mapes? How kind, indeed. Another time perhaps. They had to get home. Marcelle was cooking her ragout. Ah, the charming Parisian wife? Kendall remembered her well.

"And the family name is . . . ?" he asked Doug.

"We are the Hammonds," replied Doug, with a touch of pride.

"You're from Reno?"

"That's right. For several generations now. Over on Washington Street."

Pauline saw the way Kendall looked at his grimy overalls. There was no contempt in his gaze, only a slight pity.

"Well, I'd be happy to give the Hammonds a grand occasion to come back to the Mapes." He said he was entirely at their disposal, and he didn't propose this to all customers, only the ones he particularly favored. He held out his card to Doug, who pocketed it with a nod.

When they got home, Doug mentioned the meeting with Kendall Spencer, saying he had been friendly, and that was it. He discreetly threw away the calling card and Pauline added nothing. She wasn't going to tell her mother Kendall had been quite taken with her, nor was she about to admit she felt flattered. The only person she related all this to was Billie-Pearl. Frankly, she didn't expect to hear from Mr. Spencer again.

—»»»—

The phone started ringing a few days later, during dinner. Marcelle answered. It was Kendall Spencer's assistant. Mr. Spencer wished to invite the entire family to the Mapes, to visit the hotel. *How had he found them?* Pauline wondered. Then she remembered Doug had mentioned Washington Street. Their number and address were in the phone book. Marcelle rejoiced. Her plan had worked. Her daughter had caught the eye of the assistant director, that handsome and promising young man. She accepted the invitation, which was a Wednesday evening after work and school. Jimmy was thrilled at the idea of venturing behind the scenes of the prestigious hotel. Only Doug remained wary.

Their tour of the Mapes Hotel was engrossing, and Kendall impressed them all, even Doug. He seemed to have the answer to everything. He began by telling them the hotel was thought up by the Mapes family back in the forties, inspired by the Chrysler Building in New York. His boss, Charles Mapes Junior, the present-day manager, made sure the hotel was staffed with born-and-bred Nevadans. No expense had been spared ten years earlier when the Mapes was built: with genuine ceramic tiles, real chrome and stainless steel fittings, and state-of-the-art household appliances. But prices stayed reasonable, he added, so convenience could be within everyone's reach.

Pauline noticed what a fuss Kendall made of Jimmy and Marcelle, and how quickly they took a shine to him. Yes, there was a certain magnetism to him, she had to admit. They started with the three huge kitchens on the ground floor, where the chef and sous chef were already hard at work with their teams getting ready for dinner, not only in the Sky Room, which seated two hundred and fifty guests, but also in the Coach Room and the Coffee Shop, as well as room service for customers who wished to dine in the privacy of their suites. Jimmy was given a candy apple on a stick. Then, they visited the boiler room, where workmen were on tap monitoring pipes and cisterns; the laundry rooms, where they had never seen so many washing machines and dryers spinning at the same time; then the telephone operators facing their switchboards, each in their own cubicle.

They went down to the casino—which was yet another world, with its checkered flooring, gilded ceiling, mirrored pillars— and were greeted by the haze of cigar smoke and the smell of liquor, while clients flocked around the tables, taking a shot at playing craps, blackjack, and roulette. A security guard spotted Jimmy, dashing forward, as children weren't allowed in, but Kendall waved him away and he backed off deferentially. They had a peek at the main safes, which Kendall said he showed to no one, not even important clients.

Everywhere they went through the Mapes, Kendall Spencer was nodded at respectfully. His eyes were always on the go, checking every detail, every position of the staff, and sometimes uneasy glances were sent his way, noticed Pauline, as if some feared him. He moved swiftly and silently, like a feline, slicking back his hair, a tiny smile on his lips. He was a man of power within these walls, and he knew it.

When he bade them all good-bye, he took Marcelle's fingers in his and held them to his lips for a trifle too long.

"You have a lovely daughter, Mrs. Hammond. And I see where she gets her looks."

Just before Christmas, Pauline was doing some last-minute shopping at lunchtime on West Second Street at the Byington Building, in one of Marcelle's favorite boutiques, *The Parisian Dress Shoppe*. The saleslady didn't speak a word of French, but the clothes really did come from France—it said so on the labels. Pauline settled for a fuchsia silk scarf, which the lady was wrapping up for her when the store's bell tinkled and the familiar minty scent made its way over to her.

"Well, well...if it isn't that pretty Frenchie..."

There he was, wrapped up against the cold in a well-cut coat, a felt hat sitting rakishly on his blond hair.

"Good day, Mr. Spencer," said the saleslady. "Getting mighty cold out there, isn't it?"

Kendall Spencer was looking for a present for his aunt. He was tempted by the silk scarf Pauline had just purchased.

"What about a nice cup of hot chocolate at the Coffee Shop?" he said later, as they stepped outside into the cold.

The Mapes was around the corner. He gazed at her keenly, with the same tiny smile and she felt she couldn't refuse. It wouldn't take long, after all, not even thirty minutes, and she looked forward to the lush comfort of the Mapes, in the company of this man. No one had ever looked at her like that before and she didn't quite know whether she enjoyed it—she felt naked. But she also told herself how proud her mother would be, knowing her daughter was capable of attracting a man such as Kendall Spencer. In Marcelle's eyes, Kendall Spencer was the ideal son-in-law. He seemed well-mannered, thoughtful, and refined, not like those coarse ranchers whistling at Billie-Pearl and her. He held the door for her, letting her enter the Mapes before he did, and Pauline, once again, saw the glances cast toward him from the staff. The boss was back.

She was doing her best not to show her nervousness, but her fingers were trembling as she held her mug of hot chocolate. Kendall asked her questions and she answered timidly. Yes, she was enjoying the holiday season. She enjoyed spending this time with family. Her hobby? Horses. She rode them on a ranch near Wadsworth, with her best friend. Yes, she was indeed French, born in Paris, but she now had American citizenship and she had grown up here. Paris seemed far away to her. And did she have a job? Or did she go to college? She remembered, unnerved, that she was supposed to be almost twenty, since she had lied about her age. It seemed impossible to admit that she was still in high school, so she stammered she was studying French at the University of Reno. He in turn spoke of his well-established family from Nevada and of his work, which he was dedicated to. His job was a challenging one because the director was often away, and Kendall had to take care of everything in his absence. This hotel was enormous—she had seen it for herself—and there were a thousand details to attend to and endless problems to resolve. It never stopped! She listened to him with pleasure; his voice was gentle, but slightly ominous, as if its delicacy concealed a darker side.

As she was about to leave, he said, "It strikes me that I didn't show you my office during your last visit with your family. Mine is the largest at the Mapes, even bigger than the director's himself!"

Pauline hesitated. It wouldn't take a minute, she thought.

"It's right nearby, on the second floor. I'll introduce you to my team, they're great. Come on up!"

Curious to see where he worked, she followed him into the elevator, but when they got to the second floor, the place was deserted and there were no team members at their desks. Ah, yes, lunch break, he had forgotten. Introductions would be for another time, right?

"And here is my lair," he said, opening the double doors wide to a large room painted in coffee and rust tones, lined with garishly colored carpeting. Pauline saw shelves filled with trophies and sports cups, a teak corner desk, and two leather couches.

She came in, her coat over her arm, and Kendall took it, hanging it on a hook with his.

There was silence.

She looked out the window, toward Virginia Street, covered with a thin layer of snow, where passersby jostled along, laden with gifts.

And Commander suddenly appeared at her side, as if he were placing himself as a protective barrier between her and the young man slowly coming closer, a gentle smile on his face.

SEPTEMBER 1960

---✦---

Reno, Nevada

Pauline was changing in the basement floor dressing room when Mildred Jones came running in.

"She's back!" she said tersely before taking off again, but Pauline knew exactly who she meant. Mrs. Miller had been gone nearly ten days and each morning had brought a new scrap of gossip. Her mysterious escape to Los Angeles had fueled speculation of all sorts: There were talks of her being admitted to Westside Hospital for a breakdown, and other sources claiming she had been trying to see Montand one last time at the Beverly Hills Hotel, after his interview in the *Los Angeles Times* with gossip columnist Hedda Hopper in which he had offhandedly declared that Marilyn Monroe's feelings for him could be compared to a mere schoolgirl's crush. But the next day, Pauline heard that Mrs. Miller was better, consulting her therapist, Doctor Greenson, having her hair bleached by her loyal hairstylist, Pearl Porterfield, and somebody else added the actress even flew to San Francisco to see friends for a couple of days. Another rumor was going round suggesting Marilyn had been designated as the scapegoat, that her personal difficulties had been amplified to cover up for Huston's failure at sticking to his budget. It had become impossible to keep track of what was true. Meanwhile, Clark Gable made the most of the break to go home to Encino, Montgomery Clift to New York, and John Huston's out-of-control gambling addiction was the talk of the town. Pauline heard he spent night after night at the craps table, losing colossal amounts of money. The general consensus was that the movie would never be finished if this went on.

That morning, as Pauline was approaching the Mapes, a big bed was being hauled out of a mover's van into the lobby. The guys at the front desk were cracking up with laughter and Pauline asked them what was going on. Apparently, Montgomery Clift's sleep was so terrible that he had his own bed shipped all the way from Manhattan to Reno. Wasn't that nearly three thousand miles?

When Pauline got to Suite 614, Mrs. Miller was standing in the living room, chatting to Rafe. She was barefoot, wearing white slacks and a cream-colored blouse, and Pauline noticed a radiant glow to her skin, how her hair no longer had dark roots and was back to platinum, and how much slimmer her figure seemed. Mrs. Miller was telling her masseur about the lovely welcome she got last night at Reno's airport and how it warmed her heart.

"Good morning," Pauline said to them both. "Welcome back, Mrs. Miller."

"There's our pretty Pauline! *Bonjour!*" said Mrs. Miller, and her French made Pauline smile all the more.

Mrs. Miller went on talking to Rafe as Pauline got to work.

She was telling him things were going to be different from now on because she had settled certain issues, and she felt stronger. She was back on track and had replenished her energy when she was in California. She added there were still problems, however, and they had to get this darned film over with. Rafe was mentioning the small part he played as an ambulance driver in the rodeo scene. He was curious to see himself on screen and Mrs. Miller teased him, saying the real star of the movie was him.

The doorbell started to ring and it was just like the old days: Whitey and Agnes turned up, overjoyed to see Mrs. Miller, and May arrived with the morning mail. While Pauline cleaned up, they all conversed merrily.

All of a sudden, a connecting door opened and Mrs. Strasberg appeared as if by magic, making everyone jump and laugh. She now slept in a room adjacent to Suite 614.

"I got rid of Grouchy Grumps!" cried Mrs. Miller. "Looks like I got a good trade with Paula."

"Yes indeed, dear, but don't forget we have a film to finish," said Mrs. Strasberg. "Grouchy Grumps is still going to be on set."

While she dusted the furniture, Pauline listened to the conversation. She felt at ease with this small group of people she had come to know. There was a knock at the door and she went to open up. Mildred Jones stood there with Harper, one of the maids. Mildred asked her to step out into the corridor.

"You need to go pick up your daughter. Harper will take over for you."

Pauline felt herself go white.

"Did something happen to Lily?" she asked faintly.

"No, don't worry, she's fine. Mrs. Abigail's mother had a

stroke and she needs to be with her right now. I'll explain the situation to Mrs. Miller's secretary. I won't go into detail. You should leave."

Pauline knew she couldn't turn back to say good-bye to the Happy People, as Mrs. Miller called them. She felt a pang of sadness as she left, and one of envy, as well, thinking of Harper mingling with them. Downstairs, she changed back into her clothes and rushed over to Pickard Place, wishing the distraught Mrs. Abigail all the best for her mother.

"And I have you all to myself, Lily babe," she crooned, scooping her daughter into her arms.

She loved looking after her little girl. She spent the rest of the day at home playing with Lily, singing her favorite songs (some were French songs Marcelle used to sing to her as a child) and baking cookies for her. Lily was easy to please, always giggling. She did have quite a temper, though. At times, it was quite impossible to put her to sleep. The nighttime story no longer did the trick and, at that point, only Doug's gruff voice was able to get the little girl to bed. Sometimes, Pauline worried about how she was going to manage bringing up Lily as a teenager. She was fully aware Kendall would not pull his weight for his illegitimate daughter. She'd have to do this on her own. The prospect seemed challenging.

Later on, Mrs. Abigail rang to say her mother was in the hospital, pulling through, and Pauline could drop off Lily the following morning, as usual.

The next day, Pauline was back at work in Suite 614. Mrs. Strasberg was already up, wrapped in a black kimono and drinking coffee in the living room. She was busy reading over the screenplay, so Pauline didn't disturb her, saying hello from afar.

When Mrs. Miller came out of her bedroom, it was obvious she hadn't had a good night's sleep; her face was puffy and pasty again. Pauline thought she was going to walk right past her, but she stopped to speak to her.

"Is everything okay, Pauline? Mrs. Jones told us you had a family problem yesterday."

For once, she wasn't naked, wearing a short nightdress that revealed her shapely legs.

"Thank you, Mrs. Miller. Everything is in order. It had to do with my daughter's nanny."

Mrs. Miller's eyes went wide.

"Your *daughter*?"

Pauline bit her lip. Too late. She nodded, embarrassed.

"You have a daughter?"

"Yes," choked out Pauline.

"And no husband?"

"That's right. A daughter, and no husband."

Mrs. Miller's eyes, of an unusual blue-gray, changed with the light and the colors she wore. This morning, they were indefinable—two little lagoons shrouded in mist.

"What's your daughter's name?"

"Lily."

"How old is she?"

"She's three."

"So you were..."

"Eighteen."

"You're a mother...."

Mrs. Miller seemed moved. She touched Pauline's cheek tenderly with a finger. She told her she absolutely wanted to meet Lily, to get to know her. She adored children; it would make her so happy. Did Lily like dolls, or any other kind of toys? She wanted to give her a present. She had to see her! Only for a short moment. It would be so wonderful.

Pauline was speechless. She had no idea how to react to such a request. But while Mrs. Miller was showering in the bathroom, Mrs. Strasberg, who had overheard their conversation, confirmed the actress's love for children. She hasn't been able to have any, as of yet. It was complicated, she added, carefully. Marilyn had been so sweet to Mrs. Strasberg's daughter, Susan, who was now Pauline's age.

"It will light up her day if you bring your child one morning, and she needs it badly, believe me."

Pauline recalled reading about the actress's miscarriages in her mother's magazines. She told Mrs. Strasberg she didn't quite know how to go about it—just turn up with Lily? She was worried about how her supervisor would react. Mrs. Jones was not an amenable person.

"I'll handle Mrs. Jones. Bring Lily in tomorrow. We'll be waiting. You'll make Marilyn so happy."

—⤜⤜⤜—

The following morning, Mrs. Sheldon, the neighbor who drove them each day to Virginia Street, said she thought Lily had a lovely frock.

"That's because I'm meeting one of Mommy's friends," said the little girl. "It's my best dress."

Lily looked adorable this morning, with her dark, shiny hair pulled into two pigtails.

"A friend?" asked Mrs. Sheldon, enchanted by the child.

"A lady from the Mapes," said Lily, importantly.

Marcelle was still asleep when they took off in the morning, so she hadn't seen Lily wearing the pink-and-white dress with lace trimmings, or she would have asked questions as well.

"You're awfully pretty, Lily," said Mrs. Sheldon. "Your mommy must be so proud of you."

Luckily, she didn't add anything about Lily's father. Pauline prayed they wouldn't run into him at the Mapes, but it was early still. Kendall didn't get in until nine thirty at least. They had time. Pauline decided to avoid the service entrance, not wanting to meet any of her coworkers. She wasn't wearing her uniform either; she'd change later.

But when Pauline and Lily walked into the lobby, all the staff's eyes were upon them. There was sincere kindness in those smiles, Pauline noted, as she took her daughter to the elevators. She realized she had not brought Lily here before. The little girl was dazed by the size of the place. Pauline braced herself, expecting to behold Mildred Jones's disapproving face, but she was nowhere to be seen. They went up in the lift, and Casper made Lily laugh by twirling his red pillbox hat.

"Is she yours?" he asked, although, of course, everyone here knew about her situation.

"Yes, she's my daughter," said Pauline, proudly.

And she did feel pride at holding Lily's hand here, for the first time, in front of everyone.

It felt strange ringing the bell at Suite 614 and not letting herself in with her pass key. Mrs. Strasberg opened the door, a wide smile on her face.

"Well, now! I see a young princess is here to visit us. How lucky we are."

And suddenly all the "Happy People" were there, flocking

around them, with cries of welcome and joy. Pauline feared her daughter might become shy with all the attention, but Lily seemed to enjoy herself. They went into the living room, and Agnes handed Pauline a cup of coffee.

"Where's the lady? Your friend?" Lily asked her mother.

"I guess you mean me," said Mrs. Miller. "Hello, Lily. I sure am happy to meet you."

She knelt down on the floor to be at the child's level, telling her it was so nice of Lily to come. What a beautiful dress! Pink and white were her favorite colors too. And what lovely, glossy hair Lily had, and such a gorgeous smile!

Mrs. Miller and Lily were getting to know each other by chatting. The gift was a dainty dollhouse and May whispered to Pauline that Mrs. Miller had called the toy shop to choose it herself. Pauline looked on as her daughter touched the small, wooden structure, the miniature furniture, fabrics, and tiny carpets in awe. Would she remember these moments, she wondered, as Mrs. Miller's pretty, slim fingers touched Lily's. After all, Lily was only three. But the dollhouse was going to last; it was going to stay in Lily's room as proof of an unexpected encounter.

The morning light, softer in September, lit up a bouquet of white roses set on the table. They looked like mother and daughter, thought Pauline, reading the same thing in the faces around her. Why was it so difficult for Mrs. Miller to have children? Pauline hoped Mrs. Miller might yet have her own one day. Then she recalled the tension with Mr. Miller.

"Do you like it?" asked Mrs. Miller.

Lily nodded.

"Say thank you, Lily babe," whispered Pauline.

"Thank you, ma'am," said Lily.

"Oh, please call me Marilyn, darling."

"Thank you, Marilyn."

"Can I hug you?"

Again, Lily nodded.

Mrs. Miller gently put her arms around the little girl and closed her eyes. There was silence. She seemed so desperately unhappy that Pauline had to look away.

"My dear, we have to be on the move," said Mrs. Strasberg, quite firmly. "Whitey and Agnes need to start."

Mrs. Miller pulled away from the child. There were tears in her eyes.

"Why are you crying?" asked Lily.

Mrs. Miller forced herself to smile. Why, she wasn't crying at all! She just had to get to work, that was all, like her mommy did too. They all had to get going.

Lily held the dollhouse close.

"This is mine," she said.

"It is indeed," said Mrs. Miller. "It's all yours. And nobody can take it from you."

While everyone was saying good-bye to the little girl, Mrs. Miller took Pauline to the other side of the room. She wanted to thank her for bringing her daughter, and Pauline said it had made them both happy.

Then, Mrs. Miller said, "You don't have to answer, honey, but what is the situation with her dad?"

Pauline felt her face redden, but no stutter came. She said Lily's father was married and had kids. That was the situation.

"I see," said Mrs. Miller. "Does he help out? Give you money from time to time?"

"He does."

"Does he see his daughter?"

"Not very often. His wife is jealous. Apparently."

Mrs. Miller raised her eyebrows.

"Is he from Reno?"

"Yes. And you've already met him."

"I have?"

Pauline looked over to her daughter, who was being cuddled by Agnes. Why was she telling Mrs. Miller all this? Because she trusted her.

"His name is Kendall Spencer. The Mapes's assistant manager. You saw him in the Sky Room, the night of the power failure."

Mrs. Miller said she remembered him perfectly.

"Has he acknowledged paternity of your child?"

"No. Lily bears my name."

"Is he giving you trouble, Pauline?"

Pauline remained silent.

Mrs. Miller said there were men who were nasty pieces of work, even if they swaggered around in their elegant suits. They treated young women badly. Pauline didn't have to explain, but there was one thing she needed to know: She had to learn to stand up to him. She had to assert herself even if it wasn't easy; it was the only way.

Mrs. Miller certainly knew what she was talking about. She had endured many sordid situations, from too many men.

Pauline could feel Mrs. Miller's hand gripping her arm.

"Now remember this, honey, you put up a fight from now on. Promise me."

"I promise, Mrs. Miller."

"Oh, that's enough with the 'Mrs. Miller' business. Call me Marilyn. Please."

The filming of the movie had resumed, more or less smoothly. Some days, Pauline never crossed paths with any of the "Happy People": they were all on set, but the whims of the weather, and vagaries of transportation and logistics meant she often ran into Marilyn, Mrs. Strasberg, and the rest of the gang. Now that she also cleaned Mrs. Strasberg's adjoining bedroom, who often left her door ajar, Pauline unwillingly caught her morning phone conversations with her husband, Lee, and her daughter, Susan, and that was how she found out Kay Gable was expecting a baby next year, the couple's first one. Mrs. Strasberg seemed worried about Clark, who was going on sixty, and who had several tough stunts lined up in the coming weeks. She didn't feel the actor was in peak condition, but then no one was, shooting this particular movie. Sometimes, she told her husband, little miracles occurred, like Montgomery Clift and Marilyn, who proved to be positively prodigious in a long dialogue between Roslyn and Perce filmed behind a saloon, on a heap of empty cans and junk, with insect spray to keep the flies away. Huston had been nervous about the scene because of Marilyn flubbing her lines, and Monty being so vulnerable, but it had only taken three takes, and everyone on set had been bowled over by the sincerity between the two actors.

Mrs. Strasberg's conversations proved to be just as interesting as the cafeteria gossip, but whatever Pauline learned, she kept to herself. She had finally let Billie-Pearl into the secret of her friendship with Marilyn, the happiness it gave her, telling her how she had told Marilyn about Lily's father and the advice the actress had given her, which Billie-Pearl firmly agreed with. Those words had not left her, and when she had bumped into

Kendall a few days later, she did not acquiesce when summoned to his office. She told him, perfectly politely, that she didn't have time for any hanky-panky. Incredulous, he tried to grab her arm as she walked away.

"Let me go," she had ordered, raising her voice.

Kendall tried another tactic. "You know how much I adore you! How much I care for you and Lily!"

"Tell that to your wife," Pauline had snapped, and she had relished hearing him gasp.

"Did you really say that?" marveled Billie-Pearl.

"I sure did."

"Mademoiselle has come a long way."

Billie-Pearl wanted to know more about Marilyn, what she was really like, her little quirks, but there was no way Pauline would betray this precious friendship. Every morning, she found herself immersed in the movie star's daily life, making her bed, putting away her belongings, and journalists kept trying to bribe her. She held fast while most would have given in to the pressure, she was sure of it.

"I've noticed that ever since you started to work in Suite 614, you hardly stammer anymore. And you are much more determined."

Yes, Pauline was aware of a change, that she was at last able to stand her ground: It had come little by little, without her being fully conscious of it. When her mother had recently stumbled upon the dollhouse in the girls' room, she had wanted to know where it came from. Lily had said it was a present from "Marilyn" and Marcelle had shrugged her shoulders in disbelief. Pauline had calmly added it was indeed a gift from the actress.

"So she knows you, then?"

"Yes, *Maman*, she does know me. I've been cleaning her suite for nearly two months."

"But you never tell me anything!" Marcelle wailed.

"I don't tell anyone anything because I respect her."

Marcelle seemed to be on the brink of tears. She would have loved to have known her granddaughter spent time with Marilyn, and Pauline was depriving her of all that. It wasn't fair. Pauline had explained to her mother that she understood, but that's the way it was, and she didn't discuss her relationship with Marilyn Monroe with anyone.

"Surely you talk about it with Billie-Pearl? Or your coworkers?"

"Billie-Pearl knows, but she prefers mustangs to Hollywood. A bit like me. My coworkers? I keep quiet. And I'll go on keeping quiet."

An expression Pauline had rarely seen on her mother's face was emerging behind the disappointment—a certain form of admiration. She was still thinking about that look on her mother's face when she let herself into to Suite 614 with her cart.

Mrs. Strasberg was on the phone in her bedroom, telling someone she'd be down in a moment. Marilyn was having her morning massage, May told Pauline as she left. Shooting was stalled for this morning because John Huston was suffering from bronchitis and could barely breathe. They'd take up filming later in the day. She left, soon followed by Mrs. Strasberg in a hurry, and when Rafe finally took off, Pauline was alone with Marilyn, which didn't happen that often, as the "Happy People" were usually there, keeping Marilyn company, listening to her, or working on her hair and makeup.

Marilyn came out of her room in the nude, dashing into the

bathroom, and she stayed in there as Pauline vacuumed away. When she appeared again, she was wearing the Mapes bathrobe. She gave Pauline a little wave, and went back into her bedroom, starting one of her long phone conversations. She closed the door.

Later, Pauline was dusting the living room when Marilyn's voice made her jump.

"I was wondering..." The actress stared at her quizzically, as if she was trying to figure something out. "Don't mind me," she said, as the young woman paused, uncertain of what was going on. Then she came closer, leaning nearer to Pauline's face.

"Those eyes are quite something."

"Thank you," said Pauline, blushing.

"I'm just thinking..."

"Yes?"

"Can you come here for a minute?"

Marilyn led Pauline into her bedroom, drew back the curtains, and peeled off the dark blinds.

"Just sit here, will you?"

She sat Pauline down in front of the vanity table, turning her toward the mirror.

"You need to bring those eyes out more."

"I'm not much good at makeup," admitted Pauline.

"Well, I'm very good at it."

Marilyn laughed and Pauline couldn't help laughing with her. She seemed carefree, happy, far from the suffering of the past few weeks. Pauline sat still as she applied foundation, blusher, eye shadow, mascara with sure, deft touches, and brushed Pauline's brows, drawing over them. All the while, she hummed a little tune, raving about those fine features, high cheekbones, delicate nose. Pauline just needed to believe in herself a little more, to gain confidence. She was such a promising young girl.

"Now admire yourself in the mirror," Marilyn said.

Pauline discovered a stranger with large, slanting green eyes, thick lashes, arched eyebrows, and luscious, red lips.

"Oh!" she said, taken aback.

Marilyn's fingers were now touching her hair, unclasping the clip that held her ponytail.

"Let's do something about this. You tell me your mom is a hairdresser?"

"And I'm no good at hair either. To my mother's despair."

"Such a lovely, thick, glossy mane! I'm going to twist it up like this...pin it up....There....With a little backcombing here.... And I'll leave just a strand or two tumbling down in front.... Look at you!"

Marilyn clipped a pair of gold hoops on to Pauline's ears.

"I don't recognize myself," said Pauline, stunned.

"Isn't this fun? Wait...I have an idea."

She flung open the closet. Green was definitely Pauline's color, she was saying, and she herself didn't wear much green (even if she did possess a lovely lime-green Pucci top); however, black was the thing, black was always elegant, and Pauline should remember that. You could not go wrong with black, Marilyn went on, picking out a figure-hugging cocktail dress with a plunging back.

"Slip into this, honey, will you? Don't make that scared face, there's just you and me here."

Feeling as if she had entered a kind of living daydream, Pauline turned around, took off her uniform, and slithered into the black dress. It was tight on her, but not too tight. And not too short either.

Marilyn looked back at her, all smiles.

"Spectacular! I thought so. Oh, wait, hold on."

She rushed back to the closet and dropped to her knees, rummaging around.

"My guess is you don't wear heels often because you think they make you too tall, right?"

Pauline nodded.

"What's your shoe size, honey?"

"Size eight."

"I'm size seven, and these might do, they're a bit big on me."

She tossed Pauline a pair of white-and-black slingbacks, helped her fasten them on, and then took Pauline to the full-length mirror.

There was indeed a stranger standing there—a tall, sophisticated creature she had never seen. Marilyn put her palms on the young woman's shoulders from behind.

"Be proud of who you are, Pauline. Put your shoulders back, yes, that's right. Look at that splendid neckline! Lift your chin. Smile. I see a goddess!"

There was an impish glow in Marilyn's eyes; she said she just had an idea. A terrific one. Could Pauline wait for her in the living room? She'd be there in a few minutes. She added, flinging her arm upward theatrically, "We're going to strut around the lobby in style. And nobody will know who we are. Just you wait."

Pauline caught a glimpse of herself in the entrance mirror and froze. She really did look like someone else, she thought, as she twirled around. A very elegant someone else. It was unreal. But she was curious as to how Marilyn was going to go unnoticed in the main hall, and a bit nervous, as well.

"It's all a question of attitude," came Marilyn's voice from the bedroom. "And how you move."

The woman who strode out of the room looked so unlike Marilyn that Pauline had to blink. She held herself with a slouch, wearing a scruffy pair of jeans, a shapeless blouse, and flat sandals. She had short, black hair styled in a blunt pageboy and unfashionable dark glasses.

"Hi! I'm Zelda Zonk," the woman drawled, holding out a limp hand. "Nice to meet you!"

Pauline shook her hand, incredulous.

"Is that...you?" she faltered.

Marilyn pointed to the wig with a grin. She explained Zelda Zonk was a nickname she invented for herself when she moved to New York over five years ago. She'd discovered that a black wig and loose-fitting clothes allowed her to go unnoticed, so she often booked plane tickets using the disguise, and she had to walk and talk like Zelda Zonk, and not like Marilyn Monroe, but being an actress made that part easy.

"And that's what we are going to do with you, honey. You have to learn to move like the new person you see in that mirror."

"I don't know how," mumbled Pauline. "I can't do it."

"Of course you can. Just watch."

Marilyn sashayed across the room, swinging her hips. This would take a bit of practice, she warned Pauline, especially with the heels. Pauline had to imagine she was just as graceful as Audrey Hepburn in one her movies, like *Sabrina*, or *Roman Holiday*. Yes, she had to see herself, swanlike, in Audrey's style, with the same class, the same poise. She took Pauline's hand and made her march up and down, again and again, until Pauline mastered the swaying walk and the straight shoulders. It wasn't easy, but she did her best, and even reveled in it, after a while.

"Zelda and Audrey are now going down to the lobby."

Pauline felt fluttery with trepidation, watching as Marilyn tied a scarf around her own head, then handed her a pair of sleek dark glasses and velvet gloves.

"The final touch," she whispered. "Remember, it's all in your mind."

In the lift, Marilyn slumped against the partition and chewed her gum noisily, inspecting her nails. Casper wasn't on duty, and Pauline felt relieved. The person working today was an older guy who seemed half asleep.

When they got to the lobby level, it was full as usual, and Pauline heard the noise and chatter even before the doors opened. Marilyn took her arm, and began to lead her around, going by the flower shop and the beauty parlor.

"You're beautiful. Look at them staring at you."

Everywhere they passed, people pivoted to admire Pauline, and she couldn't get used to this new power, one she felt she never possessed. The flower shop manager bowed her head as if confronted with royalty, and the ladies in the beauty shop seemed hypnotized. Fern, vacuuming the carpet, drew back to let them pass, eyes roving over the black dress, and the grooms, bellboys, and front desk staff stared as politely as possible. Lincoln muttered something into Ernesto's ear, which Pauline caught: "drop-dead gorgeous."

And all the while, no one looked twice at Zelda Zonk, and Pauline couldn't quite believe that either.

"Let's go outside! Just for a minute or two."

"But..." began Pauline.

"Is your mom's shop far from here?"

"Why?"

"Honey, she won't recognize me. You, she might, so you'll stay in front and wait for me."

Pauline stopped short, tottering on her high heels. Here too, in the street, everyone was looking at her. Marilyn pulled down her dark glasses so Pauline could see her eyes.

"You trust me, don't you?"

"I do."

"Then tell me how long it will take us to get there on foot."

"Twelve minutes. Maybe longer in these shoes..."

"Are you up for it?"

"Yes! I am! But my mother is an utter fan of yours. She's bound to see beyond Zelda Zonk."

"Wanna bet?" said Marilyn, plonking each foot heavily on the ground and sinking her chin into her chest.

Marcelle's shop, on the corner of Winter Street and West Second Street, was packed with ladies under helmet dryers and others having their hair shampooed. Pauline knew her mother's two assistants well, Bunny and Donna, who were certainly busy that morning. Marcelle had been able to recreate the same atmosphere here as in her salon on rue Bréa in Montparnasse, and she ruled in her pink French kingdom, in a soothing Parisian ambiance that swept her away from Reno.

They halted on the sidewalk on the other side of Winter Street and, from there, Pauline could see her mother was busy dyeing Casey Smith's hair. Her most important client, the wealthy wife of a casino owner, she explained to Marilyn.

"Perfect. She won't even see me. Stay here. Act like you're waiting for a beau."

Her eyes hidden behind her dark glasses, Pauline watched Zelda Zonk push open the glass door to her mother's store, entering with a clumsy gait. For a couple of seconds, Marcelle raised her head, away from the reddish goo covering her client's head, scrutinizing Zelda Zonk's appearance while Pauline held her breath, then she resumed her task, totally uninterested in the newcomer. Bunny approached Zelda with a welcoming smile. What was Zelda Zonk telling her? Pauline couldn't tell, but when Bunny brought her nail polish samples, she saw that, while examining the different tints, Zelda boldly drew near Marcelle, under Pauline's anxious and delighted gaze. But Marcelle was engrossed with Casey Smith, and indifferent to the drab brunette who left the salon without buying anything.

"There!" said Marilyn, chuckling at Pauline, who was dumbfounded. "Now let's get back in time before that dragon Mildred Jones swoops down on us."

"You are...so..." Pauline couldn't find her words, and finally whispered, "extraordinary."

"No, Pauline. I'm only an actress accustomed to taking on roles. The extraordinary person is you. Except you don't know it yet."

1957

Reno, Nevada

Over and over again, Pauline read the letter from Mount Shasta that a smiling Doc had handed her, in which Doctor Hicks confirmed he was expecting her that summer so she could begin her internship at his California equine clinic. He had been impressed with her application letter, but also by what the Doc had to say about her, and Pauline's profile perfectly matched what he was seeking when he recruited his interns. In her carefully worded letter, she had explained her motivation was driven by her love for horses, ever since she discovered mustangs when she arrived in Nevada at seven (she had even penned a quasi-lyrical paragraph about Commander) but also by the high expectations of such a profession—its rigor, the opportunity to meet people from all walks of life, to be in the field, and all the while learning more, improving herself. For the past four years, she'd been assisting Doctor O'Brian at Velma Johnston's ranch, and she now realized she wished to devote herself to horses, not only mustangs but all horses. The animals needed her, but somehow she needed them as well. Healing them meant a good deal of patience, kindness, and mercy, and she knew now it was interacting with the horses that bequeathed an innermost force she had never fathomed she possessed. And she had finished her letter by adding that she was born in Paris, and it was coming to Nevada that had changed everything for her, opening her eyes to another universe and a new way of life. The little Parisienne had become an American. She wished to remain in her new country, to take root, and build her future here, and she wasn't afraid of working around the clock.

"It's all coming along nicely," said the Doc, congratulating her. "I guess you've discussed this with your parents? They must be proud of you."

Pauline didn't dare admit that her parents knew nothing about the internship. She dreaded broaching the subject with Marcelle, who had only one preoccupation these days: ferreting out a worthy groom-to-be for her daughter. And truth be told, she was convinced the deed was done. She embellished the situation, gloating, laying it on thick, already hinting to her clients at a forthcoming marriage. After all, Kendall Spencer was doing a lot more than just hanging around her daughter; he phoned her, had flowers delivered, gave her small, tasteful gifts, and sent her dinner invitations to the Mapes. Irritated, Doug had to rectify the situation with Marcelle: their daughter was underage, she needed to pass her end-of-year exams, concentrate on graduation and commencement, and certainly not on Mr. Spencer's bouquets and trinkets.

But no one knew what was going on in the secrecy of Kendall's office on the second floor of the Mapes, when Pauline, torn between fear and desire, went to those clandestine appointments he set at lunchtime. His method had been a slow and gentle one, without ever rushing her, or scaring her. He said over and over that she was beautiful, and she could see the effect she had on him. At first, they exchanged a few mild embraces, but slowly, she had let herself go, relinquishing to his mouth, to his expert fingers; no one had ever touched her like that, and Gus's fondling seemed clumsy in comparison.

Kendall kept telling her how much he respected her, how much she mattered to him, and, often, when they lay naked together, he spun parallel, intoxicating existences, describing torrid rendezvous, romantic candlelit feasts, unforgettable trips, saying he'd discover Paris thanks to her, dreaming of an ardent kiss at the top of the Eiffel Tower. He'd give her jewelry, fine gowns, stays in the finest hotels around the world.

Pauline listened to him, and with all the naïveté of her eighteen years, she believed every word he said, resigning herself to this fate so she might reassure her mother, reassure herself. Becoming the fiancée of such a promising young man would not be so unpleasant, and her mother would at last be proud of her. A slight apprehension, however—would Kendall agree with her going on an internship in California this summer, if they became engaged in the meantime? Whenever she tried to talk to him about horses, about her future job, she found he was not interested. The only thing that interested him was her body, which he worshipped during lovemaking sessions that ended up winning her over, even when she perceived the oily trace of his hair grease on the tips of her fingers, and she couldn't decide whether she felt pleasure or repulsion at his touch. She had the impression he was playing her as if she were an instrument—all he had to do was strike the chords and her responses were titillated mechanically, like a reflex, and she was aware she was under the grip of an unhealthy and indefinable yearning, a drug to which she surrendered, in spite of herself.

Back at the ranch, Billie-Pearl didn't mince her words. Why the heck was she dating this slimy fella? Had she fallen for him? What was she expecting? To become his wife? And when Pauline said that, yes, she was perhaps considering it, Billie-Pearl blew her top. His *wife*? Was Pauline half asleep or something? He was already more or less engaged to some posh society girl, an heiress from one of the richest Nevadan families, Evaline Steward. It was common knowledge. Pauline listened, alarmed.

Billie-Pearl grabbed her by the shoulders. "Please don't tell me you're in love with him."

"I'm not."

"Then what is it with him?"

"I can't explain. He makes me feel..."

"What?"

"I don't know, really. The way he touches me, I guess."

"God almighty...and what about poor Gus? Does he know?"

Pauline looked away. Gus knew nothing. No one did.

"Has Kendall proposed?"

"No, he hasn't. But he keeps saying he adores me, that we belong together. He means it."

Billie-Pearl let out a roar. "How can you be so gullible, Mademoiselle? He's a lying, scheming cheat. Why can't you see it?"

She felt like going into hiding as Billie-Pearl went on, unrelenting. Was Pauline really that blind? And what about those trysts in his office—just what was going on there? Pauline's face turned pink, but she knew she could confide in her best friend. She said Kendall had promised her he knew how to "be careful," as he was an older, experienced man. Billie-Pearl blew up again. They had both seen mustangs mating over the years, surely Pauline had a rough idea of what happened with humans as well. An "experienced man" could knock her up, no matter what he said.

"If you're not in love with him, and he's in no hurry to get himself engaged to you, then this circus has to stop."

Crestfallen, Pauline knew her friend was right. She had to do something now; she couldn't wait any longer. Summoning up her courage, she did her best telling all this to Kendall, and even went so far as to confess she had lied about her age—she was only eighteen and still in high school. She went on to say she intended to become a vet, that she had landed a summer internship. Then she'd go to college, and she knew she'd have to study for at least six more years. And finally, she confessed, she had a boyfriend. Gus was her age and she liked him very much. She felt awful cheating on him this way.

Kendall listened patiently, stroking her bare shoulders and arms as they lay on one of the couches. "I understand all that. Of course, I do. But why do you want to put an end to our delightful relationship?"

Pauline stared at him. She felt raw and stupid.

"B-because you are marrying someone else," she stammered.

"You mean Evaline?"

She nodded.

He got up, lit a cigarette, only wearing his boxer shorts. He had a fit, tanned body he was proud of.

"We've been engaged since we were teens, you know. It's a family thing. Like a tradition. A pact. Maybe you have that back in France. I'm not in love with her. You're the one I'm crazy about, angel."

"I don't get it," she blurted.

He said it was simple: Evaline was to be his bride because an association between the Spencers and the Stewards had always been expected, for all sorts of complicated reasons he didn't want to bore her with, like property, estates, managements, farming. But it was matrimony just for show, with no feelings involved, and Pauline had to think of it as a business transaction. That's all it was. And as for her boyfriend, honestly, the less Gus knew, the better. If no one found out, no one got hurt. Now, could she come back to the couch and resume what she had been doing to him just a few minutes ago? His little Frenchie was getting good at it. He went to sit down, put out his cigarette, and patted the cushion next to him. She told herself, as she submitted once again, that this simply couldn't go on. There would be no more encounters in his office. This was going to have to be the last one.

That same evening, at the table, after a moment's hesitation, Pauline told her mother that Kendall Spencer was engaged to an heiress, and that she was going to stop dating him. Marcelle stormed. Surely Pauline must have said or done something silly for Kendall to back off? She had indeed heard the stories about Evaline Steward, but if he was truly in love with Pauline, he would end up marrying her, not Evaline. Pauline didn't have the nerve to tell her that Kendall wasn't backing down. There had never been any talk of marriage, he had been leading her on, she had been incredibly gullible, and he had taken advantage of her, but she could tell by the look in Doug's eyes that he had it all figured out. He approved of her decision. And he was happy to hear that she had accepted an internship in California with a reputable veterinarian. Pauline took the full brunt of her mother's disapproval, which she found completely unfair, just like Doug.

But the following day, February fifth, there were other things to talk about at the Hammond dinner table. There had been a gigantic fire in downtown Reno, probably due to a gas leak on Sierra Street at West First Street. Buildings had exploded and caught fire. Two people had died and dozens were injured, and several stores were destroyed in the blast. Marcelle wasn't able to get to her salon for several days. After last year's devastating floods, she sighed, fate was being decidedly cruel to Reno.

———≫≫≫·—

The weeks slipped by, and Pauline focused on her upcoming exams, spending Saturdays and Sundays in Wadsworth, where she saw Gus. She sometimes wondered if he suspected her past liaison. She tried, in their moments of intimacy, not to reproduce the sensual gestures she had learned from Kendall. And she made him understand she wasn't ready to go all the way. But the truth was she feared he might discover she was no longer a virgin. She cared for Gus and felt ashamed, but she wasn't in love. And what she had experienced in Kendall's arms wasn't love either. It was over; the affair was behind her, forever. No one would know she had been Kendall Spencer's mistress for a few months. Soon, even she wouldn't be thinking about it.

There were other, happier, diversions. In May, Commander came to visit them at the ranch, flanked by several foals, and it appeared that most of his mares were about to calve.

"What a scoundrel!" Velma laughed. "He's certainly been sowing his seed."

Commander marched around the ranch as if he were its proud owner. Up close, Pauline saw he had new wounds on his side, some of which were still bleeding, but she knew he would not be coaxed into having them treated.

"He must have crossed paths with another stubborn stallion," Billie-Pearl said.

Later, after lunch, Pauline suddenly felt unwell.

"Are you okay, Pauline?" Velma asked, as they were putting away the dishes. "You're quite pale."

"I'm just tired. Nothing serious. Thanks."

She went into the bathroom. Her face in the mirror was undeniably drained of all color. Waiting for the nausea to subside, she drank some tap water.

But later on that fine sunny day in May, as she drove back to Washington Street from the ranch, she started to ask herself those first, hard questions. What hadn't she wanted to see? How had she pushed it all away, thinking it wasn't possible, that it wasn't going to happen to her? But it was. It was happening. And she had never felt so afraid in her life.

She was tall and slim, and she hadn't felt anything different, except some guy at school had recently teased her that the beanpole had filled out. She hadn't paid attention. As for her periods, they were most often irregular. When she had felt queasy in the mornings, she had put up with it and gone to class. He said he had "been careful," that he was experienced. She had trusted him. Now, it was high time to face the facts. The affair had gone on from the end of December to the beginning of February, just before the gas explosion that had destroyed an entire block downtown. She hadn't seen him since then. She had ignored his phone calls and, after a while, he had given up phoning. Counting on her fingers, shuddering, she counted five months.

Reeling from the shock, Pauline cowered in the Buick, white-knuckled, hands gripping the wheel. She had parked a little farther off from the house on Washington Street, and from there she could see Doug mowing the front lawn with his usual attention to detail. Marcelle was at the hair salon, as this was Saturday, and Jimmy was no doubt watching TV.

It seemed to be an ordinary spring day in Reno, but for Pauline, it was the day everything changed. It was the day her life turned upside down.

She was carrying Kendall Spencer's child.

DECEMBER 14, 1957

—⟫⟫⟩—

Washington Street, Reno, Nevada

Dear Billie,

I miss you. You have no idea. I know you're busy traveling with Velma, and how important this is for the mission, for the mustangs, but you've been gone for weeks now and not being able to talk to you on the phone, as you're on the road all the time, is tough. I'm sending this to your dad's ranch as I have no clue where you are and when you'll be back.

(You know, I realize this is perhaps the first letter I've ever written to you, although we've been best friends for over five years. So hang on to it!)

When I look back at this summer and everything that happened, I sometimes find it hard to breathe. I don't know what I would have done without you.

Lily is doing great, nearly five months now. She's already grown since the last time you saw her. She's the sweetest baby.

She doesn't look like him. Thank God. He still hasn't met her. He says he's been meaning to. (I know what you think. I can almost hear your voice.)

Each month, I get a check. A good enough amount. He found a nanny as well. A seamstress on Pickard Place. At first I was worried about leaving Lily with a stranger. But she's a warm, gentle woman and she has raised four kids. And she makes no comment about my situation.

He got me a job at the Mapes Hotel as a cleaning lady. I started last week. I clean the small rooms, not the suites. It's harder work than you might think. The good thing about housework is that you can see the effects right away. My mother, like yours, doesn't have any help. We do it all ourselves. So cleaning is not new to me. What's new is their protocol. You're trained to clean up in a specific order. You've got to stick to it.

How long will I be stuck doing this? (I can hear you asking.) He says it's temporary and he'll find something more interesting for me soon, like in the bookings department for instance. Can I trust him? (I know you don't.) We'll see.

He says his fiancée is the jealous type. That she must never ever hear about Lily or their wedding will be ruined. You know, sometimes I get the itch to write to Miss Evaline Steward in her mansion, sending her a photo of Lily and spilling the beans about her "perfect" husband-to-be.

I can't imagine working at the Mapes for long. I'll be twenty in two years, and I can't bear thinking I might still be stuck here. It's so hard to plan right now. I was supposed to become a vet. Now I guess I won't.

My boss is called Mildred Jones and she's the spitting image of a wicked witch. She is not well liked, I can tell you that. She rules with an iron fist. The other girls are okay. They feel pity for me, I can sense it, and I hate it. Everyone knows I had his baby. They've stopped asking questions because I don't answer. There is a kind girl, though. Her name is Kitty. I think we might become friends, but not best friends!

Working at the Mapes is like being in a busy little town of its own. Each day I discover something new about the place. There's never a lull. It makes your head spin. I'm getting to know the staff, from the grooms to the Sky Room team, from the room service department to the operators. Isn't it ironic to think we had dinner at the Mapes last year on July Fourth, in our prettiest frocks, and he showed up at our table and did his thing?

I'm writing this to you while Lily sleeps peacefully in her cradle next to my bed. I can hear my mother in the kitchen getting dinner ready. She still gets wasted. More so, it seems, since all this. I won't forget the way she screamed when she found out. She went ballistic. She said I had ruined her life. Everything she had worked so hard for.

That time, Doug didn't stand up for me. He was in total shock. His little Pauly had really let him down. I flunked all my exams, I didn't graduate, there was no more internship with Doctor Hicks, no more vet school, and on top of all that, I was going to have a baby. A pregnant dropout. Not quite what he expected.

Now that he's digested the shock, he's become his old self. He's very fond of the baby, and he doesn't mind the way the

221

neighbors look at us when we take her out in the pram. My mother does.

You know what I discovered? One of the administrative assistants told me that my mother rushed to the Mapes just after Lily was born, this summer. She sat outside his door until he agreed to see her. She made a scene. Apparently, she broke down, pleading for him to marry me. She was hollering so loud everyone could hear. He told my mother he was sorry, he was already engaged (and I can just imagine him saying that to her while neatly handing her a Kleenex) but that he'd work things out. There would be no marriage to me, but he'd help in his own manner, whatever that meant.

(Oh, and I forgot to tell you he had called me just after my mother's visit. He asked if the baby was his. I said yes. I said I'd never slept with my boyfriend. He knows I'm no liar.)

Jimmy worships Lily and wants to take care of her the whole time. As a result, my mother has softened a bit, watching them. She now cradles her and sings her the French lullabies she used to sing to me. I know deep down my mother isn't so bad. She's just unhappy in Reno. And I guess I made things worse.

When I told you about the pregnancy, you didn't scream or lose it. You didn't sigh, saying I told you so. You uttered holy shit, or something like that, you took me in your arms, and I could feel all that marvelous strength coming from you, wrapping itself around me, shielding me.

I won't forget what you said to me as I stood there bawling my eyes out. You said I had to learn to be strong,

*that I was going to have a child, and I needed to protect
and love that child. You told me that whenever I felt scared,
I had to close my eyes and think of Commander. Think of his
power. Take that power. I even had to imagine I was riding
Commander. But you said it yourself, no one ever rides
Commander. So I use his strength to build up mine. And
you know what? It works. Not every time, but I'm getting
there. I think.*

*I guess I learn things the hard way. When I think of the
future, I sometimes feel dragged down. I want to bring up
this little girl as best I can. I want her to know her mother
is a decent person, and not some easy lay. The look on Gus's
face when he found out. I'll never forget it. He seemed so
disappointed, so hurt. He left the ranch last fall, and I have
not heard from him since. I probably won't.*

*Billie, will I ever find a nice boyfriend after all this? I'm
soiled goods. Who will want me now? I'm only eighteen and
it seems like my life is over. (Oh, I can hear your voice again
swearing at me and telling me to snap out of it.)*

*I had to bring the Doc up to speed. He was really decent
about it. He said he'd explain the situation to Doctor Hicks
in the best possible way. Velma and her husband didn't
overreact either. Not like most of the people in my class and
some of my teachers—they were awful.*

*There are a couple of other things I won't forget, like
when you rushed me to Saint Mary's Hospital that day in
late July when she was born, more than a month early, and
you stayed there all night, in the waiting room. (My mother
didn't want to be there; she got very drunk, and Doug had
to look after her.) And you were there, nearby, watching*

over me, like you always have. And giving those nurses and doctors hell for any judgmental glances.

As soon as she was born, they let you in, remember? You looked down at her tiny face and you said she was perfect. And when she had to stay in an incubator for a couple of weeks because she was so teeny, you came to see her with me each day.

And then this—you said I had to get back in the saddle, fast. So while Lily was still at Saint Mary's, you and I went out on Dustin and Hook. And we rode hard, just like we used to. And it felt so good.

Whenever I feel my strength going and my stammer taking over, I close my eyes and think of Commander. It does help. Sometimes.

You often tell me I need to gain confidence, to break out of my shyness and self-doubt, but I don't know how to do that, Billie. I don't think I ever will. I wish I could be like you. You're strong and confident, everything I long to be. (Don't sigh when you read this, please!)

I must be going now. Lily needs to be fed. Come back soon! The horses miss you. I do too. Commander has had a couple of foals that are to die for. I really hope you'll be here before Christmas.

You're the best friend a girl could ever have.

Mademoiselle

OCTOBER 1960

Reno, Nevada

At first, Pauline thought she hadn't properly heard what May Reis was telling her. She asked her to repeat her comment. The slim, black-clad silhouette breezed through the living room of Suite 614, paperwork in one hand, a pen in the other. May spoke again: Marilyn had left the Mapes for good yesterday, checking in at the Holiday Hotel across the way, a modern building that held less prestige than the Mapes. Pauline knew where it was. Its square shape, with a green and pink façade, stood on Mill Street, just above the Truckee River, a stone's throw from the Mapes on the opposite bank.

The young woman found herself unable to say anything. She hadn't expected such abrupt news. She felt like sitting down.

"Mrs. Strasberg is staying on at the Mapes," May went on, not noticing Pauline's state. "Her husband, Lee, and their daughter will be arriving in Reno soon. They'll be staying in this suite."

"I see," said Pauline at last, doing her best to get a grip on herself.

She wouldn't see Marilyn ever again. She kept saying that to herself as she began her cleaning procedure like a robot. It was over. It was all over. She wouldn't hear her voice or her laugh; she'd never smell her perfume; she'd not lay eyes on her again. Some other maid would look after her stuff, make her bed, straighten her room. She had to consider the entire adventure as if it had been a sort of dream; she had to draw away from it, not let herself be affected, but she was forced to admit to herself there was a pit in her stomach and she felt the overwhelming impulse to cry.

May was on the phone, dealing with the final details of the actress's transfer. The general manager must have been disappointed by the sudden departure, thought Pauline, and Kendall too, no doubt. They would surely have wanted to keep Marilyn Monroe longer, until the end of the movie. It was great publicity for the Mapes, after all.

May called someone else on the phone. Yes, Marilyn was now staying at the Holiday Hotel. Less stylish, of course, but quieter and away from tensions and the squabbling! No, no communication concerning that, it had to remain under the radar. Paula and Frank, the producer, had come up with the idea. Indeed, they should have thought of it from the start, May sighed. Gable and his wife were renting a separate house, bordering Washoe County Golf Course, and they had been right. It was silly to have wanted to cram everyone into the Mapes! Marilyn was now in Suite 846 at the Holiday, if anyone needed to reach her or deliver anything to her. Arthur was in a neighboring suite, 850. Yes, he had wanted to be near his wife. No comment about that either! Everyone was trying to get along a little better. The movie was late enough as it was. It was becoming absurd. It had to come to an end. Yes, Rafe was now at the Holiday as well, Marilyn had asked for him to be there. No one else was moving for the moment.

May hung up and went to sit at the table to go through the mail and sort it out. With tears in her eyes, Pauline worked in silence. This was the last time she'd be here, in this suite, she thought, where it had all started. That July morning, when she had stepped in for Pilar at the last moment, and when she had come across "Mrs. Miller," seemed so long ago. Of course, Marilyn had forgotten all about her. Just because she'd given Lily a present or had transformed Pauline by doing her hair and makeup, didn't mean she was thinking about her. Marilyn had bigger fish to fry, seriously. Pauline had to pull herself together. She clenched her teeth, briskly rubbing at the hard water stains on the kitchen sink. There was nothing else to do except get to work and throw herself into it. But all of a sudden she felt the weight of her humdrum life bearing down upon her; her shoulders buckled, and she inwardly groaned with the agony of it.

"Pauline?" came May's voice. "Can you come here for a minute?"

Pauline drew herself up straight, the way Marilyn had taught her, wiped away the tears on her face, and went into the living room.

May said she was in charge of handing out tips for the Mapes staff. She had made a list. And Pauline's name came out first.

Pauline had done a wonderful job, she went on. She had been discreet, efficient, and had brightened up Marilyn's stay during a particularly painful time.

"So this is for you, Pauline. With our sincere thanks."

The tip was a generous one. But there was no note inside the envelope, nothing personal. Pauline knew she couldn't ask May if she might pop over to the Holiday Hotel to see Marilyn again, she would sound like the worst of those clinging fans. She murmured, "Thank you very much," and slid the envelope in her apron pocket.

Like a sleepwalker, she went back to her tasks, submerged by a strange feeling of numbness and, at the same time, she longed to run away from the Mapes right now, cross the bridge over the river, rush into the Holiday, and go up to Suite 846. Marilyn couldn't slip out of her life this way. It was unfair. But in a corner of her mind, she could almost hear the jarring chorus of Linda and Kendall's voices sneering at her: What was she expecting, really? As if Marilyn Monroe cared two hoots about a chambermaid! She imagined them roaring with laughter; she could see them doubled over. Oh, poor little Frenchie! Did she really think a movie star was going to become her best buddy? Such exaggerated self-importance! How pathetic could she possibly get?

Pauline scoured the bathtub vigorously, tears spilling once more. She wiped them away in anger.

Suddenly, she saw a smiling May standing there, holding out a pad and a pen. "I nearly forgot! I've got so many things to do this morning. Would you jot down your home number, please?"

Pauline dried her hands and stood up. She wondered why her

number was needed. Some sort of administrative procedure, no doubt.

"Of course." She complied.

May thanked her. Then she said, still smiling, that Pauline was invited to attend the filming of one of the final scenes of *The Misfits*, in the desert near Dayton, about an hour from Reno. She needed to make herself free for an entire day, and she'd leave early in the morning with Whitey, Agnes, Rafe, herself, and their chauffeur. May would call her soon with more details.

Overwhelmed with joy, Pauline could hardly breathe. May patted her shoulder kindly and added, "This was Marilyn's idea. She thought you'd be pleased."

—⟫⟫⟫⟫.-

May had arranged to meet her in front of the Holiday at eight o'clock the following Tuesday morning. When the time came, Pauline had already dropped off her daughter with Mrs. Abigail, a little earlier than usual. The old Buick Doug used to lend Pauline was on its last legs, so he insisted on driving them.

Pauline had called Billie-Pearl on Monday evening to tell her all about it.

"What are you going to tell your boss?"

"I simply told her Marilyn Monroe had invited me to the set. She sure was impressed."

"Well done, Mademoiselle. You wouldn't have dared a couple of months ago. They're shooting near Dayton, right? I heard stuff about a section with mustangs. Do you know anything about it?"

"I don't."

"It just so happens Velma was tipped off by the ASPCA. Apparently horses were rounded up for a movie shoot and it wasn't done gently. A stallion, a couple of mares, yearlings, and a foal."

"What are you going to do?"

"Well, Mademoiselle, you can expect me to turn up tomorrow to do some poking around! See you then!"

Pauline loitered in front of the hotel. May had told her to wrap up. It was now mid-October and a strong, cold wind blew, and the snow covering the mountain peaks was thicker. A leaden, threatening sky hung low. Excitement fired through her as she waited. She had never been on a movie set before and knew nothing about filmmaking. The joy of seeing Marilyn again warmed her heart, although she had been warned by May that today was the day she had to tackle her biggest scene, the most important one in the entire movie, the one she couldn't possibly fail. Listening to her, Pauline felt even more curious about the scene and wondered what it entailed. May added that Paula Strasberg usually established a secure perimeter around Marilyn so Pauline had to understand she may not be able to speak to the actress today, let alone approach her.

"Can I come?" Marcelle had pleaded this morning over breakfast, and Pauline had felt a stab of pity. Maybe she should have asked May if her mother might be allowed to tag along. Perhaps it wasn't too late; there was still time to call May. But then she'd realized with a pang she didn't want her mother there. At all.

"This is Pauly's special treat," Doug had said to his wife, kindly. "I'm sure you understand, *chérie*."

Against all odds, Marcelle had said she did understand, and the small flicker of admiration in her eyes that Pauline had noticed before was back. She imagined her mother telling her swooning customers that her daughter, *her Pauline*, had been personally invited by Marilyn Monroe to the movie set of *The Misfits*.

Rafe was the first to show up, greeting her with a wave. So this was Pauline's first time on a set? She was going to discover another world, he said, a world of make-believe, fascinating to watch, even if it meant a lot of waiting. Pauline asked what it was they had to wait for. Waiting for the right light, the right sound, the perfect take. So many things could go wrong. A film was like a succession of tiny miracles, especially this one. They were already a month over schedule.

Marilyn, in jeans, jacket, and white shirt, came out of the hotel, escorted by her husband and May. A limousine pulled up and Mrs. Strasberg got out of it, as well as a balding middle-aged man wearing a cowboy outfit and polished boots.

"That's Paula's husband, Lee," said Rafe. "He got himself a brand-new get-up so he could blend in."

Rafe's comment was tongue-in-cheek, but without malice. He explained that Lee and Paula Strasberg had been Marilyn's coaches for the past five years in New York. They worked using a particular "method," which consisted of asking actors to dig deep within themselves, to draw out their personal feelings to flesh out their characters in the best way. Some swore by this technique, others were less convinced. Hence the controversy, added Rafe in a low voice.

Whitey and Agnes were making their way toward them as the limousines started to gear up. Their chauffeur motioned to them.

In the end, May was going to ride with Arthur Miller, going by the Mapes to pick up John Huston. Most of the team was already on set, said Whitey to Pauline, since the crack of dawn!

Filming had been taking place for the past week at a site called Stagecoach, located about twelve miles east of Dayton, on Highway 50. It was an hour away. Sitting comfortably in the spacious limousine between Whitey and Agnes, and facing Rafe, Pauline felt like she was meeting up with old friends.

"I missed you all so much!" she told them.

It had been several weeks since she had seen them. Agnes wanted to hear about little Lily—what an adorable child! Pauline replied that her daughter hadn't let the dollhouse out of her sight. No one was allowed to touch it. As they sped along the open prairies, Whitey wanted to know if Pauline was planning to go on working at the Mapes Hotel, saying that surely a bright girl like her had a more promising future in mind. He meant it nicely, but her unease must have shown plainly on her face because he said he was sorry and put a fatherly hand on her arm. He thought she was great and that perhaps she deserved better; that's all he meant. Pauline stared down at her jeans, rubbing her palms along them, then she admitted that she had indeed planned things differently; she had dreamed of bigger, better things, but she got pregnant. And everything had ground to a halt.

"And what were those dreams, sweetheart?" asked Agnes.

She hesitated for a beat or two, and then she told them about her love for horses, about becoming a vet, and the internship in California the summer of fifty-seven, which was supposed to kick off her studies. She hadn't attended because Lily was born.

She had let her chance go by. Whitey said that surely, she could reapply. Pauline said it was too late. And besides, how could she ever pay for childcare while she attended the internship in California? She couldn't afford it, neither could her parents. She couldn't put herself through college at this rate. That was why she was stuck at the Mapes. She didn't know what Marilyn had told them about Kendall Spencer, so she didn't bring him up. Whitey said compassionately that he was sure she'd work something out, that he was pretty certain she'd become a vet. She had to believe in herself, added Rafe, she was capable of that, he knew she was; she just had to build up her confidence and she had already started doing so and it was showing. Agnes chimed in; she added the young woman needed to believe in her lucky star. Lucky stars were so important. And as she listened, touched by their solicitude, Pauline was struck by the fact that she had never thought about lucky stars. Even when she was a kid.

They were coming up to the site called Stagecoach and Pauline saw a signpost reading BREAK-A-HEART ROAD.

"I keep hoping Marilyn doesn't see what's written on that signboard," frowned Rafe as they drove by.

The driver slowed for a few miles; the road was rock-strewn and full of potholes. After crawling along, they finally reached an immense depression that looked like a bone-dry moon crater. A strange glow filtered through the silvery clouds, enhancing the dreamlike whiteness of the place.

A grayish dust flew into Pauline's eyes as she got out of the car, and Agnes told her to slip on her dark glasses, or she'd be in trouble. That darned dust made the filming even more strenuous, she complained, especially for hair and makeup. Had Pauline brought along a scarf? She had no other choice, with that long hair of hers and that gusty desert wind. Pauline didn't have one. Agnes rummaged around in her bag and handed her a red one that Pauline tied around her head, thanking her.

Intense activity unfolded all around: On one side, she saw several paddocks containing horses, from which restless whinnies could be heard; on the other, she noticed a battalion of semitrailers, caravans, and limousines, and dozens of people bustling about carrying spotlights, equipment, chairs, planks, and crates. A small plane rested on the sand, near the vans.

The young woman wasn't sure where to stand; she didn't wish to get in anyone's way. Rafe had disappeared on his way to the limousines, and Whitey was heading toward a semitrailer. Agnes took her under her wing. Yes, a movie set was a little unsettling, in the beginning. Everyone rushing around, all those wires, cables, projectors, cameras. She took her to a van where a smiling woman handed out coffee.

Agnes pointed to a bunch of people standing near the cameras—that was the directing team, she said. There was John Huston, cigar clamped between his teeth, and his assistant, Carl. There was Frank, the producer, his assistant, Edward, and there was the script supervisor, Angela. Pauline noticed Arthur Miller joining them. But there were loads of others, added Agnes. A little farther on were those indispensable persons who dealt with light and sound: John, gaffer; Charles, key grip; Eddie and Harry, camera operators; Russell, director of photography. And if that wasn't enough, those three trailers over there were full, she added. Jean Louis and Shirlee for costumes;

Sydney, the hair stylist other than her; and two more guys, both called Frank (very confusing, she giggled), for makeup. Had she forgotten anyone? Of course she had! Billy, wrangler for the horses; Jim, roper; and Loren, stuntman. And, oh, dear, she nearly overlooked the photographers from the Magnum Agency. There were two new ones on set every week. There had even been a Frenchman, his name was Henri Cartier-Bresson, a polite gentleman who wore tweed like an Englishman. Agnes said that the small woman right over there with the salt-and-pepper bun and striped sweater was one of Marilyn's favorite photographers, Eve Arnold. They had become close over the years. Marilyn loved her work. Next to her was a tall, dark, curly haired woman Pauline had already seen in Suite 614, who was now talking to Arthur Miller.

"That's Inge Morath, another photographer, she's from Austria," said Agnes. "And that makes a whole lot of folks on set, if you add the assistants, catering, drivers, stable boys. Nearly a hundred people, give or take."

"And what about the actors?" asked Pauline. "Where's their spot?"

"Good question! They're right over there, just beyond the director's crew. You can make out Monty, with Clark sitting right next to him. See? Eli is farther up. He's the one wearing a baseball cap."

Pauline wanted to know why Marilyn was nowhere to be seen; Agnes replied she was in Paula's limousine, going over her lines and having a neck massage by Rafe. She came on set at the last minute. After a while, Agnes left her to catch up with the team and Pauline found herself alone, coffee in hand. She dared not sit down and felt uncomfortable standing idly by in the midst of this constant hive of activity.

A young man of her age came up to pour himself a cup of coffee. He wore a blue sweater and oversized jeans.

"Hi!" he said to Pauline. "You're new, aren't you?"

She answered that she was and told him she'd been invited to attend the filming.

"I'm Cooper. I'm a bit of a do-it-all guy."

"Pauline. Nice to meet you. So what is it you do then, exactly?"

"I run around like crazy and get cold sweats. Basically, I'm the assistant to the producer's assistant, the one who gets yelled at all the time. Get the picture?"

She couldn't help but laugh. With his snub nose and dimples, he cut a comical figure. Today, he told her, they were going to shoot one of the most decisive moments of the film. The four actors were going to spill their guts, but it was especially "Miss Monroe" who was going to put her heart into it. Pauline asked him why, admitting she knew little about the storyline, only its main theme.

"Let's say Roslyn, her character, makes a terrible discovery concerning Gay, her lover, played by Gable, and his friends Perce and Guido."

"What kind of discovery?"

"It has to do with mustangs. Yesterday we shot with the wrangler, the stuntmen, and the horses. The stallion gave them a whole load of trouble. The wrangler was injured, quite seriously. That horse is seriously off its rocker."

They looked toward the enclosure.

"That's him over there, see? The big one, with a white marking on his muzzle."

"What's his name?"

"He doesn't have a name. He was rounded up two days ago in the foothills with his mares and colt. He has only one idea on his mind, to get the hell out of here. And to wreck everything in the process."

Pauline watched the stallion spin around in the too-small paddock, neighing in fury, and rearing up on his hind legs. He was Commander's twin, with the same enraged gestures, impressive mass, and magnificence.

"It was hell to get him out of the pen yesterday," Cooper muttered. "The wrangler had a rough time, believe me. But for the big Monroe scene, we're not going to need him, thank God. They're using the old mare and she gives them far less trouble."

"But mustangs are wild horses," Pauline pointed out, "not circus animals."

He glanced at her. "What do you know about mustangs?"

"I know a thing or two," she said smiling and blushing at the same time.

Cooper grimaced. "We already have the ASPCA on our backs. They declared the horses had been brutally captured and not tended to properly."

She was careful not to tell him they were going to have Billie-Pearl from the "Wild Horse Annie" league on their backs as well. She changed the subject, asking why Roslyn had to get so upset, and Cooper said it was because she discovers the mustangs rounded up by her pals are to be slaughtered for dog food.

"That still goes on in Nevada. Mustangs still end up as canned food."

"I didn't know," said Cooper sheepishly. "That's dreadful." Then he said, guardedly, "Are you an activist or something?"

"No. My best friend is. I love horses, deeply. I care about them."

"So does Miss Monroe, apparently. She hates any kind of violence done to animals. Is this the first time you'll see her in real life?"

"No. It's not."

"So you've met her? Like, talked to her and stuff? Jeez! I've yet to see her up close."

Pauline hesitated, then said, "She's the one who invited me here today."

His expression changed. "You should have said you're her friend. I feel dumb now."

"I'm not exactly her friend. But she did invite me."

"Not exactly her friend? I don't get that."

"I work at the Mapes Hotel as a cleaner. I do her suite. That's how I got to know her."

Cooper seemed impressed. But just as he was about to ask more questions, someone hollered his name.

"Oops, better get going. That's Carl, the assistant director. He hates to be kept waiting."

Time was ticking by and Rafe had been right to warn her. There indeed was a lot of hanging about, but she was far from bored. Cooper came back to get her, found her a stool, and sat her next to the sound engineers, Charles and Philip.

"This is Pauline, a personal friend of Miss Monroe," he told them, solemnly.

Marilyn's body double, Evelyn, was in action for sound and

lighting checks and Pauline was struck by her patience. She'd stand there for what seemed like ages, wearing the same outfit as Marilyn—jeans, a white shirt, and boots. From time to time, she was handed a glass of water. Two enormous searchlights had been erected around where Evelyn stood, casting an even paler light on the giant crater hemmed in by the jagged ridges of the distant Sierras. Pauline recalled that the film was not being shot in color, to the displeasure of Paula Strasberg, and she wondered what this dramatic backdrop would look like in black and white.

She gathered from the mounting excitement that filming was finally going to begin. The elderly mare, meek and weary, was led in front of the cameras; the wrangler roped her back and front legs together and slid a long rope with a tire at the end around her neck. He forced her to lie down on the ground in front of her confused and startled foal.

Pauline felt her pulse pick up when she saw the four actors were now on set: Clark Gable and Eli Wallach were positioned near the prostrate mare, with Montgomery Clift a little farther away from them. Marilyn stood against the truck. Pauline could see how focused she seemed, without the hint of a smile.

Rafe slipped down by Pauline's side. "You found yourself a good spot," he whispered. "This is her big moment."

"She must be nervous."

"She is. They're going to take it up from where they left off yesterday: the three men discussing how much they'll sell the horses for. Then it's her time to come in. Here goes."

A firm voice cried out, "Picture's up!"

And then, after a short pause, "Quiet, please. Stand by to shoot."

Pauline heard the sharp bang of a clapper board and another voice yelling, "Rolling!"

Then Philip, just by their side, called out, "Sound!"

And John Huston's booming tones sliced into the silence, "Action!"

As Clark Gable and Eli Wallach talked money, crouching near the mare, Pauline watched Marilyn's face crumple, contort, then, throwing her head back, she swiveled, running out into the white sands, her legs pumping as fast as possible, her arms flailing. Then she halted and stood there, a good fifty yards away.

"Cut!" yelled Huston.

He reshot the running away part three times. Pauline couldn't understand what was going on. Why was Marilyn filmed from so far off? Her face could barely be seen. What was the point?

"Just wait," said Rafe, as if he guessed what she was thinking. Then he leaned over toward Philip, asking him for a headset, which he handed to Pauline. "Put these on. You'll hear it all."

Mrs. Strasberg was now standing close to Marilyn. Pauline caught the conversation though her headset, and listened intently. Surely all the sound engineers were listening to this as well, which didn't seem to bother the coach in the least. Mrs. Strasberg was urging Marilyn to let it all out, to acknowledge the fact it all came from deep inside, Marilyn knew how to do that. Mrs. Strasberg's voice was soft and persuasive, almost hypnotic: Marilyn was the greatest actress. The greatest, ever. Those poor mustangs. It made Marilyn sick, she knew. Those guys rounding them up, slaying them, Marilyn was going to strike them with her own hate, her own scorn, but now, she had to look up to the sky and breathe deeply. Now, she had to move her hands up and down, like a bird. Pauline watched as Marilyn, all the way across the sand dunes, fluttered her hands like wings.

"That's part of the 'method,'" whispered Rafe. "Pretending to be a bird and hand flapping. But it works. You'll see."

Marilyn was left alone again, gearing up, fists pressed to her chin, looking like a wrestler waiting to go into the ring. Pauline picked up the actress's ragged breath, as if she were standing right next to her. It was the most peculiar sensation. She couldn't make out Marilyn's expression, but she could see she was standing with her legs bent, her chest slanting forward, her fists balled up.

"Action!" bellowed Huston.

The shrieks that ensued gave Pauline goosebumps. This was a vocal range fans wouldn't know, one Marilyn Monroe had not used in those "dumb blonde" movies she had filmed up until now, of that Pauline was certain. But this was precisely the voice she'd discovered in the secrecy of Suite 614, the day Marilyn had broken down, the day she had concentrated all her fury toward Arthur Miller. And here it was again, the gut-searing hatred, the mighty wrath for all to see; she was screaming at the top of her lungs that they were butchers, killers, murderers; that they were liars, all of them; that they were only happy when they saw something die. The hysterical, disheveled creature shouting herself hoarse was the one Pauline had heard in Suite 614, not the pink-clad temptress of *Gentlemen Prefer Blondes*. Pauline understood why Huston had chosen to film her from a distance, appearing as a tiny mouse roaring through the sand, swallowed whole by Nevada's huge, ashen wastelands.

Never had she witnessed anything so powerful and overwhelming. A few tears ran down her cheeks, and she felt relieved to be able to hide them behind her dark glasses. Rafe was all smiles; Marilyn had made it. She was the best. Huston had gotten up to speak to the actress, who was now surrounded by people. She was given hot water with honey and lemon while Whitey touched up her makeup and Agnes, the wig. From what Pauline was able to make out through the headset, she understood they had to go on, shooting over again, even if everyone seemed satisfied with the actress's performance. She asked Rafe why, and he told her the directors wished to have a choice, that's why they insisted on multiple takes. Pauline wondered how Marilyn was going to be able to reproduce such intensity, but under her astonished gaze, she did just that, four times in a row, without faltering, with the same heartbreaking tone, on-edge emotion she seemed to draw from deep within herself, and that rang out with such veracity. Marilyn left the set in a state of obvious exhaustion, supported by the Strasbergs, and Rafe got up hastily.

"She'll be needing me now," he said.

Pauline handed the headset back to Philip, thanking him. She also felt drained.

"Hey, Pauline!" called out Cooper. "There's a girl over there who knows you."

As she made her way to the corrals, Pauline made out Billie-Pearl's silhouette, busy chatting with the horse handlers. When she saw her friend, her face lit up. There was her own little Mademoiselle! How was the filming coming along? Pauline described Marilyn's amazing performance.

"Yeah, I know, I missed it," Billie-Pearl sighed. "I got there right after."

Her gaze fell upon the panting, white-muzzled stallion flinging himself continually against the stalls.

"Doesn't he remind you of someone?" she asked.

"Commander would have cleared off. He wouldn't have wasted a minute."

"You're right."

She told Pauline she had spoken with the ASPCA representative on site. The way the film crew had captured the mustangs and penned them here hadn't been the best. Apparently, Marilyn Monroe herself had been concerned about their well-being. The good news was that filming would wrap soon, and the horses would be set free. Billie-Pearl had offered to look after the aging mare and her foal at the Double Lazy Heart Ranch. Everyone seemed to think it was a great idea.

"Are you going to see Marilyn again after today, Mademoiselle?"

Pauline admitted she wasn't sure. She hoped she'd be able to say good-bye at some point, but she had no idea how. Marilyn may have already left the set, for all she knew. The day's acting must have been taxing.

Billie-Pearl had to get going and report back to Velma, and Pauline watched her walk away with her determined stride. She didn't quite know what to do with herself. Were they going to film any more scenes after lunch break? Maybe she could ask Cooper for information. She went back to the trailer where she had her coffee.

The photographer with the bun and striped sweater Agnes had pointed out beforehand was there sipping water, camera slung around her neck. She introduced herself as "Eve," with a deep voice, almost like a man's, which was surprising as she was tiny. Her hair was gray, but Pauline thought she was still in her forties. She had bright, shrewd eyes and a warm smile.

"Are you having a good time?" she asked.

"I am," said Pauline. "I'm discovering all sorts of things. It's quite thrilling!"

"You're not in the movie business?"

"Oh, not at all. I'm a cleaning lady. I work at the Mapes Hotel."

"A nice place. I'm staying there too."

"I cleaned Mrs. Miller's suite."

"So she invited you today."

"That's right."

"That doesn't surprise me. Few people know how generous and kind Marilyn is."

The photographer looked at her closely. "Do you mind if I take a picture of you? I'm here for Magnum. I saw you with the horses earlier on."

"Of course, you may. But I'm not photogenic, I'm afraid."

Eve asked her to remove her scarf, stand with her back to the trailer, looking over to the set. She didn't have to smile, she said, she just had to forget Eve was there, that's all she had to do. Pauline did just that, and while Eve clicked away, she thought about the irate stallion who looked uncannily like Commander.

"There you go! That was good. What's your name?" Eve asked,

taking out a pencil from her pocket. "This is for my files. I won't print anything if you don't want me to."

"I don't mind if you do. I'm Pauline Bazelet." She spelled her last name.

"A French name perhaps?" Eve asked.

"A French name indeed. Our own little Parisienne," came a familiar singsong voice, and Pauline turned around to see Marilyn standing there with Rafe, Whitey, and Agnes.

"Did you enjoy it, honey?" asked Marilyn.

Her eyes were hidden behind dark glasses, but Pauline could tell how tired she was; her skin seemed even whiter than usual.

"I certainly did," said Pauline, feeling the stammer creep back into her voice just as she quickly stopped it from happening. "I was so impressed and so stirred by that scene..."

She found it difficult to explain her feelings without sounding like a gushing fan and it wasn't easy finding the right words, the right tone, while everyone laughed and talked, while the wind blew and tossed her hair about.

"I thought you were just wonderful," she blurted out lamely, feeling like an idiot.

Suddenly, her moment with Marilyn was over. The actress was whisked aside by Lee Strasberg, and Pauline hadn't had time to say everything she wanted.

And as she saw her drawing farther and farther away, she suspected with hollow dread that she'd never lay eyes on Marilyn Monroe again.

Her hunch proved to be accurate. As October slid away, Marilyn was nowhere to be seen. Was she still in Reno? No one knew, and there was no one Pauline could ask. The Strasbergs had left Suite 614 and all the "Happy People" had vanished into thin air.

In the cafeteria, she heard of a joint birthday party held for Arthur Miller and Montgomery Clift, both born on October 17. It was held at the Christmas Tree, a restaurant on Mount Rose highway, outside Reno. Marilyn was reportedly there, and she hadn't wanted to sing happy birthday to her husband. Pauline was also told that, by the end of October, the entire crew was due back in Hollywood to film the scenes that didn't require Nevada backdrops.

Back at home on Washington Street, Doug, like most of their neighbors, was engrossed in the presidential debates on television between Democratic Senator John F. Kennedy and Republican Vice President Richard Nixon. Never had political debates been followed live before, and by so many viewers around the country. Pauline sat and watched the third bout with her stepfather, but sometimes Marilyn's face would pop into her mind; the candidates' heated voices became fuzzy, and she was propelled into Suite 614.

The only things she looked forward to nowadays had to do with her daughter, who was thrilled about her upcoming Halloween costume, and working on the ranch with Doctor O'Brian. For the past years, every weekend, and on her days off, she continued to assist him. The Doc often took Pauline along while he visited nearby ranches, farms, and clinics where she saw surgical operations being performed—the gelding of colts, broken legs treated, and the dreaded colic. He compensated her every month for her help, a small sum, but it added to the salary she earned at the Mapes and gave her a feeling of independence, even if she knew there was still a long way to go.

How dull her life seemed! All the excitement had fizzled out of it. She had been so pleased when Cooper, the cute guy from the movie set, had invited her on a date. They had a pleasant evening. But once he found out about Lily, he hadn't called again. And to add insult to injury, she was now back scouring toilets in the main floor ladies' room. Wringing her hands, Mildred Jones had announced the news most apologetically, confessing she couldn't understand why Mr. Spencer had suddenly requested this change, as Pauline had worked hard in Suite 614 and everyone was pleased with her. It was incomprehensible. Pauline knew precisely why. For weeks now, she had been carefully avoiding Kendall, not only within the Mapes, but also not answering any of his messages or calls either. Her attitude must have irritated him, and he had taken revenge. And when she had tried to confront him, going to the second floor to speak to him in person, he gave her a taste of her own medicine: He ignored her, and his office was barred to her. His secretary and assistants saw to that.

One morning, watching Pauline slip into her old burgundy uniform, Linda hissed, "That business with Mrs. Miller was a very short moment of glory."

The other girls in the changing room tittered. Pauline could have chosen to ignore her, to grin and bear it, as usual. But things were different now. She turned to confront Linda's mocking smirk.

"Can you repeat what you just said?" She remained calm, holding herself straight, shoulders back, closing in on Linda, and in the latter's expression, she detected fear.

Linda mumbled she only said that for fun, no need to get into such a huff, but Pauline continued her approach, while Linda shuffled back, ending up with her shoulder blades glued to the lockers.

Who was this tall young woman with glinting green eyes who was suddenly taking up so much space?

"Cut it out. I was joking."

"You were joking?"

Linda shrank farther away, finding Pauline's smile anything but friendly. A joke, really? Indeed, she'd been banished to the facilities and that was truly scandalous because she didn't deserve it, that was a fact, but she wasn't going to take this lying down. She wasn't going to be pushed around by anyone, neither by her managers nor by the likes of Linda. She certainly wasn't going to spend the rest of her life buried alive in the Mapes Hotel bathrooms. She was worth more than that. She was going to get out of there.

"And as for the 'business' with Mrs. Miller, as you put it, it's my 'business' with Marilyn."

Yes, she did call her "Marilyn," not Mrs. Miller, at the actress's request. This was blowing Linda's mind, wasn't it? And, anyway, what did Linda know about Marilyn? Zilch! Nothing more than cafeteria tattle and nonsense from gossip magazines. Pauline was incredibly lucky because Marilyn had let her into her life, albeit for only three months. She wouldn't talk about it; she wouldn't go into details. But those three months had meant everything. And yes, Marilyn called her by her first name. Yes, Marilyn had known exactly who she was. Yes, Suite 614 was a private memory she'd treasure for the rest of her life, locking it up in her imaginary personal vault, where she could play it back whenever she wanted. No matter what happened, Suite 614 remained a place where Marilyn had shone a special light on her. On her, Pauline. And no one, no one on this earth could take that away from her. Not even Linda and her jealousy.

Linda kept silent, red-faced, and the other girls weren't giggling anymore. They glanced at Pauline with a certain esteem. Pauline left the changing room on her way up to the main floor. She felt power surging through her, that new potency she'd built up over the past weeks like a fortress, brick by brick, standing thick and strong.

She was going to leave this place. She didn't know how; she had no idea where to begin, but she was going to get away.

As she passed through the reception area, Lincoln called out to her. He said he had something for her. "She left this for you." He handed her an envelope.

Her heart skipped a beat when she saw her name penned in the inimitable loping, uneven scrawl.

She already knew the answer, but she felt compelled to ask, "Who left this for me?"

"Mrs. Miller's secretary. She came by last evening and told me to make sure it was delivered straight into your hands."

There was awe written all over his face. "Aren't you going to open it, Frenchie?"

She clasped it to her chest. "Oh, don't worry. I will."

She felt the need to be alone, far from the young man's inquisitiveness. She slipped away, across to the bridge spanning the Truckee River. She hadn't taken her coat and the sharp cold ran through her. She opened the envelope hurriedly, discovered a typewritten letter first, then another smaller envelope that she didn't open right away.

Miss Pauline Bazelet
Mapes Hotel
10 North Virginia Street
Reno, Nevada

Thursday, October 20, 1960

Dear Pauline,

We left in a considerable rush and Marilyn, like me, is sorry for not having been able to say good-bye. I am writing this to you in haste as we have to fly to Los Angeles shortly. We will not be coming back to Reno. The movie is almost done.

The day you came to the shoot, we learned your dream was to become a veterinarian and to attend an internship in California, and that you weren't able to do so. Marilyn was touched by your story and wants to help you. She sends you this, in the enclosed smaller envelope.

From the bottom of my heart I wish you every success in your projects, and Marilyn joins me in doing so.

We were happy to get to know you.

Sincerely,
May Reis

Pauline read the letter a second time, clutching it tightly between her fingers against the blustery wind. She ran back to the Mapes, opening the smaller envelope in the shelter of the lobby, not wanting to risk having the precious missive blown away and ending up in the river.

On the envelope, she saw her first name, followed by the mention "personal," both written by the hand of the actress. She discovered a check, for an amount that made her feel dizzy, and a note.

Dear Pauline,

The time has come for you to spread your wings.
I hope this will help you do just that.

Love,
Marilyn

"You okay, Frenchie? Looks like you're going to pass out."

It was one of the waiters, Pedro, holding a tray in his hands.

Pauline was unable to answer him. He asked her if she wanted a glass of water, or to sit down. She collected herself, told him everything was fine. Then she stared at the phone booths to the right of the entrance.

"Do you need to make a phone call?"

"I do."

"Are you sure you're okay?"

"Say, can I borrow a dime? I don't have my purse on me."

Pedro fished around in his pockets and handed her a couple of coins. He watched her, puzzled, as she made her way to the phone booths, and then he left, heading for the kitchens.

She knew the Double Lazy Heart Ranch number by heart, but her fingers were shaking so hard she had to dial it twice. Her heart kept pumping in her ears like a loud drum blocking out any other sounds.

Charlie picked up just as she was about to hang up. His breath sounded raspy and short. He hadn't been well for the past year. Billie-Pearl was out with the horses and wouldn't be back until later. Could he ask Billie-Pearl to please call her at the Mapes? And could he take the number down? He did, wheezing down the phone.

The only thing to do while she waited was to get back to work. Every time she heard footsteps clicking on the tiles, she started, hoping it was someone coming to tell her she had a call, but it was invariably a client. The hours dragged by. At last, it was time to go home, to pick up Lily, and take the bus.

All evening, she hoped the phone would ring, but when it did, it was for Marcelle, or for Jimmy. She helped her mother with dinner, gave Lily her bath, fed her, and told her a story before she put her to bed. It wasn't until Doug got home and they had nearly finished their meal that the call finally came through.

She found it difficult to speak in front of her family, as she hadn't told them anything yet, and all the pent-up excitement nearly made her stutter again. The right words were not coming to her; they kept tumbling from her lips in a muddle.

"Whoa!" said Billie-Pearl. "Slow down, Mademoiselle. Start over."

Pauline took a deep breath and began her story again, as calmly as she could, as Marcelle, Doug, and Jimmy stopped to listen, transfixed.

On the other end of the line, Billie-Pearl let out a long admiring whistle.

"Mademoiselle, no more moping around at the Mapes waiting for better days. This is your time to move forward. You can't miss this. The Doc is still here. I'm going to catch him before he leaves. I'll call you back."

Pauline placed the phone back on the receiver and turned to face the three pairs of eyes staring at her. Doug was the first to speak. "She left you a check?" he asked, round-eyed, getting up.

"She did."

"Can I see the letter?"

Pauline went to fetch it. She noticed Marcelle went on sitting there, frozen, hand clasping her drink, while Jimmy was dancing around the room. Doug read the letter out loud, and the note as well, his voice getting hoarser by the minute.

Then he took Pauline in his arms and hugged her tightly. She noticed he had tears in his eyes. Jimmy was in a state of excitement: What had she decided? Was she going to leave? And go where? And Lily? It was all so crazy. He was so proud of his big sister. And she deserved it all.

Marcelle finally broke her silence. She lit a cigarette with trembling hands.

"What will you do now?" she asked her daughter in a colorless voice.

The phone rang again. Pauline answered it and heard Doctor O'Brian's Irish accent. He congratulated her warmly, saying that, from now on, everything could happen fast. He had already left a message for his colleague, Doctor Hicks. Pauline shouldn't be waiting around any longer. Marilyn Monroe's generosity toward her was a formidable foot in the door. That sum would allow her to find accommodation, and have her daughter looked after during her internship, because yes, she absolutely had to begin with an internship, which she could do for several months, even a year.

She should aim for a scholarship to finance the rest of her studies. Those studies, Pauline knew, would last at least six years. Never mind that she didn't get her high school diploma, she could take a GED test, which, as she was probably aware, allowed adults to graduate from high school. She was going to have to work twice as hard, but she was capable of it, of that he was certain. And he had something else to add, something important: Velma was going to write a letter of recommendation as well. This was excellent news, according to the Doc. Now that Velma was a celebrity, read about in *Reader's Digest* and even in magazines published abroad, there were only very few vets in the USA who hadn't heard of "Wild Horse Annie." And Velma had a lot of things to say about Pauline from the past eight years she'd known her.

"Doctor Hicks probably won't get back to me before next week," said the Doc. "But in the meantime, you have work to do, Pauline, like every Saturday. So I'll see you then, first thing Saturday morning."

Pauline had indeed planned to spend that Saturday at the ranch, and she was bringing Lily, who had made friends she looked forward to playing with. Doug had been right when he took Pauline to the Johnstons' ranch that first time, that children of the area came to play all year round and were welcome. They were looked after by a close-knit community of local folks, taken for treks fishing in the Truckee River, or playing games on the lawn. Lily loved it. She had even started horseback riding with Billie-Pearl.

By the time Pauline finished her conversation with the Doc, she realized her mother had left the room. Her bedroom door was closed.

"She's just tired," said Doug, ruefully. "She's so happy for you, Pauly."

Pauline didn't get much sleep that night. She kept going over the day's events—the letter, the note, the check. Things were going to happen in a rapid chain of events, the Doc said, and she sensed he was right. She was ready.

But she kept seeing her mother's tense face, the red-nailed fingers gripping her glass, the closed door. And she thought back to Marcelle wearing her pretty blue suit, standing on the platform at the Reno train station, with her beret and her hatbox. The hopeful war bride for whom the American Dream had gone so wrong.

Dear Pauline, the time has come for you to spread your wings.

NOVEMBER 1960

—»»»—

Reno, Nevada

Pauline paused in front of the door to Mildred Jones's office; she could hear she was in there, griping on the telephone, so she waited a moment. She wasn't nervous, but the hammering heart was back.

She raised her fist and knocked.

"Come in!" came Mildred's shrill tones.

She was sitting behind her desk, glasses perched on the end of her nose, and she looked up inquisitively. Pauline had practiced what she had to say several times, to Billie-Pearl, to Doug, and to herself while she was in the shower, addressing the orange bathroom tiles. She said that, in the first place, she wished to thank Mrs. Jones for everything she had learned here, mostly thanks to her. She had decided it was time for her to move on. Therefore, she would be quitting her job at the Mapes.

"Here is my resignation letter, Mrs. Jones."

She placed the letter on the desk. Mildred glanced at it, then back at her.

"You're quitting?"

"Yes, ma'am. I'm going to California, to train in a veterinary clinic. I've just learned that my application has been accepted."

"That's what you want to do, become a vet?"

"Yes, ma'am."

Mildred said nothing for a bit. Was she disappointed? Angry? It was impossible to tell.

"Have you told anyone else from the Mapes?"

"You're the first to know, Mrs. Jones."

"When does your internship start?"

"In ten days."

"I see."

Another silence.

"And your daughter?"

"She's coming with me. I've found a place for us to stay and day care for her as well."

Pauline could see Mildred was racking her brains trying to figure out how Pauline could afford this, as well as how she might ask her without sounding rude or nosy. Had Lincoln told anyone about the letter May Reis had dropped off? She did not bring it up. It was no one's business. She had already written to Marilyn via May at the Beverly Hills Hotel, because she learned they were headed there after leaving Reno. She hoped her thank-you letter would get there safely; it had taken her ages to write it. And when she had been to the bank, to put the check into her account, the lady behind the counter had nearly fainted when she noticed it had been signed by Marilyn Monroe herself.

"You can be proud of yourself, Pauline. Well done."

Pauline had been expecting anything but Mildred Jones's approval.

"There's a week's notice, according to your contract. Pilar is back with a mended wrist and I'm not understaffed. I even hired a few new girls."

"Fine, Mrs. Jones."

Mildred checked the calendar pinned to the wall behind her.

"Today is Friday, November fourth. So your last day could be Friday the eleventh."

"Very well, Mrs. Jones. Got it."

She wondered how she was going to hold out for another week but had prepared for the likelihood of a notice. As she was leaving, Mildred detained her.

"Wait a minute. Let me fix that."

Pauline wondered what she meant. Fix what?

Mildred picked up the phone, dialed a number. "Hello, Lucinda? It's Mildred."

Pauline knew Lucinda was the payroll clerk, whose office was also on the second floor. She handled the wages of the entire Mapes workforce. While she asked Lucinda how she was doing, Mildred was filling out a form. She told her she was about to send Pauline Bazelet along, as Pauline was leaving the Mapes. Yes, it was sad, because she was a fine employee, but Pauline was going to become a veterinarian, in California, yes indeed. She had to be paid her November salary on the spot, including one week's notice, until November eleventh.

Mildred handed her the form.

"There's nothing holding you back here."

"Thank you, Mrs. Jones. Thank you from my heart."

"Don't look at me with those wet eyes, girl, or I might end up bawling as well. Go get your check and run."

Mildred blew her nose loudly.

"Yes, Mrs. Jones. Good-bye."

"Wait. You said a vet, but what kind of vet?"

"Equine."

"Does that mean a horse vet?"

"It does indeed."

"Good. Off you go now, Pauline. Lucinda's waiting for you. You're free as a bird."

Yes, she was free. She couldn't believe it, nearly hopping and skipping down the corridor to Lucinda's office. She handed over the document Mildred gave her and was given an envelope in return. Her last paycheck.

"You're going to California to become a vet?"

"That's right."

"Best of luck, Pauline."

Kendall's office was on the opposite side. She might as well go there now and bid him farewell, as she was leaving sooner than she thought, with Mildred Jones's blessing.

When his secretary caught sight of her, she announced flatly, "Mr. Spencer is out."

Pauline pointed to Kendall's coat and hat hanging up. "I don't think so," she said.

"Well, he's not available," muttered the woman, whose name Pauline never remembered. Something like Ethel or Bertha.

"Is he in a meeting?"

"He's not available."

Pauline stared at the door. So many things had happened behind that door. Things she didn't want to think about anymore.

"Please leave," said the secretary.

Ethel. Pauline was sure it was Ethel.

"I only need a few minutes of his time, Ethel."

"You should go. And my name is Bertha, if you don't mind."

"Is he alone?"

"I've already told you. Mr. Spencer isn't available for you."

"We'll see."

She went up to the door and flung it open in spite of Bertha's protests. Kendall Spencer was on the phone, at his desk.

"I'll be damned! I asked not to be disturbed!"

"I apologize, Mr. Spencer," Bertha whimpered, "but this person broke into your office despite your orders."

"I'll call you back," Kendall barked down the phone and hung up. Then he pointed his chin at Pauline, asking her to come in and shut the door.

She hated coming back here, as she hated the smell that reigned in this place, a blend of cold tobacco, leather, and mint-scented aftershave.

He lit a cigarette and smoked it irritably, glaring at her.

"You have some nerve, showing up after ignoring me for the past few weeks. I take it you're here to complain about your demotion?"

"I came to say good-bye."

Kendall sat up.

"Excuse me?"

"I'm going away. I'm leaving Reno."

He stubbed out his cigarette in haste. What was she on about? Leaving Reno? And going where? What was going on?

"Lily is coming with me."

She told him where they were going and why. Kendall did his

best to remain calm, but he was having a hard time doing just that. Round and round the room he paced, running a nervous hand through his hair. He kept saying she couldn't do this. She couldn't leave. She had to stay in Reno. How was she going to support herself? Pay rent? There was no way she'd mention Marilyn's gift to him, so she answered she had planned it all out.

"I resigned. It's done."

Her words stunned him. He nearly wailed. How could she do this to him? He was about to land her a great job in the bookings department, he had it all set up, and it was going to be a wonderful surprise. How could she ever hope to become a vet? Come on! She hadn't even graduated from high school. She needed to wake up. And what about Lily? She was his daughter as well; he had a say in the matter.

"Lily doesn't even bear your name. There isn't a single paper anywhere stating you're her father."

As usual, he tried another method, a tactile one, the one she loathed most of all: putting his arms around her, planting humid kisses on her face, stroking her, but the difference was that she no longer stood there, putting up with it, imagining she was miles away; now she pushed him away.

"That's enough, Kendall."

He jerked her arm. What did she mean by *that's enough?* Who did she think she was? She was getting all high and mighty just because a movie star called her by her name. Well, he had news for her, she was only a maid. One of those insignificant females no one really noticed, even if she had a pretty face. That's all she was.

Noticing how cold and stiff she had become, he quickly went back to his previous tactic. He was so sorry; he hadn't wanted to be mean. It was just that she meant so much to him, and Lily as well. She had to understand how deeply he adored both of them, how much he cared.

"You often use that word— 'adore.' You 'adore' us."

He hugged her again. That was exactly it, he adored them. Madly. And that was why the two of them had to remain in Reno. Things were complicated with his wife, but he was convinced Evaline would end up understanding how important Pauline and Lily were to him.

He spoke to her using a deep, caring voice, the one he'd used many times and that she'd fallen for, time and time again.

"You never said you love me. Or Lily."

"Oh, but I do, my angel. I do!"

"It's too late, Kendall."

"Please give me another chance, I beg you. Trust me."

She said she was still young; she had all her life ahead of her, and for once, her future seemed brighter. She'd leave Nevada to build a better tomorrow for her and for Lily and nothing or no one was going to stop her. Not even him.

He grabbed hold of her with a kind of desperate frenzy, attempting to kiss her; she fought him, shoving him off.

"You don't have the right to leave. You belong to me. Lily belongs to me. You're mine."

She burst out laughing, and she seemed different to him, another Pauline he didn't know. She went on: What did he have to offer her apart from being the woman in the shadows, the invisible mistress he visited behind his wife's back? The prospect of that existence horrified her.

"You're breaking my heart," he said, with a sob that sounded so real she almost congratulated him.

She opened the door and in front of the dazed secretary and assistants, she said, "Good-bye, Mr. Spencer. Be well. Something tells me we won't be seeing each other again for a long time."

As she left the second floor, she couldn't believe what she had managed to do. The hesitant young woman had flown away; in her place was a warrior. And she saw herself in armor, spear in hand, hoisted on Commander's back. She almost laughed, but the image delighted her.

She went to the basement floor to put her clothes back on, slipping her uniform into a bag she left behind. She would never wear it again. It was now time to say good-bye to all the Mapes people, her entire world for the past three years. She took her time doing this, not wanting to miss anyone—from Ernesto the doorman, to Dan up in the Sky Room, as well as Addie, her favorite operator, and Pedro, from room service. Casper was so upset, he nearly cried, and Marty let out a candid, "Oh, no, Frenchie, you can't just take off!" Lincoln said she was doing the right thing. But she'd be missed, he added. Fern, Kitty, Harper, and Maud were genuinely sad to see her go, but happy for her. Only Linda had nothing to say, but Pauline was not surprised.

It was such an odd sensation, leaving the Mapes for the last time, walking out of it, and turning around to see its massive tower up behind her like a silent giant, wishing her well.

———⫸———

It was her last weekend at the ranch. When would she come back here? She wasn't sure. She had gone about her chores with joy, assisting Doc O'Brian, helping Velma with paperwork, lending Billie-Pearl a hand with some new arrivals.

"Seen Commander lately?" she asked her friend.

"I think he's been injured. Probably a new fight."

He seemed to limp, staying away from the ranch, letting his colts and mares come up to the fences. Was Billie-Pearl worried? Not really. He could fend for himself. But she bemoaned the fact he kept his distance and could only be seen from afar.

"He likes playing hard to get."

"I know. But I would have liked to say good-bye."

"He's building the legend."

Commander's colts were less reserved, at times mingling with the other mustangs. His offspring were easy to pick out: They had their begetter's powerful elegance. Billie-Pearl had found perfect names for them—Captain, Major, Scout, Athena, and Storm.

On Saturday afternoon, Velma came rushing up as they were cleaning out the barns.

"Clark Gable had a heart attack! He's in the hospital. I just heard it on the radio."

Mrs. Strasberg had been worried about his health, Pauline recalled. He had gone on a strict diet for his part as a cowboy, losing a lot of weight. Velma said she heard through the grapevine he was a heavy smoker and drinker. Like most people on that set, added Billie-Pearl sardonically. Some were whispering the film was already doomed, even before it hit the big screen, but Pauline couldn't wait to see it.

"I thought you didn't care much for movies," said Billie-Pearl.

"Well, that was before Suite 614," grinned Pauline.

Velma wanted to know more about her internship at Mount Shasta, so Pauline gave her details: Doctor Hicks's wife had been awfully helpful with finding a place to live, right by the clinic, as well as a good person to look after Lily.

"When are you taking off?" asked Velma.

"In a couple of days."

"How are you getting there?"

"Doug is driving us. I have to find myself a car later."

"And how is your mother taking all this?"

Pauline knew she could tell Velma and Billie-Pearl the truth, that her mother was taking her departure badly, but she decided not to go into it.

"She's not thrilled," she said, carefully.

And she felt remorseful thanking Clark Gable for having had a heart attack, because she knew, at dinner tonight, Marcelle would have something else on her mind other than Pauline's Mount Shasta internship.

Indeed, when Pauline got home, Marcelle was glued to the television and the radio for updates on her idol. Apparently, John Huston and Marilyn Monroe had been implicated by Gable's entourage, both accused of putting him at unnecessary risk to perform his own stunts and keeping him waiting for hours in the baking desert heat.

"It seems he complained very little," said Marcelle. "A remarkable man."

But even Clark Gable's distressing health condition could not distract the household for long from Pauline's departure, scheduled for November 9. Everything was prepared: her suitcase, her daughter's suitcase, the tiny Eiffel Tower she had kept all these years, as well as the dollhouse Marilyn had given Lily. No snow was forecast and the weather would be fine going up to Mount Shasta. They had a four-hour drive ahead.

When Marcelle appeared at breakfast on the morning of the departure, Pauline noticed her haggard expression, her unkempt hair with gray roots sprouting, which was surprising, as her mother attached so much importance to her appearance. Her unmade-up face seemed crumpled, older, and, in Pauline's eyes, suddenly poignant. Under Doug's worried eye as he poured her coffee, she seemed lost, moving about uncertainly.

Lily filled the room with her chatter, excited to leave, to discover another home, different friends, as Marcelle huddled in front of her cup.

"Any news about Clark Gable, *Maman*?" asked Pauline over Lily's babble.

Marcelle looked up. There was sadness in her eyes. She said she didn't care about Gable. What she cared about was her daughter leaving. And her granddaughter. She spoke in French, which cut Doug and Jimmy straight out of the conversation, and when Pauline answered back in English, Marcelle tenaciously stuck to her native language. She said she couldn't bear the idea of this house, this town, this state without Pauline, without Lily. She was going crazy, just thinking about it. How would she ever survive without them? She wasn't going to make it. She felt like closing her shop, selling it, moving back to Paris with her sister. Nothing had worked out for her here. And, without her daughter, she was going to go under.

Pauline knew her mother amplified things, making them better, or in this case, worse. Marcelle reveled in her own theatricality.

"We need to get going, Pauly," said Doug.

He didn't need to speak French to understand his wife's turmoil. He put a comforting hand on Marcelle's shoulder. Pauline and Lily were going to be okay. It was a normal part of life, to see children leave the nest. That's what Marcelle was feeling right now, a sort of emptiness. It was the natural order of things and

Marcelle had to learn to face it. He added he was going to check the car tires and left.

Marcelle started to cry while Jimmy looked on, perplexed. He had witnessed many things linked to his mother's sharp tongue—her drinking, her clumsy remarks—but never such grief. He took Lily out of the room, suggesting they play one last game before leaving.

Usually, Pauline comforted her mother by listening, patting her hand, and nodding. This morning wasn't the same, she knew. She held her mother's hand, firmly, forcing her to look up. She spoke to her in French, with an intensity she'd not yet used with Marcelle. Doug was right. She and Lily were going to be fine. But now Marcelle had to get a grip on her own life. This couldn't go on. The drinking had to stop. It was time for Marcelle to take care of it, to talk about it. When she had been at the hospital for Lily's birth, she'd seen posters in waiting rooms. There were places Marcelle could go to get help without making an appointment.

"I'm not an alcoholic. I have too much once in a while. That's all."

"*Maman*. Face it. Please."

Marcelle lowered her head, letting out a whimper. "I'm ashamed. I'm so ashamed."

"*Maman*, listen to me."

Marcelle had to become aware of certain things—of her own luck, of doing a job she loved and did well, of being successful; she should rejoice in having all those good customers, but above all, a loving and devoted husband, and a bright son. Yes, Marcelle's life was beautiful. She had to look at it and find joy in it.

Her mother interrupted her in a broken voice, "I can't live without you, my darling daughter. I'm not going to make it."

Tears streamed down again. She'd been too hard on Pauline, she knew that. She hadn't ever told her how proud she was of her, and how wrong she'd been to wait so long to do so. She had been unbelievably clumsy with her daughter. As a child, Pauline had been able to adapt to this new country, its language and ways. Pauline succeeded where Marcelle had failed. And as for the mustangs...what a fool she had been to hold Pauline's passion against her. Not seeing who her daughter really was, not believing in Pauline. She had pushed her into the arms of that vile young man, and she wouldn't ever forgive herself, even though Lily had been born out of that disaster and she loved Lily more than anything. She had failed. She had been a pitiful mother. She was ashamed of that as well.

"Stop it, *Maman*," Pauline cut in, stroking Marcelle's damp face. "Stop putting yourself down."

"The idea of your empty room kills me."

"You probably left home too one day, didn't you?"

Marcelle wiped her cheeks.

"As a matter of fact, I did. And I do recall your grandmother was in tears. You know what they call Nevada? The leaving state, because people come here to divorce, to lose their money in the casinos, and leave. And now you're leaving."

"Now, now! We're only four hours away, not that far."

"It's time to go, ladies," said Doug, from the porch.

Marcelle called out for Jimmy and Lily, and they all made their way out into the cold November morning.

A shiny blue Ford Thunderbird was parked in front of the house. Doug handed Pauline a set of car keys.

"Surprise," he said quietly. "This is to help you fly along."

She gasped, nearly losing her balance on the front steps. Doug had obtained a good deal from a workfellow in another garage, and he had worked on the T-Bird himself. She was secondhand, but in tip-top shape. Pauline's luggage was already in the trunk. She was going to drive herself and Lily all the way to California.

"Did you know about this?" Pauline asked her mother and brother.

They had. And they approved. Pauline could guess how much this car had cost him; how much of his savings had gone into it. She flung herself into his arms, murmuring her thanks. This morning, she had made up her mind not to cry, but there was no way she could fight the sobs.

"Take her for a quick spin to get to know her," said Doug, also struggling to keep his eyes dry. "She'll be a change from the old Buick."

Pauline sat behind the wheel, the Thunderbird's engine making a pleasant roar.

"You rock, Pauly!" Jimmy said with pride.

Their neighbor, Mrs. Sheldon, cup of coffee in hand, opened her door to greet them.

"Have a good trip!" she cried.

"It's Mommy's new car," Lily yelled, overwhelmed with excitement. "We're going to California!"

When it was time to go, Doug put Lily in a small harness in the backseat and told her to stay quietly in it. Pauline hugged her brother, then Doug, and finally Marcelle.

"Call me when you arrive!"

"I promise, *Maman*."

Just as Pauline and Lily were about to leave, the telephone could be heard ringing from inside.

"Let me get it!" said Jimmy, dashing back in.

He returned a couple of seconds later, a wry expression on his face. "It's for you, Pauly. Kendall Spencer."

She didn't hesitate. "Tell him I've already gone."

As she pulled away, she watched them wave in the rearview mirror: Doug clasping Marcelle to his side, Jimmy blowing kisses.

She waved back until they faded from view, until Washington Street disappeared.

———⋙———

Pauline headed north to Route 395. The traffic was smooth, and a pale November sun was coming up, igniting the silvery mountain peaks with a rosy glow.

When they reached the highway, Pauline said, "How about some music, Lily?"

She turned on the radio, and the first song they heard was by Ray Charles, "What'd I Say." She turned the volume up. How could she not think of Marilyn dancing to that same song during the blackout up in the Sky Room, when forest fires raged around Reno? It was like the smallest of signs.

In twenty minutes, they'd reach the border, leaving Nevada to enter California. She thought of everything she was leaving behind, just like she had when she was seven years old and boarding that ship to America. And she remembered one of her first summers at Lake Tahoe, when she had clambered to the top of a craggy boulder and the water below seemed too far to jump, and she became frightened. Doug, already in the lake, shouted out for her to come, telling her to make sure to spring away from the rock, while Marcelle, sitting on her towel on the shore and holding Jimmy, fretted that her daughter might slip and hurt herself. She had hesitated for a while, her stomach churning with fear, then leaped into the water; when she bobbed back up, as Doug and Marcelle applauded, she had never felt such pride.

Today, all those years later, she was taking another plunge. And she was no longer scared.

Pauline picked up speed, feeling the Thunderbird throb through the steering wheel under her fingers.

"Watch us, Lily babe. We're spreading our wings."

RENO, NEVADA

————≫≫≫——

Sunday, January 30, 2000, 8 a.m.

The crowds had fallen silent, and during those long minutes during which no one spoke, the biting cold seemed to intensify. Turning away from Pauline, the journalist and her cameraman zoomed in on the doomed building. It was past eight o'clock and still no signs of an implosion. Was there a snag with the detonators? In front of her, a woman wearing a black-and-white headscarf blew her nose.

At last, Pauline heard the rapid fire of a string of explosions, similar to a handful of firecrackers thrown by children, and for a couple of seconds, the hotel stood its ground, stoic. Then, during a new burst of blasts, mightier this time, the east wing of the brick structure wavered like a curtain teased by the wind, and warped, dragging the bulk of the hotel in its wake, tumbling forward onto Center Street.

It lasted only five or six seconds, but Pauline had time to look up to the sixth-floor corner suite facing southeast, and to the

Sky Room windows, before the entire façade twisted under the weight of an invisible grip, falling apart with unsettling grace and a loud, crackling whoosh.

How could it be that a section of her life, of Reno's life, could be wiped out so effortlessly? She thought of the thousands of customers who had spent nights there since 1947, of everything that had taken place within those rooms: joys, surprises, and plights unraveling between walls that no longer remained, only debris that would not endure, unlike the vestiges of ghost towns visited in her youth. And now more personal reminiscences ebbed back to her—the creamy thickness of the wall-to-wall carpeting adorning the hallways, a faulty tap's drip in the ladies' restrooms, the sweetish smell of the basement changing area, the grainy texture of the leather sofas in Kendall's office, the hasty cigarettes smoked with Kitty and Harper in the employees' entrance near the coffee machine. The Mapes Hotel was gone, but images of Suite 614 lingered on like neon leaving markings on her retinas: the vase of white roses on the low table, the scattered bottles of Nembutal, the platinum hairs trapped in the hairbrush, the earrings under the bed.

Enormous billows of golden dust began to rise, like unruly tendrils unfurling through the icy air, toward the river and the crowds gathered along the streets. People began to cheer, clapping and whistling, even shouting, and Pauline couldn't understand their delight, as the bitter smell of smoke and powder stung her eyes. She remembered Nick's warning, how he had said her feelings might overwhelm her, and he had been right. In the heart of that pile of rubble and memories lay a part of herself.

As if Jim had guessed at her inner turmoil, he clasped his sister's shoulders. There were not just jovial faces amid the onlookers: The young woman with the blue beanie whose father used to work at the Mapes casino was wiping away tears while the distraught old gentleman holding the red rose kept bringing the flower to his lips.

"Are you okay, Mademoiselle?" Billie-Pearl asked.

The camera was once again pointed at Pauline. She hardly had time to regain her composure, let alone answer her friend, but that's what they probably wanted, spur-of-the-moment reactions.

"You ready?" said the young woman, fiddling with her earpiece. "We're on."

A bagpipe's slow lament was heard, its stirring chords plucking at Pauline's heartstrings, while over the gaping void left by the Mapes, blonde dust gently settled.

MAYFAIR, LONDON

The same day, Sunday, January 30, 2000, 6 p.m. local time

The old lady with her arm in a sling was having trouble turning on her TV. She was almost ninety, and the broken limb infuriated her, but it certainly didn't stop her from clambering up the seven flights of stairs every day to her mansion flat on the top floor. For nearly forty years, she'd been living in a yellow brick Edwardian building overlooking Grosvenor Square, and she still took pleasure in teasing the guests who arrived panting at her door.

She finally called out to Linni for help. Her assistant and friend knew the old lady didn't want to miss the news from the United States, her home country, watched every evening on a cable network with a glass of wine, usually red.

Linni was full of admiration toward her longtime friend who, in spite of retiring twenty years ago, went on writing at her crowded desk, filing her archives and entertaining guests. She remained well-dressed, with rose-scented perfume, her long ivory hair tied up in a small bun, dressed in sleek trouser suits and bright-colored silk scarves.

Linni switched on the television, found the right channel, and went to fetch the wine, drawing the curtains against the chilly London night.

"How about Cabernet?" she asked from the kitchen.

"Perfect," came the low growl, which sounded almost masculine.

The phone rang during the newscast: It was a neighbor enquiring about how the broken arm was doing. The old lady's eyes remained on the screen during the conversation.

At one point, to Linni's surprise, she told her neighbor she'd call her back and hung up.

"Linni, can you turn that up?"

It was a recorded broadcast, as far as Linni could see; a building destroyed in clouds of dust. The red caption under the footage displayed *"The Mapes Hotel checks out forever. Reno, Nevada."*

"Did you know this place?"

"Yes, and I even slept there," the old lady answered, watching carefully. "A long time ago."

The journalist explained the Mapes Hotel had had its claim to fame, once considered one of the classiest Reno venues before being outshined by Las Vegas's glittering casino-hotels and shutting down in the eighties.

"How pretty it was," sighed Linni, as ancient photographs of the red-bricked structure rising above the city appeared.

The journalist was now back on the screen, and a woman in her early sixties stood next to her.

"We are in Reno, Nevada, in front of the Mapes Hotel, or

rather what is left of it, in the company of Doctor Pauline Bazelet, veterinarian from California. Whereabouts in California?"

"Mount Shasta."

"Just before the implosion, you were telling us that during the summer of 1960, you were employed at the Mapes Hotel as a cleaning lady and you met someone there who changed your life. Can you tell us more?"

"Yes, of course. One morning, in July 1960, I thought the suite I was working in was empty, but it turned out it wasn't. I woke up the guest with my vacuuming."

The journalist smiled.

"Did you get into trouble?"

"No. That guest was so kind to me. And I had no idea who she was, at that point."

"And who was she?"

"Marilyn Monroe. She was staying at the Mapes for the filming of *The Misfits*."

"You mean you did *not* recognize her?" the journalist asked the woman by her side.

"No, I didn't. She was different with no makeup."

The old lady chuckled, sipping her cabernet.

"Very true!" she told Linni. "The Millers were heading to divorce by then. Marilyn was already taking too many pills. In the mornings, she did not look good."

"Of course, you were there!" exclaimed Linni. "How could I have forgotten?"

"I certainly was there. And I remember it clearly. Such suffering on the set."

On screen, the journalist went on with her questions, "How

long were you around her at the Mapes? And what was so special about her, in your opinion?"

"Marilyn was special because she was interested in people you never notice, like me, the cleaning lady. She even wanted to meet my three-year-old daughter. She was the one who requested that I take care of her suite. And for a couple of months, I saw her almost every day."

"Tell us about one of your best memories with Marilyn."

"It's hard to pick only one . . . but there was the day she invited me to the movie set." She smiled: Yes, that was a wonderful memory. Marilyn had played her most difficult, moving scene. An unforgettable one.

The woman's face suddenly lit up on the TV; she ran a hand through her short, gray-streaked hair and the camera filming her in close-up caught her large green eyes.

The old lady slapped her knee with her free hand, startling Linni.

"Gadzooks, I know I've seen that woman before! I remember those eyes. That smile. Can you write down her name? It's up on the screen now. Quick."

The journalist went on.

"So you met Marilyn Monroe at the Mapes Hotel, while she was going through one of the most challenging moments of her career. Did you become close?"

"In a way, yes. But I never saw her again after she left the Mapes."

"That's Doctor Pauline Bazelet," said Linni, writing on a pad. "Veterinarian from Mount Shasta, California. Got it."

"And how did Marilyn change your life? What did she do for you, exactly?"

"I was trapped in a dreary routine. I was young and had no

idea how to break free from it. She showed me how to believe in myself, how to stand up for myself. And she gave me a gift."

"What was it?"

"It's very personal. I'd prefer to keep it to myself. Let's just say her present was like a stepping-stone. That was the summer I took flight."

"So the Mapes must have been quite a unique place for you. What was it like when you watched it come down minutes ago?"

"Like watching a whole part of my life vanishing."

"Thank you, Doctor Bazelet."

The old lady got up with energy.

"Now, Linni, listen. I can't do anything with this stupid arm. Please go to my files and get everything marked Reno, Nevada, 1960."

Linnie went to look.

"There must be seven or eight folders," she shouted from the nearby office. "Do you want them all?"

"Yes, I want them all."

"What are you looking for?"

"You'll see. You know how much I love going through my stuff, finding things I'd forgotten, thumbing through archives of memory."

Linni gazed at her affectionately.

"Well, I certainly love that merry smile on your face."

"I could use another glass of Cabernet, dear, as I'm not planning on going to bed. Neither are you. It's back to Nevada tonight, and you're coming along for the ride."

RENO, NEVADA

———⟫⟫⟫———

The same day, Sunday, January 30, 2000, 8:30 a.m.

"Frenchie! I thought it was you."

No one ever called her that anymore. A woman her own age was tugging on her sleeve, as crowds went on moving around them, and Pauline lost sight of Jim and Billie-Pearl. She looked at her blankly, doing her best to recall who this person was.

"It's Kitty. Remember me?"

"Kitty!" exclaimed Pauline. "Of course I remember you."

Kitty grinned, flashing suspiciously white teeth. Well, yes, she'd altered her hair, she'd had more than several nips and tucks over the years, a nose job, her chin redone, and other bits and bobs. She waved long red nails: Pauline hadn't changed one bit, she'd picked her out right away, tall, slender, such class! Kitty had had three more kids after Pauline left. And two more ex-husbands to boot. But what about Pauline? What had happened to her after all this time? She hadn't forgotten her friend Frenchie. And those ridiculous girls who were green with envy because of Mrs. Miller.

"You did well in that interview. Were you nervous? It didn't show. Say, you never saw her again?"

"Mrs. Miller? No. She died two years later."

"You know, when I heard the news, I thought of you. The week you left Reno, Clark Gable kicked the bucket. And then Montgomery Clift in 1966. Talk about an ill-fated movie."

Kitty's voice now sounded familiar to Pauline, as well as her eyes, unchanged in an unnatural, frozen face. It seemed daunting to sum up forty years in a moment, but Kitty was just as much of a chatterbox, which made her smile, telling her the tale of a chain of cataclysmic divorces, dwindling alimonies, and five kids to bring up on her own. It had certainly been a hard sweat! And now, things were better and Kitty was a happy granny. The implosion saddened her; she had been sure the preservationists would save the hotel at the last minute. Weren't those bagpipes haunting? Kitty had stayed on at the Mapes until it closed down, and then she went on to work at a hotel in Carson City, where she moved with husband number three. Did Pauline know Mildred Jones passed away not that long ago? She had become mellower with age, and always had a kind word for Frenchie.

All Pauline had to do was answer Kitty's questions: Yes, she still lived in California. No, she didn't come to Reno that often, now that her stepdad and her mother rested in Mountain View Cemetery. No, she had not married, had not had more children, and for a long time had just had passing flings.

"Yikes, that's kind of gloomy! All work and no play."

"Yes...but...I did meet someone, recently."

"Tell me more?"

"Well, just when I wasn't expecting anything ever again, after that string of sad romances and letdowns, I met this man at a friend's dinner party I hadn't planned on going to."

"*And?*" encouraged Kitty, sounding so much like her younger self that Pauline had to giggle.

Kitty offered her a cigarette and, in that gesture, Pauline felt again like she was thrown back to their past, to their twenties, wearing their Mapes uniforms.

"There he was, this quiet guy, sitting in a corner, sipping his wine. Sometimes, he'd say something, just a couple of words, and everyone would crack up laughing. A terrific sense of humor. A rare thing. As you know."

"Go on. Sounds fascinating."

"We spent all evening just talking to each other. I think the other guests were quite annoyed with us. And there was this immediate attraction, but there was more to it than just that. I could tell, and he did too, that this was serious. From the start."

"What's his name? What does he look like?"

"His name is Nick. He's tall. Dark hair. Hazel eyes."

"Frenchie, are you blushing or what?"

Pauline hooted, "Me?"

"You are! You're definitely blushing. You must be in love. Sounds like it to me."

"Yes, I am, for the first time. Madly in love. At sixty-one!"

They burst out laughing.

"And what about your daughter? Such a cute little girl."

Lily was now a woman of forty-three, married, and the mother of two, working with Pauline at her equine clinic.

"So you made it, Frenchie! You became a vet. Your dream!"

Yes, she had made it, but by dint of hard work, she told Kitty.

She had gone the extra mile from the start and, when she left Reno to attend her internship, she had understood right away there would be no slacking, that she needed to earn money with French lessons and waitressing. In that first year, she passed the GED test, obtained her diploma, and applied for a scholarship to UC Davis.

"Did you get that scholarship?"

"I did, and I moved to Davis with Lily."

How on earth had Pauline managed? Forty years ago, most folks would have frowned upon a single mother attending college. Pauline admitted she got lucky. Doctor Hicks, the terrific veterinarian from Mount Shasta with whom she had completed her internship, happened to have an equally terrific daughter who taught at UC Davis, called Cleo Hicks, who owned a house near campus. She rented rooms to students and took in Pauline and Lily.

"And how long did you live at Davis?"

"For four years, the time it took me to complete the first chunk of my studies. Lily started kindergarten there."

During her specialist training, she had returned to Mount Shasta, where she rented a house and collaborated with other local equine vets. When she finally became a full-fledged vet, she decided to stay on.

"And now? What are your plans?"

Pauline was already thinking about her retirement. She had taken on Doctor Hicks's patient base fifteen years ago and the clinic was flourishing. But she felt like making the most of her free time, planning a trip to Paris with her partner, and bringing her grandkids as well. She wanted to get back in touch with the French part of herself.

"Your mother was so Parisian to me. I can still see her gliding into the Mapes, with her stylish dresses and hairdos."

"She wasn't happy here. She missed France too much. It broke my stepfather's heart, I think. He never mentioned it, but I felt it."

Kitty pointed to Billie-Pearl, who was in conversation with Jim and other people.

"Is that the friend you used to go horseback riding with? She has not changed one bit either. Honestly, what's your secret, both of you? Don't tell me it's mustangs."

"That's Billie-Pearl, all right. She's an activist, devoted to protecting mustangs, like Velma Johnston was. She's the one who brought me here this morning. To tell the truth, I wasn't sure about coming."

"Is that because of . . . ?"

Kitty's voice dried up as a silhouette appeared next to them and Pauline glanced up to see Kendall Spencer standing there, alone.

A bubble of silence settled around them, while Kitty backed away, leaving them alone, and Pauline was aware of an uncomfortable hush. He wore the same cologne, which she picked up despite the air still thick with clouds of dust circling above their heads. From close up, she saw how much older he looked.

"It's been a while," he said.

She remained quiet, curious to hear what he might say next. How was it that this man had once held her under his dark spell? He appeared insignificant, and she felt nothing for him, glancing at the hands that had caressed her, at the lips she had kissed in the secret of his office; there was a glint of pity, which no doubt showed on her face, because he seemed to bow his head as if in shame.

"The years have treated you well, Pauline."

She could see his eyes halting at the silver ring she wore on her left hand. Nick's ring. He appeared to wonder. The abyss of unsaid words stretched between them. She could walk away, like she already had, in 1960. But she was a different person now.

"Don't you want to get to know her?"

He seemed thrown by her question. "To know her . . . ?"

"Lily. Your daughter. And your grandchildren. You already have a whole bunch, but you have two more."

She opened her purse, fished out a scrap of paper and a pen, and jotted down a number. Lily's cell. It wasn't too late to give her a call, to get to know one another. Did he know what a wonderful person their daughter was? Funny, bright, brave. Raising her kids beautifully. Married to a delightful man called Howard. Adored by her friends. She also had quite a temper, which reminded Pauline of Marcelle. What was he waiting for, anyway? Did he really want his daughter to remain a stranger? Wouldn't he kick himself for it?

She told him about Ryder, who was ten years old and fascinated by trains. You could ask him any train question and he'd have the answer. He was awesome. And Brooke, age eight, wanted to become a writer. She spent her time filling the pages of her diary and reading books, even at night, with a flashlight under the sheets.

Kendall listened intently, and Pauline noticed how weary he seemed. She knew nothing of his life. Had he been happy married to Evaline? How had he felt, watching the Mapes go down?

Kendall Spencer was now an old man with mournful eyes. At one point, she thought he was going to say he was sorry, which she hoped for, but he never did—he just stared at her, clutching Lily's number in his hand.

"Good-bye," she said, turning away.

He said, "Tell Lily I'll be in touch."

She did not believe him for one minute. As she walked off, he called her back. The expression on his face was unfamiliar to her, a blend of remorse and tenderness. He said he had this image of her stuck in his mind that never left him.

"When I think of you, that's how I remember you. Dancing up there in the Sky Room. With Marilyn Monroe."

FRIDAY, FEBRUARY 4, 2000

Mount Shasta, Siskiyou County, Northern California

Starling kept quiet, letting Pauline examine him without making a fuss. The colt was putting up with the splint and didn't need screws or a plate. His overall condition was satisfactory and he'd be out of the woods in a couple of weeks, Pauline thought. Another patient worried her much more, a dressage mare named Velvet, suffering from a lipoma in her small intestine, who had had to be urgently operated on as soon as Pauline returned from Reno. The surgery lasted nearly four hours, and her teammate, Doctor Merrill, had assisted her, as well as an anesthetist and a nurse. Velvet was still on stall rest, on a drip and closely monitored. Her recovery would take a long time.

Under her probing fingers, Starling's golden hide shivered.

"You'll soon be up and about, buddy. I'm not at all worried about you."

She gave him one last pat and left the stalls. It was early still, and the sun had just come up, illuminating the abundant snow that had fallen overnight. She took a moment to admire the beauty of the winter sky. A pair of arms lovingly wrapped themselves around her waist.

"There's fresh coffee," said Nick, kissing her.

She followed him to the cozy kitchen, where a fire crackled, the smell of toast filled the air. They sat and had breakfast, looking out to the white-coated fir trees. She treasured this morning ritual, starting the day under Nick's tender gaze, watching him read the news, spreading butter and jam on his bread. For years, there had been no man at her breakfast table. And before that, she had looked after her daughter, who was always late, and those mornings had been rushed.

"I've been meaning to tell you. You've been very quiet since you got back from Reno on Monday."

Pauline bit into her toast. "Well, that emergency colic surgery was hell. Haven't dealt with such a tough one for years. I hope Velvet makes it."

Nick was waiting for Pauline to tell him about the implosion. He didn't know much more about it apart from the fact she had seen Kendall Spencer. *Was she all right?* he wondered. He was even a bit concerned.

She could tell him he shouldn't worry, that she was dead tired, that was all, but she didn't like the idea of lying to him. Their relationship was still young; she wanted to nurture it. She finished her toast, poured herself more coffee.

"It isn't easy explaining how I felt."

Nick nodded. She felt sad, was that it? No, *sad* wasn't the right word; more like a blend of several feelings she was struggling to sort out and define.

"It must have been weird to see him again. Your daughter's father."

She no longer resented him, that was for sure. Gone was the urge to slap him in the face. She felt sorry for Kendall; he seemed wizened, remorseful, almost endearing. The ambitious young man had disappeared. Yes, she was flooded by persistent nostalgia since the implosion, and on the way back from Reno, during the drive with Billie-Pearl to the mustang sanctuary, her friend had noticed the same thing: Why did she look like she was down? Billie-Pearl had insisted upon arrival that Pauline should go on a horseback ride.

"And did it do you good?"

"It did. I rode Dansa, and it was perfect."

"Perhaps you need a horse to ride and love, instead of horses to heal. Your own horse."

He had a point. Her own horse. A mustang, of course, one of Commander's descendants. Billie-Pearl would be in charge of choosing it, breaking in it, bringing it to her. She loved the idea.

There was a busy schedule for today, so there was no more time to loiter. Doctor Merrill would be arriving any minute and they were planning to assess how Velvet was doing. Nick was heading to Dunsmuir, where he worked. He'd be back tonight, and it was his turn to make dinner. He gave her a kiss and went out into the snow. She watched his tall silhouette cross the garden to his car. She had been single for so many years, committing herself heart and soul to her work; she had thought she'd end her life without knowing anything about love. And here she was, discovering it, at her age. This belated romance was a small miracle. Was she right to believe in it, to give herself entirely to it? She was taking that risk.

The morning flew by; other horses were expected, with more or less serious ailments, and they needed to be welcomed, and their owners reassured. Velvet was pulling through pretty well, but Pauline knew she had to remain on her guard, and it was too early to celebrate victory. She had, after all, removed eight feet of Velvet's small intestine. Dr. Merrill was confident; he thought Pauline had done a fine job and risen to the occasion in a critical situation most vets dreaded. But, he added, he thought it was time Pauline took a breather. For years now, she had been such a hard worker. Pauline answered that it was on her agenda, she was even thinking about her retirement and her future trips.

At noon, Pauline went back to the kitchen, her favorite place in the ranch. When she moved in fifteen years ago, taking over Doctor Hicks's clinic, she had added her own touch with books, colorful rugs, paintings by a local wildlife painter, furniture belonging to her parents, all the while preserving the place's unassuming, rudimentary character, which added to its allure. The ranch appeared smaller than the Double Lazy Heart, or Billie-Pearl's, but it had one unique characteristic—it wasn't a single-storied place, like most buildings of the kind. It had an upper floor, which doubled its surface area. She loved the view from her bedroom, from which she could see over a waterfall all the way to the meadows lost in the rolling hills, the magical, remote forest, and overlooking it all, the monumental icy cone of Mount Shasta, the subject of a number of myths and legends. She knew now how much she needed nature, fresh air, majestic trees. Living in a town was not for her. Nick had understood this from the start.

She began to prepare a meal in the kitchen, expecting Lily to come in as usual. Why couldn't she shake that lost feeling? As if something were missing. But she couldn't figure out what it was. Her daughter had lunch with her on Fridays, when they went over the week's schedule ahead. People occasionally asked her if it was tricky for a mother to employ her own daughter. And it was, from time to time, because Lily had quite a fiery temper, and they occasionally argued. But now that she was in her forties, Lily had softened, and she had begun to watch over her mother.

The front door banged, and Lily walked in holding a parcel she set down on the table. For a split second, Pauline saw Marcelle there with her dainty figure and dark hair swept up in a ponytail. Lily had looked like her grandmother from the start, and over the years, the resemblance had become even more striking.

She had told her daughter about her conversation with Kendall Spencer the day of the implosion, adding she would be surprised if he ever got around to contacting her. Lily had said she wondered, in the end, if she wanted to get to know a father she had no recollection of, the most notable absence in her life. She had done without him for ages; he had become a ghost. Perhaps it was better that he stayed that way.

They had a quick meal since they had to start up again right after their break.

"Oh, I almost forgot!" Lily went to get the parcel she had brought with her. She opened it with care, taking out a dollhouse. Mrs. Miller's gift. She had searched for it high and low, distressed at the prospect of not finding it. She remembered that she had not wanted to let her own daughter play with it, for fear Brooke might damage it, and had preferred to store it in a safe place.

"I thought maybe you would want to see it again."

The dollhouse's colors had faded. Its tiny curtains were tattered, but it was still in one piece, and Pauline marveled as she peered into it. Did Lily have any memories of Marilyn at all? Lily frowned. No, she didn't, she was only three, but some things did come back to her, like wearing her best dress to meet "Mrs. Miller" and going to the Mapes.

"What was it like, seeing the Mapes blow up? You haven't told me much about it. And when you arrived home, you had to tend to the Velvet emergency."

Pauline held the dollhouse in her hands, trying to find the right words for the wavering state she was still trapped in. She longed to light up a cigarette, but her daughter was trying to get her to quit, so she refrained. She replied that she felt a kind of inner loss she couldn't understand nor bridge.

"A loss of what, Mom?"

How could she explain to her daughter the Mapes Hotel had been the last link connecting her to Marilyn? She gave it a shot. She said she hadn't often spoken about the actress to Lily, nor to those close to her. All this time, she'd kept the events that had taken place in Suite 614 to herself, and the pictures, scents, and sounds had never ceased to accompany her, preciously stored in her memory. And now the proud Mapes reigning over the Reno of her youth, where she and Marilyn had met, was nothing but a pile of rubble.

"I understand. Did you feel that way when you heard she had died?"

"No, that was different."

Her death had been a total shock, like it had been for almost anyone on that Sunday morning, August 5, 1962, whether or not you were a fan of Marilyn Monroe.

"Weren't we living in Davis then?"

"We were, but that weekend we were in Reno."

Lily was five years old then. They had gone to spend a couple of days with Doug, Marcelle, and Jimmy. Pauline recalled getting up early, going to make breakfast in the silent house. She had turned on the radio, with the sound low so she wouldn't wake anyone, and she heard it on the news. She remembered stopping in her tracks, nearly dropping the coffeepot. Marilyn Monroe had been found dead in her Brentwood home, aged thirty-six. Pauline had forgotten about breakfast, about coffee. She sat down to listen, stunned. Doug had been the first to spot her when he came out of his room, asking her what was wrong. Unable to speak, she had pointed to the radio. The journalist was in the middle of providing a list of sordid details: The actress had been found in bed, naked, facedown, hand clasping the telephone. The cause of her death was probably due to a barbiturate overdose. A likely suicide. Marcelle came to join them, a little later, and she had shed a few tears. Pauline remembered the onslaught of headlines. For a long time there had been talk of suicide, and then other books published in the seventies and eighties mentioned the Kennedy brothers, the Mafia, insinuating Marilyn Monroe might have been murdered.

Pauline didn't buy any of the assassination theories, refusing to believe Marilyn could have been killed because of her affairs with the Kennedy brothers. Over the years, she had seen many snapshots of the house at 12305 Fifth Helena Drive, Marilyn's last home. It didn't look at all like a movie star's palace, set in a quiet residential area, of Mexican style with wooden beams; it seemed surprisingly humble. The previous owners had had a

Latin motto engraved in the tiles: "*Cursum Perficio*" meaning *here ends my journey.*

"How ironic!" gasped Lily.

Pauline went on. She had also seen the black-and-white photographs of the night Marilyn died, especially the notoriously gruesome one of the actress still sprawled between her sheets, tousled peroxided hair on the pillow, and a cop's index finger pointing to the nightstand and the all-too-familiar jumble of pills. An unspeakable snapshot of Marilyn in death at the morgue was published in a book. Pauline wished she had never seen it.

She often thought about those prescription drugs the actress had been taking for ten years, or so she'd read. That was the Hollywood trend at the time, popping downers to sleep and uppers to wake up, the lot swallowed with liquor, and Marilyn had become addicted. No one had taken care of her; no one had watched over her. Day after day, her malaise was assuaged by pills handed to her like candy, without qualms, just like Pauline had seen with her very eyes.

Pauline told Lily about that moment in Suite 614 when Arthur Miller had held the young, quaking doctor accountable: Had he been aware of the amount of sleeping pills his wife had already ingested? No, he hadn't. No one had been. And that, for Pauline, was what would later lead Marilyn to her death. Incompetence. The actress had, in the past, attempted suicide several times, revived at the last minute by stomach pumps, but that night, in 1962, Pauline was convinced the overdose had been unintentional. She had learned that Marilyn's two doctors had not consulted each other concerning Nembutal dosage and the astronomical quantities consumed by the movie star. And that fateful day in August 1962, one of them had prescribed an enema with chloral hydrate, a powerful sedative, without checking the number of tranquilizers already consumed.

In Pauline's opinion, Marilyn's doctors were the wrongdoers, the ones who covered up her accidental demise, which was their fault. Hurriedly staging it to look like suicide with the help of that shady housekeeper, Eunice Murray, appointed by one of them to supposedly "look after" Marilyn. But the mystery endured. There had never been any proof, and hypotheses of all kinds still abounded, nearly forty years after her death.

Pauline read Arthur's Miller memoir when it was published in 1987, especially the section concerning Reno, *The Misfits*, and his late ex-wife. There were a couple of striking sentences in which he wrote that Marilyn's vulnerability had been too much to bear, that there were dark moments where he did not believe she knew how to survive, and when he wondered if her doctors had any idea of the mortal danger she was in from all those sleeping pills.

In February 1961, during a weekend in Reno, Pauline had gone to see *The Misfits* with her mother. Marcelle had read the unfavorable reviews to her, but they both wanted to make up their own minds. Clark Gable had been dead for three months, and Marcelle had told Pauline that Marilyn, freshly divorced from Arthur Miller, hadn't made it to the première.

Marcelle had been puzzled by the film. In her eyes it was neither a western, nor a comedy, nor a drama, and she had not approved of the black-and-white images either, which she considered outdated. To her, it was a failure, and she wasn't the only one to think so. Box office revenues were disappointing. It would be Marilyn Monroe's last completed film, but they didn't know that at the time. Lily had seen the movie on DVD with her mother ten years ago. She was fond of it because her mother loved it and knew it by heart. As a teenager, she had enjoyed hearing about the day Pauline went to the set.

But it was time to get back to work, and they made their way to the central office by the stalls. In the afternoon, Lily was on the phone when Pauline spotted a white Federal Express van entering the gates, probably a client sending X-rays for an upcoming operation.

"Doctor Pauline Bazelet?" asked the delivery driver, coming up to the office door.

He handed her a large, rigid mailing envelope. She thanked him, signing the receipt. Lily called for her attention about a request from a fellow vet, and she didn't think to open the envelope.

It was only later, when dusk was beginning to fall, that she remembered it. Lily had gone by then, picking up her kids from school.

Pauline unsealed the envelope, extracting a letter and prints wrapped in protective bubble wrap. They weren't X-rays. Intrigued, she glanced at the back of the envelope. The items had been mailed from the United Kingdom, and the name inscribed—Mrs. Linni Campbell—rang no bells. She was about to read the letter, but the first picture caught her eye. She was stunned and put the letter aside.

It was a black-and-white shot of her standing, gazing into the distance, long brown hair whipped by wild winds, with a trailer behind her, under a sky laden with clouds. And the desert all around her.

The set. *The Misfits*. That photographer in the striped sweater with the deep voice who had asked her to forget she was there, to think about something else. She had thought of Commander.

She read the letter.

Dear Doctor Bazelet,

*I apologize for this typewritten missive, but I broke my
arm and can't write by hand. I saw coverage on television
about the destruction of the Mapes Hotel in Reno and your
interview.*

  *I remembered you and looked through my archives.
Fortunately, I had recorded your name.*

  I hope you enjoy these two prints.

Sincerely,
Eve Arnold

The second photo was in color, showing a group of people standing together in front of the same trailer. With a beating heart, Pauline recognized Agnes, black scarf knotted over her white hair, and she picked out Rafe's burly shoulders seen from the side, the top of Whitey's crew cut, and from the back, a young man in a blue sweater. She couldn't recall his name.

But what she saw next took her breath away. There she was, on the left, standing next to the actress. Marilyn wasn't wearing the dark glasses Pauline remembered—they were dangling from her hand. And Marilyn was smiling back, looking straight at her.

She was so engrossed in the photograph she didn't hear Nick come in. She only understood he was there when he murmured, "That's insane."

He wanted to know where she got this extraordinary print, and she told him about the moment with photographer Eve Arnold on the set. Pauline didn't know she had snapped a photo of her with Marilyn.

"Looks like your smile is back."

He hugged her, wanting to know who the other people in the photo were. He wanted to know everything. So Pauline complied. These were Marilyn's "Happy People," that's what the actress called them. And Pauline liked to feel she had been part of that gang, for a while. That was Ralph Roberts, Marilyn's masseur, nicknamed Rafe, a tall, friendly guy, whom she had initially taken for her husband, then her lover, before understanding who he was. He followed her everywhere, massaged her several times a day. Next to him stood Agnes Flanagan, the actress's faithful hairdresser, a charming person as well, full of kindness. From behind, a young man whose name she had forgotten, one of the producer's assistants. And the person with only the top of his crew cut visible was Allan Snyder, Marilyn's beloved and equally devoted makeup artist, whom she called "Whitey." Pauline had read it was he who had done her makeup on her deathbed.

"And there's you. My beautiful you."

How young she seemed, how naïve! But then she realized it was at that precise moment in October 1960 that she had already begun to break away from Kendall's hold, to build her independence. It was all there, sprouting, ready to bloom. The stuttering young girl was no more.

Nick and Pauline stood holding each other close, staring at the photographs.

"I just remembered," she said. The day she went to the set was the day Agnes had told her something, which she only recalled now.

"What did she say?" Nick asked.

Pauline looked down at the image again. She was back there once more, feeling the bite of the cold wind, smelling the dry scent of the Nevada desert, hearing the murmur of chatter rise around her.

Here was her intimate link to Marilyn—their story was in that picture. All of it.

She smiled. "Agnes told me I needed to believe in my lucky star."

ACKNOWLEDGMENTS

The first person I want to thank is my husband, Nicolas, who believed in this book from the start.

Then, I want to thank Susanna Lea for her enthusiasm, her energy, and getting this book into the right hands.

Ten years ago, writer and editor Gérard de Cortanze suggested I write about "Mrs. Miller." Thanks to him as well.

I wish to thank Karen Kosztolnyik for her fervor and warm welcome, as well as her team at Grand Central.

My dear friends Valérie Bertoni, Sarah Hirsch, Laurence Le Falher, Gaëlle Nohant, Laure du Pavillon, and Chantal Remy were the first ones to read this book as it was being written. Their feedback was invaluable.

Dr. Nathalie Veniard, by speaking to me with passion about her job as an equine veterinarian, helped me shape Pauline's professional path.

A black mustang now haunts my dreams.

Obviously, his name is Commander...

—T.R.

PLAYLIST

"Cathy's Clown," the Everly Brothers
"I'm Sorry," Brenda Lee
"Stuck On You," Elvis Presley
"T'aimer follement," Dalida
"Les feuilles mortes," Yves Montand
"The Man I Love," Ella Fitzgerald
"Melodie d'Amour," The Ames Brothers
"What'd I Say," Ray Charles
"The Twist," Chubby Checker
"Only the Lonely," Roy Orbison
"Walking to New Orleans," Fats Domino
"He'll Have to Go," Jim Reeves
"Autumn Leaves," Frank Sinatra
"Every Day I Have the Blues," B.B. King
"Tonight You Belong to Me," Patience and Prudence

BIBLIOGRAPHY

Cauchon, Sébastien, *Marilyn 1962*, Paris: Stock, 2016.

Cruise, David, and Alison Griffiths, *Wild Horse Annie and the Last of the Mustangs*, New York: Scribner, 2010.

Cursum Perficio, www.cursumperficio.net/.

Kaiser, Hilary, *French War Brides: Mademoiselle & the American Soldier*, New York: Paris Writers Press, 2017.

Laxalt, Robert, *Sweet Promised Land*, Reno: University of Nevada Press, 2007.

Mailer, Norman, *Marilyn*, London: Hodder and Stoughton, 1973.

Malone, Aubrey, *The Misfits: The Film That Ended a Marriage*, Orlando: BearManor Media, 2022.

Mapes Hotel, www.facebook.com/mapeshotel.

Miller, Arthur, and Serge Toubiana, *The Misfits*, Paris: Les Cahiers du Cinéma, 1999.

Miller, Arthur, *Timebends: A Life*, London: Methuen, 1987.

Monroe, Marilyn, *Fragments*, London: HarperCollins, 2010.

Pepitone, Lena, William Stadiem, and Maurice Hakim *Marilyn secrète*, Paris: Pygmalion, 1986.

Plantagenet, Anne, *Marilyn Monroe*, Paris: Folio Biographies, 2007.

Roberts, Ralph L., Chris Jacobs, and Hap Roberts, *Mimosa: Memories of Marilyn & the Making of "The Misfits,"* Salisbury: Roadhouse Books, 2021.

Rosten, Norman, *Marilyn: Ombre et lumière*, Paris: Éditions Seghers, 2022.

Santucci, Françoise-Marie, *Monroerama*, Paris: Stock, 2012.

Schneider, Michel, *Marilyn dernières séances*, Paris: Grasset, 2006.

Spoto, Donald, *Marilyn Monroe: The Biography*, London: Chatto & Windus Ltd., 1993.

ABOUT THE AUTHOR

Tatiana de Rosnay is the author of more than ten novels, including the *New York Times* bestseller *Sarah's Key*, an international sensation with over eleven million copies in forty-four countries worldwide. Together with Dan Brown, Stephenie Meyer, and Stieg Larsson, she has been named one of the top ten fiction writers in Europe. De Rosnay lives in Paris, France.

For more information you can visit:
Tatianaderosnay.com
X @tatianaderosnay
Facebook.com/tatianadcrosnay
Instagram @tatianaderosnay